SEX
VIOLENCE

A NOVEL

CARRIE MESROBIAN

carolrhoda LAB

MINNEAPOLIS

Carolrhoda Lab™ is a trademark of Lerner Publishing Group, Inc.

Carolrhoda Lab™
An imprint of Carolrhoda Books
A division of Lerner Publishing Group, Inc.
241 First Avenue North
Minneapolis, MN 55401 U.S.A.

Website address: www.lernerbooks.com

Cover and interior photographs © iStockphoto.com/Ola Dusegård (tile);
© iStockphoto.com/Dmitry Fisher (water); © iStockphoto.com/ansonsaw
(water splash).

Main body text set in Janson Text LT Std 10/14.
Typeface provided by Linotype AG.

Library of Congress Cataloging-in-Publication Data

Mesrobian, Carrie.
        Sex and violence / by Carrie Mesrobian.
            pages cm
        Summary: "Sex has always come without consequences for Evan. Until
    the night when all the consequences land at once, leaving him scarred
    inside and out" — Provided by publisher.
        ISBN 978–1–4677–0597–4 (trade hard cover : alk. paper)
        ISBN 978–1–4677–1619–2 (eBook)
        [1. Interpersonal relations—Fiction. 2. Sex—Fiction. 3. Emotional
    problems—Fiction. 4. Psychotherapy—Fiction.] I. Title.
    PZ7.M5493Se 2013
    [Fic]—dc23   2012047181

Manufactured in the United States of America
1 – BP – 7/15/13

FOR AKD, MY FAVORITE BOY

They fuck you up, your mum and dad.
They may not mean to, but they do.
They fill you with the faults they had
And add some extra, just for you.

—Philip Larkin

The Lake
This girl I hardly knew, taller than I was
and skinny, who made us boys
puff ourselves up and show off how far
we could throw rocks, or how many times
we could skip stones across the choppy water;
this awkward kid I'd never really spoken to
asked me one afternoon to swim across the lake with her.
We were sitting on the dock. It was chilly, but I said
I would do it, though the other side was hazy—almost
out of sight—and it would take us until dark
to make it there and back. So we dove in and started off
slowly. As we swam, mostly breast stroke, she talked
about the lake, how old it was, what sorts of creatures
lived there now, how it had changed
over its lifetime, the depth of its ice
in winter, how the fish huddled down on the bottom
between the ice and mud. And then she asked me
what I knew, and I had to say, Nothing in particular.
And then, despite myself, I made up a story
about the stars: I heard myself singing a song
I made up as I sang, about the constellations,
and soon she was singing with me. We reached
the middle of the lake, out of breath but singing,
and realized the other side was too far. We treaded
water there, then turned and headed back, quiet now.
We were tired. We climbed out and walked our separate ways
home through the dusk light to our families
in silence. No goodbyes. And we never spoke again.

—Michael Hettich

PROLOGUE

You'd think the most fucked-up part of the last year would be the moment when I read this and thought, "Yeah, that. That sounds like the way to go."

> *The northern side of Pearl Lake is unusually deep, due to its formation during the time of the Ice Age. It is near this point that the lake links up with the Beauchant River, which has been used as a logging route since the last century. However, not all of the intended cargo made it to a lumberyard destination; many of these logs sank into the cold abyss. An intrepid diver would find many of those tremendous logs still at the bottom of the lake, in a kind of graveyard to industry. Abandoned and untouched they remain, as any microorganisms that might decompose them cannot survive at those temperatures and depths.*

You'd think that would be my low point. Not even close.

CHAPTER ONE

When I came out of the Connison gang shower, Collette Holmander was waiting for me. She was standing in the hallway, her long red hair splashing down her black jacket and white shirt, her red knee socks on her pretty legs beneath her little black skirt. Even though Remington Chase was a vaguely religious boarding school, the girls' uniforms were unreasonably sexy—practically porn fantasies.

"Check out Evan Carter, skipping chapel!" Collette said.

"So are you," I answered, all annoyed, because she'd caught me in nothing but flip-flops and uniform pants (unreasonably dorky, think dipshit caterer). While my body's not deformed or anything, I'm not one of those douchey guys who struts around shirtless. But it could have been worse—for Collette, at least—as Connison was a boys-only dorm, and lots of guys went around in just towels, sometimes less.

"I don't get you, Evan," Collette said, walking toward me. "You're weird."

"Thanks," I said, pushing by her, digging through my shower stuff for my room key.

"No, really." She was following me. "You run superfast, but only, like, 50 percent of the time." Now, as if to live up to this accusation, I was walking pretty fast. But she kept up with me, her shoes clacking on the linoleum way too loudly.

"And you ace every test in chemistry but flunk everything else," she added, when we got to my door. Her fucking perky-cocky voice echoed in the empty hallway.

"So?" I said, putting my key in the lock.

"Plus, you're decent-looking, but you won't even talk to Farrah no matter how much I tell you that she wants you to ask her out. Now the chapel skipping? What could all this mean?"

I had nothing to say about what this all meant, but that didn't matter. Collette Holmander was the kind of girl who asked you a million questions and then didn't give you time to answer half of them. The kind of girl who wouldn't stop getting in your face when she wanted something. The kind of girl sent by her friends to feel out if a guy liked them. I hated that kind of shit, as a rule. If I'm looking to hook up, I don't need any help. I've got my own tested methods, and they didn't include messenger chicks like Collette Holmander.

"Farrah *always* goes to chapel. She might think you're avoiding her."

"I *am* avoiding her," I said turning to stand in the doorway. "Her boyfriend wants to smash my face in, remember?"

"I told you, they broke up," she said.

"Try telling him that," I said. "And what the hell are you doing here, anyway? No girls allowed beyond the common room."

"Then let me in, dummy," she said, standing on tiptoes to look behind me.

So I let her in my room, against my better judgment. Collette and my roommate, Patrick Ramsey, had hooked up last year, but now they hated each other. (This was before my time, but he made sure I knew his hookup history as soon as we became roommates.) He called her firecrotch and she called him needledick and it was fucking uncomfortable.

On top of that, Collette was always pestering me about Farrah, who supposedly liked me, for no reason other than I sat by her in Spanish and I was the Fucking New Guy at this incestuous little prison of a boarding school forty-five minutes south of Charlotte, North Carolina. Apparently, for Farrah, the fact that I had a Yankee accent and shaggier hair than every square-faced Southern boy she'd grown up with made me thrilling and exotic. Or just more thrilling and exotic than Tate Kerrigan, her asshole boyfriend, who used entirely too much hair gel and who remained obsessive about Farrah to the point where he had nearly punched me out one night outside the dining hall because he'd heard we'd done a Spanish project together in the common room at Fountaineau, the junior girls dormitory.

**

So this was the context when I found myself cornered in my own room by Collette Holmander. Who was pretty foxy, actually. If you had to be cornered by a girl while skipping chapel, Collette was a good candidate for the job. Still, I was a little surprised. Messenger chicks don't usually help themselves to the guys they're sent to check out.

Collette kicked the door shut, grabbed my towel and

shower kit, and dropped them on the floor. She was so close to me that my whole body popped up in goose bumps, which was embarrassing enough, but things got worse below the belt when she reached over and touched the necklace I wore. It was this flat silver circle on a silver chain. My mother gave it to me when I was eleven, the week I went to Scout camp. She died five days later.

"What is this?" Collette asked, her voice soft, her eyes locking on mine. I could smell her perfume. Or whatever it was. She smelled like a vanilla milk shake.

"Nothing," I said, swallowing hard. "My mom gave it to me. It's just a circle."

She reached behind me and turned the lock on the door. Her other hand still on the silver circle.

"Collette . . ." I started, not sure what to say.

Then she rose on tiptoes and kissed me.

So. All right. This was the first thing about Southern boarding school I could recommend. Alone in my room, with a cute girl who had nice boobs and made all the moves and blew my mind with her long jump during track and called my douchebag roommate a needledick.

"Did you just shave, Evan?" she whispered.

"Yeah."

"It smells awesome."

There was probably ten more minutes of chapel. But I didn't want her to go. She was wrapped around me, my hands on her ass over her skirt, her boobs smushed against my chest and her hair everywhere in a big awesome mess. I thought about the box of condoms stashed in a duffel bag in my closet. The only other redhead I'd ever been with was the Cupcake Lady

5

of Tacoma, which sort of thrilled me and freaked me out at the same time. I wondered if I could even get Collette's clothes off in time.

But then she stepped back. Straightened her skirt and hair, pulled up one knee sock, checked her watch. "Chapel ends in four minutes. I'll come by tomorrow."

"Here?"

"Has to be here," she said, kissing my lower lip one last time. "Mrs. Herst patrols Fountaineau during chapel, but Mr. Feining always gets coffee in the canteen. And if you tell anyone about this, you will never fucking see me again. I mean it."

Then she whooshed out, and I stood there trying to get my dick to calm the fuck down.

***

I was lucky Collette had a sense of time, because a few minutes after I'd gotten my wood to deflate and put on my shirt and tie, Patrick Ramsey came back to the room. I wasn't particular about friends, as I've attended six schools nationwide since age thirteen, but Patrick Ramsey wasn't anyone I'd pick to hang out with. Patrick Ramsey—he told me everyone called him The Rammer—was a huge, muscular guy, with a face like a spiral-cut ham. He was from Georgia, where his parents owned a bunch of factories, and he played football in the fall and wrestled in the winter and took off sports in spring, because that was when he dedicated himself to "finding some ass to nail."

But as I transferred to Remington Chase at the end of January, I didn't have much choice where roommates were concerned. My father's job took him between Charlotte and London, so boarding school was his magnificent solution to his absence. Not that Adrian Carter had ever been really present in any sense since my mom died. My father has a Ph.D. in applied mathematics, but his specialty is computer science. What this meant out in the world was that he either taught college classes or pimped out his skills to companies (or both). What this meant to me was that he hardly spoke or did anything that didn't involve his laptop.

Patrick was now looking at me strangely, and I panicked that he knew what had happened with his ex-girlfriend. But he just smacked on a ton of aftershave and told me to clear out.

"You're sexiled, Carter," he said. "Jenna's coming over. I made it happen during chapel. You really underestimate chapel, dude. It's where The Rammer gets all his ass."

I hated the word "dude" as a rule, and I wouldn't have believed anyone would ever talk about themselves in the third person until I met Patrick Ramsey. Though I didn't mind being sexiled. I could barely sleep on the nights Patrick whispered to some dumb chick on his phone while he yanked it. At least when you got sexiled, you could get away from that shit, sit in the common room doing homework until your roommate finished his blue-balls session. But now I just nodded, trying not to smile. Because as far as I could tell, The Rammer knew fuckall about the value of chapel.

"And fucking cut your hair, dude!" Patrick yelled as I headed out. "Everyone thinks I'm rooming with a fag!"

In these modern times, there are three types of guys who use the word "fag." The first have been ignorantly brought up. The second never get any chicks anyway. And the third are secretly gay themselves.

If I didn't hear him coo into his phone in the middle of

the night on a regular basis, I might have put Patrick Ramsey into all three categories at once. He was from *Georgia*, for one thing. And I doubted most girls found it too appealing how he went around insisting people call him The Rammer, which, in addition to the whole "find some ass to nail" comment, wasn't exactly heterosexual, either. But girls are weird. I'm always amazed at the shit they put up with for a little attention.

***

It should be said that though nowhere as muscular as Patrick Ramsey, I am a decent-looking guy: black hair, brown eyes, almost six feet tall, skinny-but-okay build from track and swimming—when I could manage the timing of both sports with all the moving around. And this, along with the fact that human beings are fascinated with novelty, might explain why though I had my share of problems being the Fucking New Guy, getting girls was never one of them.

I'm not being conceited, though it might come off a little dickish. I realize common sense would tell you that getting chicks and being the Fucking New Guy don't necessarily go together. But the novelty thing—it goes a long way for girls. Just go into any mall, where 99 percent of the stuff is for women. Girls are endlessly fascinated with trinkets. Cell phone charms and hairbands and rings on their toes and scarves in the middle of summer and whatever the hell else. I never get over how much junk girls drag around, like those flea market people who haul all their shit around in conversion vans. Bracelets rattling on their arms and earrings up and down their ears and a million things crisscrossing over their shoulders—purses and book bags and backpacks and bra straps and tank tops and necklaces.

But it wasn't just being new and shiny that made me successful with chicks. The selection of the target also was important. For example: Farrah. Farrah was cute and interested in me, but that didn't make her a good target. It wasn't that I had high standards or anything. I just looked for Girls Who Would Say Yes.

Not Yes to giving me phone numbers or hanging out. That was a Yes I knew Farrah, with all her rings and her long blonde hair fluffing up everywhere, would happily say.

I mean, Yes to getting naked—or at least naked enough. Yes to sex. Because I didn't live anywhere for too long and didn't have time to mess around going on a million dates or whatever. I've got a profile of the Girl Who Would Say Yes, and Farrah, with her redneck ex-boyfriend and gold crucifix necklace, didn't fit it.

Really, the best you could hope for from a Farrah type is if you endured some spectacular nightmare prom scenario where you rented a limo and a tux and suffered through a million pictures with her friends and her parents and went out for dinner and danced with her and then at the end, maybe, just maybe, you'd get a handjob out of the deal. And Farrah looked like the kind of chick who'd keep all her damn rings on while she did it.

Even though I look fairly normal myself, Girls Who Would Say Yes tended to be left of normal. A left-of-normal girl doesn't care what you look like, beyond that you aren't a hunchback or covered in acne. Because for a left-of-normal girl, it's all about her, anyway. These chicks have certain, obvious quirks. Piercings, tattoos, hair dyed a color never intended by nature. Or—this sounds horrible and probably would put mothers everywhere on high alert—a really short skirt or low-cut shirt. Because left-of-normal girls aren't allergic to risk. Gothic or artistic hippie chicks were often a good bet. Though sometimes I picked wrong and got a girl too far down the dial toward crazy. Like stalking crazy. But then my dad would make us move, and it wouldn't matter anymore.

***

So the next day during chapel, when Collette Holmander came to Connison, I was waiting for her, happy that I'd barely done anything to get her in the first place. Though Collette herself was somewhat left-of-normal, actually, compared to other girls at Remington Chase. Maybe I'd just failed to recalibrate left when I crossed the Mason-Dixon.

Collette was from Boston. She swore a lot and constantly got demerits from Ms. Stahlman, the girls track coach. Plus she was a redhead, which, since The Cupcake Lady of Tacoma, I couldn't help but find attractive.

I locked the door and Collette flopped against me on my unmade bed and we made out until her shirt was off and I was so hard I was almost sick to my stomach. But before I could test the idea of where she was on the sex thing (I usually started with this basic hand motion toward the belly-button area and then just a little lower toward the edge of the panties, as if to acknowledge they were there, as Girls Who Said No were always touchy about things going in that direction), Collette just shoved her (ringless) hand down my pants and jerked me off. Then she popped up and put back on her clothes.

"Chapel ends in four minutes," she said, running out the door before I could even move.

These secret chapel make outs went on for a couple of

weeks. It was dangerous, because Patrick could have come in at any time, and I didn't want to imagine what he'd do if he found me with the one girl at Remington Chase who wasn't afraid to curse him out across the dining hall. So I couldn't talk to Collette except during chapel or at track practice, when I'd see her doing the long jump and get wood at the sight. I could barely look at her at all without getting wood, to be honest.

***

One night I went to dinner with Patrick and one of his friends, a tall blond guy who played basketball, whose name I instantly forgot except for the fact that it ended in III. (People at Remington Chase tended to have fancy names like that, even if this asshole looked about as aristocratic as the guy who changed my father's oil at the Mercedes dealership in Charlotte.) III was nice enough but sort of interchangeable, in the way all The Rammer's friends were. Bulky, athletic, sort of dim. Focused on giving each other shit and getting drunk and doing things like sitting around in someone's room and talking about all the pussy they wanted but instead of actually getting up and doing something about it, just watching crap old movies like *Apocalypse Now* or *A Clockwork Orange* over and over, rewinding the super-insane violent parts and spitting chew into soda bottles and farting, all activities to ensure no females would ever come near them. Some of these guys had girlfriends, but they seemed uninterested in crossing the regulated sex divide Remington Chase had built up around the dorms, like it was more fun to hang out with each other and call each other a fag every second, which was crazy to me, since all their male bonding was highly gay, in actuality.

Hanging around with guys like that did nothing to increase my chances of finding chicks, which annoyed me, as The Rammer made sure our room was regularly crammed with guys like that. And which was the main reason, before I started getting naked with Collette, that I liked to skip chapel.

III didn't have a lot to say, which was fine with me. I never liked talking about myself in a new place, but if people asked, I occasionally made stuff up. Nothing too crazy, like that I came from circus people. But boring stuff—I'd say I had three older sisters. Or that my father was a diplomat, my mother wrote cookbooks—that kind of shit. But that night in the cafeteria we just sat there silently eating our shitty meals (slopped-together biscuits and chicken for the entrée, unless you wanted to eat from the salad bar—another good way to get The Rammer to call you a fag).

I was moving around the biscuits in the rat-fur-colored gravy when Collette bounced by to ask for the relay handout for track—which she hadn't gotten because she was late again. I told her it was in my backpack downstairs in the common room.

Patrick tore himself away from his tray long enough to notice Collette. Between mouthfuls of chicken and biscuits, he said something like "Quit slobbering all over my roommate with your nasty-ass firecrotch."

Instead of recoiling in horror like most dainty girls at Remington Chase would have, Collette snapped, "Why don't you take some more steroids, you goddamn needledick!" Then in a nicer voice: "I'll be in the common room downstairs, Evan."

After dinner, I went to meet Collette, trailed by Patrick and III. Patrick hung back in the hallway, dicking around with his phone, but III stood at my shoulder, his arms crossed over his tie. Collette offered up some Lemonheads from a box, and I shook my head, though III grabbed the box and toppled it into his hand.

"Jesus, have some," Collette snatched the box back. "So, Evan. Farrah says she's sorry she can't come watch our meet," Collette said, a little too sweetly. "Her parents are coming down to visit."

"Collette, tell Farrah to stop that shit." III was suddenly all crabby. Then, as Collette rolled her eyes at him, III turned to me and said, "Come on, man, we're leaving."

I didn't say anything as we headed back to Connison. Patrick was lagging behind us talking on his phone still, probably to a girl, because he kept saying all these wishy-washy, breathy things: *Yeah . . . I don't know . . . Probably . . . That's funny.* Though for all I knew, he was talking to his mother. Of course, I didn't know how to talk to one's mother on the phone, not having one anymore.

Beside me, III breathed out a big sigh. "You're new here, and you seem like a good guy. But I would avoid anything with those bitches. Collette's always doing some dumb shit for Farrah. The whole thing last year with Patrick"—I noted III didn't call him The Rammer, either—"and now she's all up into everyone's business. And he's still pissed that she dumped him. But—*really*—stay away from Farrah. Because she's been screwing with Tate Kerrigan since Christmas break, and he's not sane when it comes to her."

"I barely know Farrah," I said.

He considered this while Patrick murmured on the phone a few yards behind us.

"Girls make a big fucking deal about stupid shit," III continued. "But so does Tate, when it comes to that blonde bitch. He's been with her, on and off, since seventh grade. Even if he fucks someone else, he doesn't want her with anyone else. And he knows she's got some stupid crush on you, even if she's just doing it to make him jealous. But it's working, trust me. Tate's my roommate, and he's been a complete asshole lately. So don't fuck with this. Really."

* * *

So I didn't fuck with it. Really. I avoided Farrah even more. But I didn't stop with Collette, and the next two chapels she let me take off more and more of her clothes. Her skin was pure white and covered in freckles. During Friday chapel, the day before our first track meet, I pulled off her skirt and was kissing her belly and she was sighing in this soft, happy way.

"Why are you doing this?" I asked.

"Because I like to."

"It sucks that it has to be secret," I said.

"That's because last year Patrick told everyone what we did together in bed," she said.

"You think I'm some douchebag who goes around telling people everything?" I asked. "I'm not that kind of guy, Collette."

This was marginally true—I wasn't *that* kind of guy. But not because I was honorable. I just never had any friends to tell in the first place. I didn't mention this to Collette, however.

"You have no idea how shitty that was, Evan," she said. "And while, no, I don't think you're a douchebag, I'm not giving anyone any more opportunities. Because now I'm the firecrotch of Remington Chase. Everyone thinks I'm so bad."

"I think you're pretty good, actually," I said. I pushed down her panties a little.

"You're alone in that," she said, breathing heavily. "Everyone else just thinks I'm a slut."

"Why are you a slut but Patrick's not?" I asked. "Or me?"

"I don't know," she said. "But if you keep doing that"—she pointed to my mouth right above her panties—"I'm going to lose my mind."

So I pulled her panties off all the way and she lost her mind. Me too.

***

Our first track meet was in Charlotte, and it went late. I sat in the back of the bus with Collette and a couple of other people. I'd won the 3000 and placed third in the 1500, so I was feeling exhausted but good. In the dark, Collette's fingers brushed mine. I looked at her and knew exactly what she was thinking. Or what I hoped she was thinking. Who can ever tell what girls are really thinking?

We walked from the field house with our gear, and the others left us to go to the freshman and sophomore dorms. Then, when it was just me and Collette and I was considering how I might get her naked, my father called. Collette leaned against the brick wall of the library courtyard while I had the same conversation with Adrian Carter we'd had since he left me at this godforsaken school.

"Everything going okay, Evan?"

"Yeah. How about you?"

"Things are not going well here," he said. He launched into

a technical explanation that I didn't care about and could barely comprehend. My father's very smart. But not smart enough to figure out when someone doesn't give a shit about what he's saying.

"Sorry to hear that, Dad," I answered, when I couldn't stand it any longer.

"You need anything?" *Anything = money.*

"No, I'm good."

"Grades okay?" *I hope you're not flunking anything.*

"Yeah, they're fine." Though I was flunking almost everything but chemistry.

"Well, good. Call me if you need anything. Good night."

"Good night, Dad."

I would never call him. It's not that my father's a dick, necessarily. He's just a little distant. Silent. I mean, growing up he seemed normal enough. But then my mother died and he got stuck raising me by myself and that turned him into whatever he was now. Not a dick. But not much of a dad, either.

"Walk with you to Fountaineau," I said.

"You can't come in, though," Collette said, her hand grabbing mine.

"Herst patrolling?"

"She's gone this weekend. But that just means there'll be a ton of people hanging around."

"Feining's never around Connison."

"Feining's new and probably banking on girls not being as slutty as I am," Collette said. "And at this school full of Jesus-freak virgins, he's probably right."

"You're not slutty," I said.

"You're sweet, Evan," she said. "But in the minority, I think."

I stopped and looked at her, barelegged in her shorts with her track hoodie zipped to her neck, and I pressed her against the brick of the library building and kissed her. Not violently or anything. But because she seemed a little sad and because she turned me on and because once we got to Fountaineau, we'd have an audience of girls.

"You can't do it with me here, Evan," she said, after a while, pushing me away and zipping up her hoodie. I had kind of gotten sloppy with my hands everywhere, because even post-race sweaty, she was still crazy-hot to me. I hoped she wasn't pissed about me getting so pervy, because the library courtyard was pretty public and well lit. But she was smiling, shaking out her hair.

"Sorry," I said. "Where can I do it with you, then?"

"Your room," she said. "This Monday during chapel. From 9:28 to 10:13."

I stopped. Because though we'd done a lot of various naked activities, we'd never done *it*.

She kept on walking toward Fountaineau. "Buy some condoms," she said over her shoulder.

I stumbled to catch up. "I have condoms."

"You're so dirty."

"You mean slutty," I said.

She laughed. "I've got to go," she said. "I'm going to catch shit if anyone sees me with you."

I kissed her again, but a minute later she pushed me off.

"Monday," she said, pressing a finger to my lips. "Focus on Monday."

***

When I came back to my room, Patrick and III—I really should have learned his name—were drinking beer. III was watching some crap on Patrick's laptop, and Patrick was dismantling the smoke alarm. I didn't even ask. I set my shit down and went to shower.

The Connison showers were sort of notorious. Not in a prison way, though I'm sure that kind of crazy hazing shit had happened. But while all the other dorms had separate shower stalls, Connison just had a big room full of showerheads and no privacy. Maybe the powers that be assumed that by junior year you could handle being naked around your classmates. Probably not even that much thought had gone into it. The shower room had a door separating it from the urinals and sinks, so at least you didn't have to bare it all while some dumbass was taking a piss.

At ten at night, no one was in the shower, so at least I could relax. Not relax enough to yank it, which was thing #476 that sucked about boarding school: no yanking it in the shower, like I was used to.

After about ten minutes, I shut off the shower, dumped all my stuff into my shave kit and wrapped my towel around myself. I hoped that by the time I'd finished brushing my teeth, Patrick and III would have passed out or gone somewhere else.

But when I opened the door, I nearly slipped on my ass. Because right there by the rows of sinks was Tate Kerrigan, smiling. Next to him was Patrick Ramsey, his ham face all sweaty. Not smiling.

"Carter," Tate said. His stupid hair was all gelled and crunchy. "Why you gotta fuck around with what doesn't belong to you?"

"Uh . . . ?"

"This is for firecrotch," Patrick said, reaching forward and grabbing my head, his hands in my hair, slamming my face against the shower door and then Tate kicked me in the stomach and I fell on the orange industrial tile and spit up a blob of blood and the last things I remembered were Patrick Ramsey calling me a fucking fag and Tate Kerrigan laughing when my nose broke open under his fist.

CHAPTER TWO

I thought I heard Collette crying. People were over me, putting things on my body, moving quickly, touching me everywhere. Everything hurt. Far away Collette was saying *No, no, no, no, please,* her voice so sad in a way I'd never heard it. Desperate and begging. I didn't know if I was dreaming or awake.

***

When I woke up I felt like I was padded in cotton, like a layer of air separated me from the world. My father appeared. Nurses appeared. A police officer appeared. It was easier to shut my eyes, because it took too much energy to open them and I couldn't see that well.

Soon I became accustomed to my father looking down at me, his usually shaved head sprouting golden blond fringe, like he'd been unable to shave it down as had been his practice since his twenties, when he'd started balding. And I became accustomed to two nurses. A woman with a daisy-chain tattoo on her wrist who smelled like caramel. And a male nurse with hair as red as Collette's. Every time he came in, my eyes filled with tears. He probably thought I hated him. Maybe that's why they brought in the shrink a few days later. But I wouldn't talk to the shrink or anyone else. There were stitches on my tongue, and it hurt to talk. It hurt to do anything with my mouth—even eat Jell-O. Once the male nurse brought me tater tots—maybe he was trying to be nice because I love tater tots—but they hurt my mouth, and I threw them up, which hurt worse.

The police officer came back; I could hear him arguing with my father.

"Just do what you have to and let us alone," my father said. "We'll come back for court. But we're moving out of state when he gets out of the hospital. Whatever that girl's family does is their business."

I tried to sit up, to ask if Collette was okay, but my chest ached, and that was when I realized that it was covered in a huge plane of a bandage. That I'd had surgery. My father said they'd removed my spleen. A little while later, the daisy-chain tattoo nurse came in to get me out of bed for a walk. I got up and walked with her, because I didn't want to be accused of being weak, but I hated it. It was embarrassing having a tiny lady who was at least a foot shorter than I was lift me out of bed. But I could barely lift my head and my chest burned. That was the incision, and also, the nurse said, broken ribs.

The daisy-chain tattoo nurse made me walk the ugly, beige hospital hallway, every day, wearing these horrible socks with sticky dots on the bottoms. A little farther each time. To the waiting lounge. To the nurse's station. To the drinking fountain. The drinking fountain day I didn't want to get up at all because I was so tired and my chest hurt—and I had won the 3000 just a week earlier. The drinking fountain day, I itched my nose and the plastic ID band on my wrist ripped open the cuts in the corner of my mouth and blood poured out all over my hospital gown, but the daisy-chain tattoo nurse didn't notice right away until I was crying. Crying like a fucking baby and then she said, "Oh, honey," and that made me cry more until she got me back to my room and re-bandaged my face.

It felt like I would spend the rest of my life in the hospital. That I would never go home. I didn't know where we lived, anyway. I had never been to the place, because my father rented it after moving me into the dorm. I thought about what I'd left behind at Remington Chase. My backpack and some books and clothes. My track bag. I thought of the circle necklace my mother gave me when I was eleven. I sat up then, and my chest hurt.

"Where is my necklace," I croaked out to my father. He tried to take my hand, but the right one was covered in a bunch of smaller bandages, the left was wrapped up in an Ace bandage. He said, "Shh. They took it off during surgery. I have it in my pocket. Shhh, Evan. Shh."

I didn't fucking *shh* until he pulled the necklace from his pocket. Then I laid back and closed my eyes.

The last day in the hospital, I took a shower sitting on a stool because I was so wiped out from walking up and down the hallway plus the actual process of undressing that I couldn't stand up. I locked the bathroom door, though the nurse told me not to, but there was no way I would have taken off the gown if just anyone could walk in. I had to be careful with my incision. It was about ten inches long and stapled together. The first time I saw it in the bathroom mirror I threw up in the sink.

When your spleen is ruptured, it has to be removed. That was what the surgeon told me. A ruptured spleen will hemorrhage, and you will die of internal blood loss. It is better to have a spleen, of course. But if it is ruptured, say, while you are assaulted in a gang shower while wearing nothing but a towel and flip-flops, then living without this organ is the way to go. The doctor showed me a picture of a human spleen in a book that he said I could keep. It was large and purple and seemed too big and important to be dismissed so quickly.

The spleen protects the immune system, is the body's defensive army, the doctor explained. But it's not very combat ready, I wanted to tell him, if a few punches from two pissed-off guys could demolish it. Later, flipping through the book from the surgeon, I learned that in ancient times, the spleen was thought to be the source of melancholy, that the bile it produced was believed to cause depression.

This was funny to me in a fucked-up way. Because by Aristotle's definition, without my spleen, I should now be happier than shit. Which might have made me laugh, but when I laughed my entire chest hurt; when I smiled the cuts on the corners of my mouth split open.

***

Home was a condominium in Charlotte. My father loved to live in condos, because he didn't have to mow or fix stuff or do anything but interface with his laptop. The Charlotte condo was like all the others: boring and beige. A couch. A kitchen table. A giant television that only I watched. In the kitchen there was nothing but takeout menus and clusters of power strips for all my dad's computer gear. My dad said one of the bedrooms was mine, but I camped out on the couch in front of the television instead. Spent my days napping. Taking pain meds. Noting the different shades of beige and tan and taupe in the condo. Imagining inventive suicide methods. Going to follow-up appointments at the clinic. Avoiding the shower and reeking like hell, until one day my father told me we were moving. And so, with my dad's Mercedes dragging a U-Haul trailer behind us, we left Charlotte and drove to Minnesota, where my father had grown up. I had been there when I was little but could barely remember it.

The whole drive, my father talked. I knew that before I would have given anything if he'd just open his goddamn mouth and say something interesting that was not about Unix, Linux, the Conficker virus, algorithms, or Google's market cap. But now the whole trip he wouldn't stop jabbering about himself, and I couldn't stand that, either. He talked about Pearl Lake, where he had spent his summers growing up. About Marchant Falls, the town nearby, where his family lived the rest of the year. About the Kiwanis Camp and swimming until dark and their dog Rusty who chased cars and got hit by a bus. About his older brother, Soren, who had made his own canoe out of a tree at age twelve.

"Pearl Lake was Soren's church," my father said. "He loved it there. He hunted and set animal traps. He could stick his fishing pole in a goddamn puddle and catch something. He never came back from fishing without a full string. He camped and canoed and fished and swam—all of it. Lived like a savage all summer long."

I nodded. I didn't know much about my family. Or my Uncle Soren. I had supposedly met him once, at my mother's funeral, which was also in Minnesota because that's where her family wanted her ashes spread. I don't remember Soren much; except after the funeral, he climbed up into a tree with me and we talked about bugs. I was into bugs when I was eleven. After that, Soren left Minnesota, my dad said. He'd been in the military, but they didn't talk. Soren traveled a lot, and no one had heard from him in years. He didn't even come to his own mother's funeral, my grandma, a lady I remember very little except that she made me cry once so I didn't like her.

My father had to talk loud, and with the radio off, because I couldn't hear in my left ear anymore. The doctors didn't know if my hearing would come back or if it was permanent. Also, it hurt my incision to sit up for long periods of time. Though the staples were removed, I still felt them, like phantoms. And the rest of me was similarly broken: the healing raw bit on my left ear where the cartilage was torn, my left hand sprained, my right hand covered in scabbed cuts that itched. Defensive wounds, the doctor called them. Though it seemed that I had put up very little defense.

We arrived in Pearl Lake, Minnesota, on the first of April. I hadn't slept well the whole trip. My father stopped at decent motels, but they all felt creepy to me because either the bathroom tile was that same industrial orange of the Connison gang shower or the doors didn't have locks, so I continued my shower boycott and just wiped myself down with a washcloth. But still I reeked, which bugged my dad, who was the kind of guy who had his shirts dry-cleaned and cleaned out his fingernails with a Swiss Army knife while sitting in traffic.

My father drove down a long gravel drive, checking the rearview often to make sure the trailer was holding up okay. He parked and we got out.

"Here it is, son," he said. "The ancestral family lake home. In all its glory."

There was no glory, but it wasn't an anonymous condo. It was an old A-frame with cedar shakes and a big blue door. It looked like the kind of place that would have little plaques that said Gone Fishin' on the walls. Cutesy shit that never was a part of any place we lived in because a) we were guys b) we didn't live anywhere long enough to decorate. There was a front deck and a balcony on the second floor, enclosing a little window. The lawn was muddy and scrubby, and an old tire swing swayed from a yellow nylon rope hanging from a fat birch tree. The lake in front was choppy and gray. On a short dock, a green fishing boat banged along with the waves.

"That boat ours?" I asked.

"I had a guy pull it out of storage and clean it up for us," he said. "We'll go out on the lake once we get settled."

"How come I've never been here?" I asked. "If this is the family cabin?"

"Melina didn't like coming here," he said.

My father didn't say my mother's name often. It was odd to hear it now. He started unpacking the car. I helped a little, but he waved me off.

"Go inside," he said. "Get comfortable. We're here all summer."

That long? I almost said. But I was too tired to even be a smart-ass.

I took the room on the second floor, because the main floor bedroom didn't face the morning sun and my father needed complete darkness when he slept. I didn't mind, though my father worried about how I would get to the bathroom, which was on the first floor. I told him I could piss out the balcony window and then he laughed and so did I. Which was a little strange, because he didn't laugh very much and never with me.

I liked the second-floor room. It was huge and the bed was beside the window and I could crawl out on the tiny balcony and look at the lake. When it was windy, I didn't stay out there long, but it was getting warmer each day, and the sun woke me up every morning.

The rest of the cabin was small but clean. There was a big front room with a fireplace and brand-new furniture, which was all black. As if my father couldn't decide on a color. (Which was probably true. He basically wore the same thing all the time—white shirt and khaki pants. He didn't like thinking about inconsequential decisions, he always said.) The walls were knotty pine paneling, and there was nothing on them. There were built-in bookshelves full of yellowed paperbacks and jigsaw puzzles, which my father said he planned to throw out. There was a wooden pipe rack, with a brown glass canister in the center for the tobacco ringed with a dozen different pipes. I asked him if he'd throw that out too, but he said no, because it had been hand carved by his brother. Which was cool—privately I thought they'd make good weed pipes.

***

Every day my father and I went out on the lake. I got good at driving the boat and liked the feel and sound of moving on the water, and I liked my dad smiling at me when I remembered to do something he had taught me. He showed me how to start the motor, how to add gas to it, how to steer and stop and uncrank the anchor and dock properly. We never stopped to fish, though he kept saying we would. We went all over the lake, looking at the crappy little trailers and the deluxe mansions. He pointed out a restaurant that he said was a good place for steak, noted the biggest house on the lake, a towering thing that looked like it should have a moat and drawbridge around it.

"That used to belong to Melina's parents," he said. "Up until a few years ago, actually." I nodded. Talking about my mother wasn't high on my list, either.

One day we approached a huge island that was ringed with boulders and surrounded with No Trespassing and Wildlife Sanctuary signs from the Department of Natural Resources. We had skirted around it before but never approached it close.

"That's Story Island," he said. "People like to fish around it, but you can't go on it, because it's a protected habitat for loons. Which are the state bird of Minnesota, by the way. When we were kids, it was a big dare to go out there. People said there was a haunted house on it. All the kids talked about going out there a lot. But the only one who ever did it was Soren."

Story Island, covered with trees and brush, looked completely wild and intimidating, fringed with dead reeds and cattails and boulders covered in a slippery-looking green scum. I'd done a little rock climbing in Tacoma, hiked around Mount Rainier a bit, but those boulders looked like a nightmare to scale. My Uncle Soren must have been a real badass kid to heave it up Story Island all by himself.

"So was there a house?" I asked.

"Soren said there was, but no one went with him, so no one believed him," he said. "But my brother wasn't a liar. He said we shouldn't bother with it, though, because climbing up those rocks wasn't easy and if we made it, we'd probably fall into quicksand and die. And that we'd just kill off all the loons if we messed around in their habitat. Obviously, he was kidding about the quicksand, but when you're young you believe what your older brother says, you know."

Like I'd know.

"Soren had a thing about the loons," my father continued. "He beat up this kid Tyson Murphy once, who was two grades older, just for saying he was going out to Story Island with his BB gun to practice on the loons. Took Tyson's BB gun too. Soren was very territorial about Pearl Lake—he loved it and knew everything about it, which I always thought was odd. But we never agreed on much, so I suppose the feeling was mutual."

There was something in his voice that made me worry he might cry. So I didn't say anything, and a few minutes later we motored off.

***

One Friday afternoon, my father came into my room where I was reading and said, "You've got an appointment in town." Marchant Falls was what he meant by "town," and it was about twenty miles south of Pearl Lake. It was small and dumpy and reminded me of Havford, the little shitty town near Remington Chase where kids would sneak off to buy cigarettes and alcohol. Everything about Marchant Falls was piddly and subpar. The grocery store was called Cub Foods and the high school mascot was a beaver and the sidewalks were covered in trash from the receding dirty snow. We passed the high school, where kids hung around the front doors, playing Frisbee and Hacky Sack. I pretended not to see them. I didn't want my father to think about enrolling me back in school.

He pulled up to a yellow house with a white door on a residential street.

"What is this?" I asked.

"Your appointment's in five minutes," he said.

"But this is somebody's house."

"It's an office."

I had thought I was going to the clinic, like always. I had some damn checkup every week, it seemed. Hearing and blood work and my sprained wrist and other stuff you need checked when you suddenly have no spleen. So I looked awful. Deranged. I barely had any hair. Unable to shake the memory of Patrick Ramsey grabbing my hair, I kept it cut super short, which wasn't hard as they'd shaved it off in the hospital to stitch up parts of my scalp. But with short hair, my ears stuck up, all pointy, like an elf, totally noticeable because of the big strip of scab on the left one. And I reeked too. The shower in the cabin was so tiny I could barely stand up straight in it and tended to have spiders crawling everywhere. Most importantly, the bathroom had a flimsy door with no lock. So I'd only washed my entire body a couple of times since coming to Minnesota, and that was in the freezing cold lake, at night and not for long, either, since the temperature made my nuts jump up my neck.

My father knocked on the door, which had a row of brass bells lining the upper part of it. They jingled when the door opened, and a short red-haired woman appeared.

"You must be Adrian Carter." She shook my father's hand. "I'm Dr. Janice Penny."

My father introduced me, and the red-haired woman shook my hand. Her hand was white and cool to the touch, like a seashell. I've never understood people whose handshakes are cool like that. I'm always a sweating ball of nerves.

We went inside, and I looked around, trying not to seem as freaked as I was. The room was outfitted in white wicker furniture and paintings of flowers and smelled like dried roses. Dr. Penny handed my father some forms and told him to take a seat in one of the wicker chairs, which creaked when my father sat down.

"Evan, please come into my office," she said.

I looked at my dad, but he was busy with the forms. I wanted to kill him. He hadn't told me I was seeing a shrink, and I knew why. Because I wouldn't have come.

Dr. Penny sat in a white wooden chair and invited me to sit too. There were two options: a little pink sofa with poofy pillows and a rocking chair. The pink sofa was so . . . *pink*. Plus it was closer to her. I sat in the rocking chair, trying not to make it squeak and failing.

"It's nice to meet you, Evan," Dr. Penny said. "How are you feeling today?"

"Fine."

"Good," she said. "I thought we'd start off by getting acquainted with one another."

"Yeah, but um, I'm not really sure I need to be here. I mean, I don't really get *why* I'm here, exactly.

"Your father is worried about you," she said. "He knows how much you're hurting."

"I'm healing up pretty good, actually," I said. "My ribs are healed, and the doctors said that . . ."

"I know physically you're doing well," she interrupted. "You're a very strong young man. An athlete, your father said. But you've undergone something very traumatic. You have fears. And with good reason. Your father wishes to help you with these matters."

"Then why doesn't *he* help me?" I asked, sounding whiny.

"Maybe he doesn't think he can," she said.

"And you think you can?" I asked. Which was dickish of me, but it just sort of came out.

"I can help you with some ways to think about your life and choices," she said. "It's really your job to get better. I'm just offering some perspective on how you look at things."

I'd never had therapy. Even when my mother died. I'd never known my father to consider such a thing. It wasn't that he didn't believe in psychological principles; he just didn't seem to think about me that way at all. About emotional things. He treated stuff like that how I'd imagine a father would treat his daughter's menstrual cycle—with caution and distance. Him talking to me about my feelings was like him buying a strange woman a box of tampons, I guess. Which I had actually done once, when we lived in San Diego. A girl I met at the mall asked me to give her some cash because she needed some tampons. Mandy was her name. She was cute and fit my left-of-normal profile. We later did mushrooms together at a movie theater, and I got so annihilated by the black-and-white tiled men's room that Mandy had to pull me out of there by the wrist.

Thinking of Mandy made me shiver. Because I had been a guy who just met girls like that. Like I'd met Collette. Though more often, I pursued them, looking for an angle to get what I wanted. It was something I was good at. At least I thought I was. I hadn't known how close to danger I'd been that whole time. Oblivious of all the history of all these places. How many Tate Kerrigans and Patrick Ramseys had I almost missed?

"Let's get started," Dr. Penny said.

Therapy with Dr. Penny was either the weirdest thing in the world or I didn't know anything about therapy. I expected her to ask me about sad things, my mother dying and all the places we'd lived and left, and how we never saw any of my relatives, because my father rarely mentioned them and my mother's side fell away from us after she died. Or I thought she'd ask whether I drank or did drugs or looked at porn. But Dr. Penny just talked about Marchant Falls and how she grew up here and how her parents had a cabin on Pearl Lake too and how she'd gone there every summer, swimming and fishing until Labor Day. How Pearl Lake was one of the oldest lakes to have settled residents. How *Marchant* was the French word for "merchant," because the town was a hub for French beaver fur traders, hence the high school mascot. How the high school had an amazing hockey team and offered AP courses. And there was a track team too, if I was interested.

I didn't say anything. I didn't want to return to school for any reason. I wanted to take the damn GED. I was done walking into new buildings and seeing how things played out as the Fucking New Guy.

But Dr. Penny didn't care that I was silent. She just kept talking. She sounded like a brochure from a travel website.

I was starting to wonder who exactly this therapy was for, when she asked me the first question.

"Have you ever written a letter to anyone, Evan?" Dr. Penny asked. "Or a long e-mail? Something that went on at length?"

"No," I said. "I used to write my mother from Scout camp. But I quit going after she died."

"Didn't you like Scout camp? Being outdoors?"

"No," I said. "I like the outdoors fine. I just didn't like going somewhere like that and . . . then, you know, how something bad could happen while I was gone."

Then I felt stupid, because my eyes filled with tears, which I didn't expect.

But Dr. Penny said, "I want you to think of someone you'd like to write a letter to. You can send it. Or not. The sending isn't the point. Just think of someone. This week, write a letter telling that person how you are now. Where you are. What you are doing."

"Do I have to bring it in?" I asked. "Like homework?"

"You can if you want," she said. "You don't have to show me. But you have to do it. Okay?"

I nodded.

"Our time is up for today," she said. "I will see you next week. Same time."

As I left Dr. Penny's office, my right hand was already in a fist. Ready to explode at my father. I felt like a giant loser for having to talk to this woman, for having to write a letter I wouldn't send, like I was in some bullshit English class. Though I'd never hit anyone before, the thought of smashing my father's face sounded pretty satisfying.

But when I got to the car, my father shocked the shit out of me.

"I know you're pissed," he said, holding up a hand. "So I'm giving you two choices. You can unload on me all you want. Scream your damn head off. Or I can just buy you a car. Right now."

He opened his wallet, and I saw a huge flap of hundreds. My father always carried around cash, but never that much. He made a lot of money, but rarely spent it and always forced me to get a job to pay for stuff I wanted. He had never offered me a car, would barely let me drive his Mercedes once I got my license.

"So," he said. "What's your decision?"

It wasn't a decision at all. I felt further tricked as I drove behind him back to Pearl Lake in my new car, a used Subaru Outback, the only four-wheel drive on the lot that I could stand, I had said, again sounding whiny. I bitched that the bumper was mashed in and the interior smelled like wet dogs. Though I actually really liked the car a lot.

My father took the scenic route back to Pearl Lake. I couldn't tell if this was his idea of letting me enjoy myself or just showing me where things were. Either way I felt mixed. I felt bought and I felt awesome and I felt like I would get a headache if I didn't do something about the goddamn rattly ski rack on the roof.

So now I had a therapist, and now I could drive myself places, in my own car. Where I would go besides Dr. Penny's office was a good question. And with who, another one.

Dear Collette,

I'm writing because another redheaded woman is currently boss-ing me around. Apparently, I have a thing for redheads. I would tell this to Dr. Penny, but she might think I was hitting on her and things are already crazy enough. Plus she's like fifty years old and wears Swedish grandma clogs. I don't think I have a thing for redheads, though I always thought you were cute. Thinking of you makes my stomach hurt, though. And not just because of the hole where they yanked out my spleen. It was all my fault, what they did to you. Makes me think of a million other things I'd like to do that aren't legal or sportsmanlike. Which I don't have the balls to do anyway. I hope you're enjoying whatever you're doing in Boston. Your new school. I'm sorry I caused this.

I live on a biologically unique lake. I've been reading all about it. The study of lakes is called limnology. "Limnos" is Greek for "lake." Pearl Lake was formed by glacial movement, as well as the result of an oxbow lake from the Beauchant River. This means one side of the lake is amazingly deep and the other is shallow. The shallow side is subject to much agricultural runoff, while the deep side is colder, ideal habitat for a large fish with teeth called a northern pike. Did you know that all lakes experience a phenomenon each spring and fall called turnover? Because of the density of water, as the temperature increases in the spring, the water from the top sinks, while the water at the bottom rises to the surface. The reverse happens in the fall. I wonder what the fish think of that shit or if they even notice, since it happens every year. If they just get used to that kind of turbulence to the point it doesn't even register anymore.

I would never send you this, Collette, because a) I doubt you'd care b) we never talked about anything, anyway. I never knew if you liked chemistry, for example. I know you thought I was good at chemistry, but it's actually not my favorite science. Beyond that you were from Boston and swore a lot, I just knew you liked track and liked me. And I liked you too, but mostly I just wanted to get naked with you, because I was miserable at Remington Chase and you were one thing I could look forward to. Because I am a dick. A slutty seventeen-year-old guy who didn't care what it cost you until it cost me something. A spleen and a left ear and a broken nose and ribs. More stuff too, but I'm too pussy to talk about it to you or anyone else.

Later, Evan

CHAPTER THREE

The Friday of Memorial Day weekend, I drove into Marchant Falls for my appointment with Dr. Penny. I passed the high school, and again, all the kids were outside. Guys playing Frisbee. Girls in short skirts lying in the grass on their backs as if they were on a beach instead of suffering through the last days of school.

I brought my letter with me, but Dr. Penny didn't ask for it. She wore a sleeveless blue dress, and her skin was creamy and freckly like Collette's. Which sort of shocked me. Would Collette look like Dr. Penny when she got old? It was hard to imagine Collette getting old.

This time Dr. Penny asked me questions. Where did I live before Charlotte? What were the names of the schools? What sports and activities did I do? What subjects did I like? Did I have a job outside of school?

I listed it all off, from the most recent: Charlotte, San Diego, Richmond, Tacoma, Washington, D.C., Oberlin, San Francisco.

I swam and ran track. My favorite subject was science. In San Diego, I worked in a mall, running a carousel in the food court, a job everyone called the Merry-Go-Round Master. In Richmond, I worked at a greenhouse. In Tacoma, I worked in a cupcake shop. In D.C., and Oberlin and San Francisco I was too young to work anywhere.

She was like a cop interrogating me, one question after another. It was a little dizzying, but I'd taken a long swim while I washed up in the lake the night before and had slept better than normal, so I kept up okay. Until she asked the next thing.

"Did you have any friends in any of those places, Evan?"

I stammered and shrugged.

"Evan?"

"I guess. But nobody really, you know. Nobody I still talk to."

"Girlfriends?" she asked. "I'm assuming something here, feel free to correct me if I'm wrong."

Like I was gay?! I thought. I looked down at my clothes. I tended to dress boring. Today I wore jeans and a grey T-shirt and flip-flops. My hair was cut close to the scalp, trimmed just this morning with my dad's shaver, any extra bits clipped away with a little scissors I kept in my shave kit. The bump on my nose where it had been broken tingled, and my elf ears burned, the wound on the left one throbbing like suddenly there was a big lighted arrow pointing at it. Even wearing a baseball cap didn't quite cover it. What about me looked gay?

"I'm not suggesting you're gay," Dr. Penny said, reading my mind. "I'm just wondering if you had any romantic attachments. It doesn't matter to which sex."

"I'm . . . I like girls," I said. I looked down, my face hot.

"Okay," she said.

"I didn't hang out much with guys," I admitted. "I had better luck . . . with girls. I mean, I knew a lot of girls. Hung out with them a lot. But not as friends, because we were usually always, you know, uh . . ."

"Physically involved?" Dr. Penny said, holding up a hand as if to make me stop. "I get it, Evan. Don't feel uncomfortable or embarrassed."

I nodded, completely uncomfortable and embarrassed, anyway.

"Do you still talk with any of those girls?"

I always deleted girls' numbers as soon as we moved. Some of them even got deleted immediately after we'd had sex. Not that some of them weren't cool girls or anything. But sometimes, I just couldn't face them again. But there was no way of saying this that didn't make me sound like a dick.

"Some of them," I lied.

Dr. Penny pressed her fingers to her mouth, like she was about to come to a conclusion, give me a lecture maybe. But she was quiet.

"I wrote that letter," I said, because I couldn't stand the silence anymore.

"How did that go?"

"Fine," I said.

"Who did you write it to?"

"A girl from my last school."

"Hmmm," she said. "How do you mean, it went fine?"

"Just . . . that it went . . . *fine*?"

"I'll be more specific, I apologize," she said. "Was it difficult to get started? Difficult to choose whom to address it to?"

"No," I said. "I wrote it pretty quickly."

"Good, good," she said, glancing above my head to the clock where she could track when the hour was up.

"I want you to write another letter this week," she said. "Same idea—you don't have to send it; you can pick to whom you write it. This time I want you to tell about the kind of person you were in just one of the places you lived. Tell the story of your time there."

I nodded, but I didn't get it. I was in therapy for getting the shit kicked out of me and my inability to shower in a human bathroom like a civilized person. And my insomnia. And probably my obsessive haircutting, but I wasn't sure that my father had noticed that, really. He probably dug it that I was almost as bald as him, actually.

"I'm interested in establishing your patterns of attachment and trust," Dr. Penny said, again somehow reading my mind. "I know it might not seem relevant, but it's something I need to understand as we go forward, in order to help you build relationships with people, Evan. Trust me on this, okay? Have a great weekend."

***

Almost to the turnoff to Pearl Lake, I heard a pop, and then the whole car started rattling even worse than usual.

I pulled over and got out to look. Flat tire. Completely stripped to the rim. Goddamnit.

I was flipping through the owner's manual from the glove box to figure out where the spare was when a giant green pickup truck pulled up behind me. Instantly I was on high alert. I unbuckled my seat belt. I locked the door. I unlocked the door.

It had looked like one guy—*just one guy, no big deal, fucking chill*—but when I looked in the rearview, whoever it was had already gotten out. So I wasn't ready. I jumped out of the car and bashed into a kid in a Minnesota Twins T-shirt.

"Whoa, easy buddy," he said, his voice that weird nasal Minnesota twang that reminded me of rednecks on helium. He was as tall as me, not as skinny, though. His hair was spiky, a blondish color, but not yellow blond. More like the color of snot in a Kleenex, the greenish tint swimmers get from too much chlorine.

"Got a flat?" he asked.

Okay. This is okay. Safe enough.

"Looks that way," I said.

"Let me give you a hand," he said. "You got the jack?"

"I just got this car last week," I said. "So . . ."

I couldn't finish my sentence. Because I was an idiot who didn't know where the jack for my own car was.

"You buy this used, by any chance?"

"Yeah."

"Thought I recognized that dented bumper. It used to belong to my neighbor on the lake. I'm Tom Tonneson."

"Evan Carter," I said. We shook hands in this very polite, wholesome way that made me think this kid did that all the time. At least Tom Tonneson was an easy name to remember.

"You and your dad are a couple doors down, right? Next to Brenda and Baker? That empty A-frame?"

I nodded. I was a little embarrassed that anyone knew us or knew what we were doing.

"My uncle used to look after the place," he said. "He's the one who tuned up the boat for you and cleaned the inside and

42

everything." Tom asked me to flip up the hatchback, where he pulled the jack and the spare from under the carpet mat on the floor. He had the car jacked up in less than five minutes.

"Thought I saw this car the other day," Tom said from the ground, the tire iron clanking. "Thought maybe they were back for the summer, but then I remembered Brenda sold it, and it was kind of early for Baker and her to be back. Me and my dad, we always fish from Mother's Day until October."

I didn't say anything. My head was jumbling with names. I had never gone fishing with my dad. I never did anything with my dad. Besides pack up U-hauls and move, of course. And never anything on Mother's Day, obviously.

"You've got a bum wing, man," Tom said, when I asked if he needed help. "Don't worry about it. What happened?"

"Skateboarding accident," I said.

I thought he'd ask me for details, which would have been hilarious, as I've never stepped on a skateboard in my life. But Tom just asked me to hand him the tire iron again. A few minutes later, the tire was changed and I stood there feeling stupid but grateful.

"You heading back to the lake?"

"Yeah," I said. "Thanks for the help."

"No sweat," he said. "Come on over for the bonfire tonight. Bonfire's the Tonneson Memorial Day tradition. Baker and Brenda have their barbecue tomorrow. But my mom's all about the Friday bonfire. She's kind of a freak, but what can you do? Tell your dad too."

"Okay."

"I've got some whiskey we can drink if it gets boring."

"All right," I said, knowing full well I'd never attend.

I didn't mention the Tonneson bonfire to my father, but somehow he knew about it. Seemed excited to go, even. He showered and tucked in a clean white shirt and put a bottle of wine under his arm, asked me if I was ready to go, which was weirder than hell. We never did anything social together; I couldn't imagine standing beside him, his bald nerd self; and me, the cancer patient/accident victim, shaking everyone's hands, both of us pretending to be normal. I told him I needed to shower, that I'd head over later.

At the word "shower" he looked a little surprised, a little hopeful. "There's lots of kids your age around here."

"Yeah," I said. He nodded, like he wanted to say more but couldn't access the proper vocabulary, and I started making myself a bowl of cereal so I wouldn't have to look at him until I heard the front door shut.

I ate three bowls of cereal and then made a fire and sat on the couch reading a book I had found on the living room shelf. It was old, and the pages were full of diagrams and figures. It was a history of Pearl Lake called *Under the Waves* written by a very dry-witted individual named E. Church Westmore in 1974. From this book I had learned about turbidity and turnover and the difference between the hyperliminion, hypolimnion, and thermocline. It didn't seem like it would be terribly interesting, but frequently old E. Church would hit on a turn of phrase that cracked me up. And the book helped me fall asleep too, which was good, because I'd slept for shit since the hospital. Before when I couldn't sleep, I'd just yank it. But now it was like a major undertaking to work myself into a sex mood. So instead, I'd read *Under the Waves* and fall asleep with it on my chest. Both were pathetic: masturbating or reading a book about the cycle of fish spawn and the habits of muskrats but whatever. It was better than lying awake thinking shitty thoughts.

I was reading about the biological aspects of the sublittoral zone when someone banged on the door. Which scared the piss out of me. Nobody ever knocked on our doors. Nobody ever came to our house besides food delivery people or the FedEx man. I shot up, put on my flip-flops, and looked at myself in the mirror above the fireplace. Elf ears, bump on the nose, that fucking cut in the corner of my mouth, baldish head. One good thing about cutting my hair every day was that it never got messy, but I still looked horrible. Plus, there was a grease stain on my T-shirt and my jeans needed washing. But the banging kept on, so I ran to answer the door.

It was Tom Tonneson—with two cute girls. Not how I expected him to roll. I mean, Tom wasn't ugly or anything, but he gave off a pretty strong Totally Regular Guy vibe. Which I didn't have a problem with, really. The last thing I wanted was some douchebag like Patrick Ramsey for a neighbor.

"What's been taking you so long, man?" Tom stepped inside. "Bonfire's been going on for an hour. Your dad sent us over to get you."

"What?"

"And he told us we could hang out inside too, because you have a fire going and I'm freezing cold," said one of the girls, who was wearing a miniskirt.

"It's like fifty degrees; don't be such a baby," said the other girl, who barged in after Tom. "Tom, did you bring the Coke?"

"No, I've got the whiskey," he said, sitting on the sofa. "Didn't Kelly bring that two-liter?"

"I wish you'd got Cherry Lick instead of whiskey," the girl Kelly said. "Cherry Lick is way better with Coke."

I stared at her. She had weirdly dark hair, like she'd dyed it black. She was pretty, but the hair made her look like she'd escaped from a burning building.

They fanned out in the living room, and Kelly Burnt Hair asked me if I had any Coke in the fridge, so I got the Coke and some glasses. Tom did all the introductions. Burnt Hair was his girlfriend, Kelly Some-Last-Name-Starting-With-K. Kelly K. knelt in front of the coffee table mixing everyone drinks. The other girl, with long brown hair, was Baker Trieste, my neighbor next door. Before I could even compute how weird a name that was for a girl—for anyone, actually—Tom explained that I had bought Baker's mother's car.

The girl named Baker laughed. "You bought her Subaru? Does it still smell like wet dogs?"

"Yeah," I said and smiled and the cut on the corner of my mouth twinged. I kept forgetting it was there, swiping it with my toothbrush, and ripping it back open.

"We've never even owned a dog," Baker said. "We bought it used too, and it came that way. Nothing could get the smell out. So, you're the night swimmer boy," she added. "Saw you the other night in the water."

"You've been swimming already?" Kelly K. asked. I took a big gulp of whiskey Coke. I didn't want to explain how I bathed in the lake. Luckily, Kelly K. interrupted before I had to respond.

"What's with your hair?" Kelly K. asked. "Do you have cancer or something?"

"Kelly!" Baker yelled. Tom looked down into his whiskey Coke all embarrassed.

"It's just short." My elf ears were burning.

"No offense about your hair," Kelly K. said. "My mom owns a salon, so I can't help it—I'm always thinking about hair. Sue me," she added to Baker, who was still looking outraged. "So, here's the thing, Evan. You moving here? It's sort of a weird sign."

"Kelly!" Baker said. "Are you completely rude or what?"

"No, God, you're not listening!" Kelly smacked her long-nailed hand on the coffee table. "I meant, it's *weird* because this cabin? Has been unoccupied for so *long*. And this year? Suddenly, there's something where there used to be *nothing*."

"Very observant," Tom said, and Kelly K. punched his arm in that harmless way that girls are allowed to hit guys but never the reverse.

"Let me finish!" Kelly K. griped. "What I mean is that we have to explain to Evan what goes on around here. So he understands what's normal and what's not. The difference between Marchant Falls life and Pearl Lake life. And the difference between all the sides of the lake, how things are here on the east side. How's he supposed to know what's expected of him?"

I gulped more of my drink. I was a little horrified to know a) I had zero privacy and b) there were expectations from total strangers.

"Kelly, you're completely fucking this up," Baker said.

I was surprised, then, because Baker Trieste did not look like a girl who would swear. It gave me a thrill, actually. Reminded me of Collette.

"Kelly's in it to win it tonight with the whiskey," Tom said and got girl punched again.

"I think what Kelly means is that here on our side of the lake, we do things a certain way," Baker said. "We're not like the north siders with their billion-dollar second homes and lame-ass jet skis, or the loadie west siders, living in ice houses and trailers and beating their kids."

This sounded intriguing. And not just because it seemed strangely hot how Baker said "a certain way." Like this was some cult or sex club and I was about to get initiated. Not that I wanted initiation in anything. Just that I was being instantly included as if I were normal. But I just nodded and kept quiet. Kept drinking.

Baker set down her drink, crossed her legs. She wore a skirt too, but wasn't acting all freezing cold like Kelly K. (Why do girls always freak out about being cold? It drives me nuts.) Baker's legs were smooth, with good muscles. I tried not to stare, but Baker was cute. Long brown hair, lots of freckles, blue eyes, a red North Face jacket. Apart from saying the f-word, she looked very regular. Like the kind of girl who was on student council and who would apply for early admission to college. I bet she had nice, neat handwriting. That her car had an air freshener hanging from the rearview and that she went out for sports. And that she was a virgin. She had that bossy, rule-obsessed way about her that so many virgin girls affect.

"Memorial Day weekend is when summer starts on Pearl Lake," Baker said. "Tom's family has the bonfire Friday, and my mom and I have the barbecue Saturday. Keir's coming this year too, when he can get a break from the sheep."

The sheep? I thought.

"And Saturday night, the kids all have a party. Which hasn't been busted in over twenty-five years."

"As far as you know," Tom said.

"I researched it," Baker said. "The last time was like 1986. And that was just because a kid drowned and the cops would have come out anyway. This year it's at Jim's, which is a few cabins down from Tom's. I'll give you the directions if you're interested."

"But you have to keep your mouth shut about it," Kelly K. said.

"He doesn't seem to have a problem with keeping his mouth shut so far," Baker murmured into her whiskey Coke.

"Are you guys drunk enough yet?" Kelly asked. "This is *sooo* not what I call being in it to win it."

"You just want to go behind the compost bin and feel up Tom in the dark," Baker said, draining her drink.

"Like you wouldn't be with Jim right now if you could!" Kelly yelled.

"Where's Jim, anyway?"

A banging knock on the door interrupted Tom's question. Baker opened the door, and two more guys and a very skinny blonde girl came in. The guys were huge, Tate and Patrick huge. The girl one of those basic blonde skinny types who everyone decides is gorgeous for some unknown reason. I nearly dropped my drink, and my chest immediately tightened in a panic.

"They told us everyone's hanging out here," said Guy #1, who was as tall as me, but with way better muscles. He wore a Marchant Falls Football T-shirt and a backwards baseball cap and had pierced ears that looked very red and uncomfortable, like he'd just had them done. He also reeked of body spray. Eau de Douchenozzle. I couldn't stand him on sight.

Kelly K. handed Guy #1 a whiskey Coke, and he asked, "This isn't Cherry Lick, is it? That shit's nasty," as she rolled her eyes and shook her head. Guy #1 parked it by Baker on the couch, while Guy #2—who was ten times #1's size, wearing the same football T-shirt and looking like he'd been breastfed steroids and corn on the cob—pulled up a kitchen chair that I worried might smash into toothpicks under his hulking frame.

Baker introduced everyone. Guy #1 rubbing her knee was Jim. Guy #2, the giant Midwestern Viking, was Taber. The skinny blonde girl also had a weird-for-a-girl name, which I instantly forgot. Kelly K. set everyone up with drinks, and they all seemed so relaxed, boozing it up in some stranger's living room. I sat down again. Then, because it was so fucking weird, I couldn't help but ask.

"So, does no one care if you drink underage here in Minnesota?"

Baker laughed, and Kelly K. got all technical: "You're dad told us we should make ourselves at home!"

Tom explained that all the adults on the east side of the lake spent most of the summer in various states of drunkenness themselves, and so as long as the kids weren't blatant about it, they looked the other way.

"No going on the boat or driving or nothing," he added. "Plus . . ."

Again, Tom was interrupted by a knock at the door. I was getting pretty anxious about this constant intrusion but Skinny Blond jumped up and got it, and two more people joined the Whiskey Coke Convention: an impossibly tan redhead and a skinny guy with super-stoned eyes. More names that I instantly forgot. Stoner Guy started rolling a joint on the coffee table, which seemed promising to me, at least, but Impossibly Tan Redhead looked grouchy about it. She also refused Kelly's offer of a drink.

"The east side is pretty loose," Baker said. "But this summer is different. It's our last one. We all graduate next week."

"Jesse doesn't," Impossibly Tan Redhead said. "He's only a junior."

"Thanks," said Stoner Guy, licking his joint.

"You want help smoking that?" Jim asked. He smiled with amazingly, blindingly white teeth.

"Can we smoke here?" Stoner Guy asked me. Which I thought was considerate, seeing as the rest of them had basically bulldozed into my evening without permission.

"My room's upstairs," I said.

"Cool," Jim and his Teeth said, and then he and Stoner Guy, Giant Sasquatch Guy, and Skinny Blond all went upstairs. I flashed to the notebook where I wrote all my imaginary Collette letters but remembered I'd left it under the bed, next to the condoms and thing of wank lotion I never used anymore. All my shameful crap, luckily hidden.

"So Minnesota football players smoke weed," I said, taking another drink and setting out my glass for Kelly K. to refresh. If I was going to be flattened by all these house guests, they might as well be useful.

"Not normally," Tom said.

"Baker's decided this is the summer of Last Chances," Kelly K. said in a bored, disapproving voice.

"Kelly, god!" Baker shook her head that Kelly couldn't get shit right. Baker turned to me. "See, Jim and Taber? They're very good at football. They're both going to Wisconsin to play on scholarships, and they've worked super hard for it. So this summer they're going to do everything they haven't gotten to do. All the stuff normal teenagers get to do. So we're all making it a thing. Everyone's got to come up with their Last Chance activity."

I nodded.

"I need to figure out mine," Impossibly Tan Redhead said, and Baker nodded in approval.

"But it's not smoking pot with my boyfriend," she added, in a voice that indicated she equated smoking pot with drinking raw sewage. "Something I've never done before."

"But we've done everything there is to do in this stupid town," Kelly K. whined.

"You and Tom haven't," Baker said, all sly, and Tom's face flared up bright red.

"That's personal," Kelly K. huffed.

"What's personal?" Jim the Gridiron Pothead asked, coming down the stairs. The Viking Sasquatch and Skinny Blond trailed behind him.

"The summer of Last Chances," Baker said.

"And no rules, don't forget that," Jim said, baring his amazing white fangs at her. "No rules was your idea." He looked annoyed about that last thing.

"Jim . . ." Baker said, like she didn't want to talk about it.

"Baker's all into *non-monogramy* this summer," Jim said, looking at me for a long time. As if it was my idea. Or he expected me to get up and protest. Mostly I itched to correct him—*non-mono*GAMY, *YOU MEAN?*—but his cartoonishly white mouth freaked me out a little.

"Where's Jesse?" Tan Redhead asked.

Nobody answered her.

"Well, there's not much I haven't done," Skinny Blond said, flipping her hair. "So I just plan on doing a lot of skinny-dipping. And not alone, either."

"How is that different from any other weekend with you?" Kelly K. said, all bitchy.

Skinny Blond leaned over all sexy, like the view of her knobby collarbone was something special.

"Well, because we'd be in the water, Kelly," Skinny Blond said. "I mean, I'd explain, but it might burn your *virgin* ears."

Kelly gave Skinny Blond the finger.

"What are you going to do, Jim?" Baker asked.

"Mushrooms," Jim said. "My brother's friend knows a guy who can get us some."

"Ooh, I'll do that too!" Skinny Blond said. "I almost did them last New Year's with my cousins in Minneapolis? But there was a blizzard and it didn't work out."

"I'm way too much of a control freak to do mushrooms," Baker said. "What's your Last Chance, Tom?"

"Isn't it obvious?" Tom murmured into his drink. And got girl punched again by Kelly K.

"True enough," Baker said. "So we'll skip over Kelly too."

"I'll skinny-dip!" Kelly shouted, as if she didn't want to be a total virgin square.

"Who cares about skipping-dipping?" Tan Redhead said. "I want to try drinking something besides beer. Or whiskey. Or Cherry Lick."

What the fuck was Cherry Lick? I thought.

"Taber?" Baker asked. She sounded like a game-show hostess interviewing all the contestants.

The giant Viking Taber leaned back on his chair, his blue eyes completely blown to red.

"Maybe a loadie party on the south side," he said. "Find some loadie chick to hook up with?"

"Ewww!" all the girls said in unison.

"God, Taber, you're so high," Baker said, shaking her head like she was his mom. "Okay, Evan, that leaves you."

I studied my drink, which was almost gone.

"I don't know what a loadie chick is, but that sounds all right," I said.

The guys all laughed; the girls looked disappointed.

"Where is Jesse?" Tan Redhead asked again.

"Let's go play Frisbee," Jim said.

"I can barely move, man," Taber said.

"No, we should get up and do something," Kelly K. said.

"Like feel up Tom behind the compost bin?" Baker said, standing up and tidying the Coke cans and glasses like a waitress trying to clear out a table. Kelly K. told her to shut up, but she jumped up to help and they both went into the kitchen and started rinsing out glasses as if they lived here. Tan Redhead helped and then hollered up the stairs, "Jesse!" until Stoner Guy stumbled down, looking sleepy.

All of this was insane. That I barely knew these people, either, and they barely knew me didn't seem to matter. I was looking forward to them vacating, when Baker tugged at my arm.

"Come on, Evan," she said. "I'll show you around."

***

It wasn't really cold, but I still shivered under the hoodie I'd thrown on as I followed Baker outside for more of her relentless, one-woman welcoming committee. She pointed out her dock and Tom's dock and the joint diving platform. Pointed farther down the shore toward where the party would be at Jim's tomorrow. Pointed east, to the sandbar, and north, toward Story Island. Explained how we shared driveways with the Tonnesons so if one was blocked by snow or a downed tree, it was okay to drive through the others' lawn.

"People on the east side don't give a shit about lawns," Baker said, walking beside me. "I only mow ours because it cuts down on the bugs. Lakes aren't about lawns. Plus fertilizer makes algae blooms."

I nodded. E. Church Westmore had said as much back in 1974.

"Now, over there, by the shed behind my cabin?" she pointed. "That's the best place for digging up night crawlers. But don't abuse it, or I'll kick your ass. I'm kidding—I think fishing's completely fucking boring. And that pallet fence over there? Where Tom and Kelly will spend the night doing everything but having actual sex? That's the adults' pot patch. They act like it's just compost, but we all know. But don't bother taking from it. Tom's dad's kind of an amateur grower, and half the time it's junk. If you need weed, you can get it in Marchant Falls from any of the dishwashers at Mackinanny's. That's a restaurant. Now, Conley's house is on the snobby side of things—don't drive on *their* lawn, if you get what I mean—but Conley's my best friend, so it's cool. Then there's Kiwanis Camp, which

55

is sort of a dividing line between the old-school cabins and the new-money bullshit construction. Taber's on the other side of that . . ."

I listened to all this, nodding down at her head that came to my shoulder, knowing I'd never remember all these names. Baker smelled like the cocoa butter lotion my mother put on me when we went to the beach, and I didn't want to think about it too much, but the smell was strangely appealing. Baker's cuteness and friendliness just made me feel stupid, though. Like I'd left my ability to talk to girls with all my stuff back at Remington Chase (along with my spleen and a half-empty box of condoms).

"Okay, I'm done talking," she said. "You're not saying anything, and my friends say I'm annoying when I talk too much."

Great. Silence usually went unnoticed by chatty girls like her.

"Uh, thanks for the introduction," I stuttered.

"We're pretty accepting over here. It's the north side you need to worry about. They're houses are sickening. Though Conley's is pretty big too."

"Who's Conley again?"

"The blonde girl? Who came in with Jim and Taber?"

I nodded. "Is she Taber's girlfriend?"

"No," Baker seemed disgusted by the thought. "Conley hasn't had a boyfriend forever. Because last summer she went out with this loadie dude on the south side? Who had a grim reaper tattoo on his chest? God, he was a freak. But her parents caught her with him and made her break up with him, and she's not over it yet."

"Pearl Lake's starting to sound like *West Side Story*," I said.

"Exactly," she laughed. "Except no violence. Or singing. Unless it's the Tonneson's Midsummer Party. That's always nuts. And Jim's party might be crazy too. I'm a little nervous about that, because he's invited way too many people. I don't get why he did that."

"Because it's the summer of no rules?"

She laughed. "Come on, I'll introduce you to everyone."

It was hard to keep track of the people I met, but I tried. Baker dragged me around by the elbow of my hoodie. You could tell she liked being social and that people liked this about her too. She could talk to everyone without pause. Old people. Moms holding sleeping little kids. Men bullshitting about boats. My father was there, too, shockingly, standing by Baker's mother—*Brenda*, I told myself, *Baker and her mother Brenda*, trying to remember—and this gay-looking guy, who was supposed to be Brenda's boyfriend, but I seriously doubted he was any female's boyfriend because he was wearing purple yoga pants. Brenda Trieste looked a lot like Baker, except she wore a long hippie sundress with hiking boots. Brenda laughed with my father, who then smiled at me while he drank beer from a plastic cup.

All of this made me nervous. I'd had no idea we were moving to a place where everyone was up in our business. But my dad never gave me any information about places we moved before, beyond what to pack and how long the trip would be. I kind of wanted to get away from this, from Baker especially, but she wouldn't leave me alone.

Finally, I said I needed to piss and went into the Tonneson's cabin to do it. The Tonneson's cabin was shabby likes ours but had way more stuff on the walls and none of it the Gone Fishin' variety. The bathroom was basically a shrine to male frontal nudity, and above the saggy living room sofa was a pretty pornographic print of a naked woman spread-eagled in a chair.

"My mom's nuts," Tom said, catching me looking at the nude lady picture.

"Your dad probably doesn't mind."

"She teaches theater arts," he said, as if that explained it. "So there'll be fairy costumes and shit at our Midsummer Party in June. I'm just warning you now."

"I hate the Midsummer Party." It was Jim of the piano-key teeth, holding a bag of Chili Cheese Fritos and shoving them into his mouth by the handful. "It's so gay."

We all went to sit down in the TV room, where Taber The Giant was stretched out watching SportsCenter.

"When's the Midsummer Party?" I asked.

"June 20," Tom said, sounding tired, as if it he was the one making the fairy costumes himself.

June 20 was my birthday. I was turning eighteen. Though I would be a senior—if I bothered to set foot in a school again, that is—I was always the oldest kid in my class, as my mother had held me back from kindergarten. My mother hadn't been one of those grasping, hovering moms—I mostly remember her as a very calm woman who was always reading—but apparently she thought me too much of an idiot to handle sitting still for storytime with everyone else. But for some reason, being held back like this made me feel stupid, so I never mentioned my birthday as a rule.

"We should do the 'shrooms on Midsummer," Jim said. "That would make it less gay."

"Looking at a bunch of glitter and rainbows isn't gay

enough?" Tom asked. "You want to hallucinate on top of *that*?"

"I can't figure out what Baker's mom is doing with that gay guy," Taber said suddenly. "I mean, he teaches yoga? To goats?"

This was very funny to me, mostly because Taber talked very slowly, like he'd taken too many hits on the football field without a helmet.

"It's a sheep farm," Jim said. "Keir just teaches yoga on the side. But they sleep together," he added. "Baker says they share a bedroom."

"Maybe they just do each other's hair?" Tom said.

"No, it's some fucked-up feminist thing," Jim shook his head. "Some shit where you act as gay as Christmas and women think it's hot. At least weird professor women like Brenda think it's hot."

"What's she a professor of?" I asked.

"History or something." Jim was all pissy, like it made him mad that people did history for a career. "I think the dumb *non-monogramy* thing was Brenda's idea too."

I was kind of loving it that he mispronounced this again and might have laughed, but I had to let it ride, since he'd been smoking weed and I was lucky to string together three words in a row when I was high.

"What does that even mean?" Tom asked.

"It's like an open relationship," Jim explained. "We're to-gether, but we can see other people. She said it's that or we just break up completely. At first, I was like, 'Okay, is this a trick?'" Jim's head lolled back on the sofa, like he was exhausted by such complexity. "She thinks it'll make it easier when we leave for college, because she doesn't believe in long-distance relation-ships."

"Where's Baker going to college?" I asked.

"Out in Oregon somewhere. But I don't think she'll hook up with anyone else. She's so fucking picky about everything. Like she'll be able to find anyone who'll do everything how she wants." He didn't sound exactly smug about this but more like he recognized that his own stellar capacity struggled to keep up with her requirements.

Aside from his super-white teeth—which were somewhat gay to me, in all their upkeep—Jim was a handsome guy. Easy to see why any girl would want him. He had normal hair—not all gelled and stupid—and the muscles I would like to have but never do because the strutting-douche quotient in school weight rooms is always too high. Still, Jim looked like the kind of guy whose favorite place to eat was a sports bar. Who'd probably grow up to be the vice president of something and make more money than was reasonable and who'd marry a superhot chick but still secretly go to titty bars. I naturally leaned toward hating such a guy—would've hated him before my elf ears and chemo hair patheticness too.

"Hey, maybe all the girls will decide to go for that . . . *thing*," Tom said, not mentioning non-monogamy, as if he wasn't sure how it was truly pronounced.

Then Kelly K. dribbled into the room, looking all girl-wasted, and saying, "*Tommmmmm . . .*" in that dragging way that girls must think is appealing but I've always found to be a dick-shriveler. I stood up to head out.

"Loadie party, dude," Taber said, holding out his concrete block fist to me so I could bump it. Then, because I suddenly felt like I would die if I couldn't get in my bed, far away from everyone, I followed Tom and Kelly out, where they staggered and veered off toward the compost patch presumably for some kind of groping that didn't involve penetration. My father was now talking to the gay, yoga-sheep-farming, feminist boyfriend, looking like he was actually enjoying himself, and I shuffled home without saying good-bye to anyone. Not that I could remember their names, to start with.

***

Back home in the bathroom, feeling panicked and a little drunk, I trimmed my hair with the scissors I kept in my shave kit, snipping a bit on my left ear, which bled like hell until I wrapped it in toilet paper. I stripped out of my shitty, bonfire-smelling clothes and got in bed, eager for descriptions of beaver dams and the sound of waves from the open balcony window to knock me into the usual oblivion.

But just as E. Church was lulling me into my coma, I realized that the only person who didn't declare her Last Chance Activity was Baker. She had asked everyone else to say theirs but hadn't spoken hers. Was that because there was too much a bossy, virgin girl like her had left to experience? I thought about how weird she was. Her name, her mix of normal and deviant. Her potty mouth, her tour guide act. Her nice legs and cute face. It was a long time before I slept.

Dear Collette,

Say it's your last summer before college. Or your last summer after high school. Whatever. Going to college for me sounds like going to Mars. Anyway. What would you do, your last summer? Your Last Chance to hang out with the same people you've gone to school with this whole time? What would you do?

Except, that doesn't really work for you and me. Because you've switched schools and so have I. Maybe you have old friends in Boston? I don't know anyone. Anyway. What would you do? Your last summer as a teenager. Kinda. WHATEVER. I'm trying to come up with something myself.

Nothing sexual, for one. That's been done, and while I'd hope to have it happen again sometime before I hit the old coffin, it's not exactly on the urgent must-do list.

And I don't need to try any drugs or whatever. I mean, I like getting drunk and smoking weed here and there, but I'm not crying out to learn what crystal meth feels like or anything.

I guess I just don't want to do anything risky with my body. Not anymore. My body is so fucked up, and I feel like an old man sometimes. So cliff jumping or skydiving or driving at high speeds (my car's a fucking Subaru, which disqualifies it from coolness in all ways) all sound like terrible ideas. I don't want to get in a fight with anyone. I think I got that experience covered.

All I talk about is shit I don't want to do. I don't even know what I like.

Later, Evan

CHAPTER FOUR

My father must have drank too much at the bonfire, because it was almost noon and he was still in bed. This was his first hangover I'd ever been aware of, and it was working in my favor so far. Across the way, I could see Baker and her mom and Gay-Yoga-Sheep Guy setting up food around a picnic table.

I went to brush my teeth and have my daily staredown with the shower. Pushing back the curtain, I didn't see any spiders, just one of those ladybug things that aren't ladybugs but some kind of exotic beetle. I smelled like hell since I couldn't go in the lake last night because of the bonfire. But even reaching out to turn the water on freaked me out. So I just wiped down my pits with a washcloth, put on deodorant, trimmed down my hair a little more, and got dressed.

Then I drove as quietly as I could up the drive and then into Marchant Falls to this place called The Donut Co-op to eat breakfast and read *Under the Waves*. I rang the counter bell, and the guy who came out gave me a two-for-one on the donuts and free refills on coffee and didn't care that I sat there all afternoon reading about the life cycle of the mayfly, as presented by my boy E. Church Westmore. I was about to mark my place in the book, when I came to this passage:

> *Formally known as Two Storey Island, later shortened to Story Island, this formation has been a distinct feature of Pearl Lake since time immemorial. Purchased in 1859 by Anson F. Archardt, it was left inviolate for over fifty years until noted lumber baron Barrett A. Archardt decided to fortify the property with boulders to prevent erosion and build his family a lake house on it. Archardt intended it as a vacation home for his wife and three young children, but tragically Archardt's wife drowned not long after completion. Archardt then leased the property to Kent County, on the strict condition it be preserved in perpetuity as a sanctuary for loons.*

I drove around Marchant Falls, killing time, wondering how long a barbecue could last. I went into Cub Foods and got a bag of chips and a soda and saw they were hiring. My father paid for the car and insurance but had said gas was my responsibility, so I needed a summer job. That was one thing he always insisted on, wherever we lived—that I got some kind of part-time job. I grabbed an application from customer service and headed back home.

Once in the drive, I could see the empty picnic table at Baker's cabin. Evidence of a barbecue but no people. I went into our cabin, flopped on the sofa and drank my soda and ate my chips. I thought about Story Island. The sanctuary for loons, the abandoned house, the motherless children. Barrett Archardt and his drowned wife. I thought of him holding her in their old-time clothing and her saying, "Oh, Barrett" all breathy, which was ridiculous, because what chick could get all worked up over anyone named "Barrett"?

The house was quiet and the sun was starting to go down and I realized that I would have nothing to do except wait until it was time to get in bed. That and the motherless children and the poor bastard named Barrett abandoning his house because he lost his wife and everything else gave me this feeling I thought of as being Almost-Weepy. Which had been happening to me since I was eleven when my mom died. Almost-Weepy was where you felt bad enough but just a little too dry to actually weep. Though Almost-Weepy was probably better than being Actual-Weepy.

There was a knock on the door. More of a banging, actually, and I jumped up. Was this another thing about life on the east side—people demanding shit of me at all hours?

It was Baker Trieste. She looked frantic and apologetic and her hair was all over her shoulders and I could see through her thin white shirt that she wore a striped bikini top as her bra and I felt thankful for that, because I hadn't noticed how nice her rack was the night before, which gave me something else to think about besides being Almost-Weepy. She was also holding a red gas can, which said she actually needed something real, not just to be social endlessly or something.

"Evan," she said. "I'm so glad you're home. I need to ask you a huge favor."

My father chose this moment to wander out of his bedroom then, looking like he'd slept in his Dockers and T-shirt.

"Oh, hello," he said to Baker, running his hand over his bald head, as if to freshen up. "I'm afraid I missed your barbecue. Did Evan here go?"

"No, actually, he didn't," she said, tipping her head and looking a little peeved at me.

"Sorry," I said.

"I'm here to ask you a favor, Mr. Carter," Baker said, in this responsible, student-council-vice-president voice. "My friends ran out of gas, and they're out in the middle of the lake stranded on their pontoon. And Keir hasn't got our boat off the lift yet. I was wondering if Evan could take me out there with my gas can."

"Of course Evan would love to help you out." My father nicked the boat keys off the hook and tossed them to me, and I was so surprised I didn't catch them. Smooth. Baker bent over and picked them up.

"We'll be right back, Mr. Carter," she said. "And some of the kids are getting together a few cabins down to watch movies tonight too. Can Evan come?"

My father grinned, like Baker had just offered him a million dollars and not a big fat lie making Jim's party sound like the polar opposite of the keg-stand pukefest I'm sure it would be.

"Of course!" he said. "Of course, Evan can go!"

I wanted to kill him, but fifteen minutes later, Baker and I were in my boat, approaching Story Island, the sun setting orange all around us. The island was almost frightening now, as the sunlight intensified how dense and overgrown it was. There was no dock access and along with the cattails, there were now lily pad-like things and fresh green reeds shooting up around the boulders, complicating everything with their little clots of bugs snarling around in the fading light.

I was thinking Story Island was more of a penal colony than a vacation home getaway, when Baker explained to me that though the party was out at Jim's, Jim and Skinny Blonde Chick Conley and Titanic Taber had gone out on Taber's pontoon for some reason. Conley called Baker from the pontoon, freaking that they were out of gas.

"Conley always has to fucking pre-party," Baker said.

I hated it when people used the word "party" as a verb, but I didn't mention this to Baker, because she sounded pretty mad. Also, I was wondering what exactly a "pontoon" was. It sounded like Minnesota slang for "vagina."

"They're around here somewhere," Baker said. "Conley said they were near Story Island."

We slowed and circled the island until we saw them, and I realized that "pontoon" didn't refer to girl bits but one of those flat-bottomed boats, a floating platform on which the youth of Pearl Lake thought it wise to "pre-party." As we neared the pontoon, I silently wished Baker would just chuck the gas can at them so I could peel off and get back to my life reading *Under the Waves* and avoiding all these fucking people, but then Taber and Conley waved at us.

"Anchor us here," Baker said. "I'll moor us to that No Trespassing sign."

That seemed like a terrible idea, but I did what she said.

My boat slid next to the pontoon, and Taber's huge blond self stood up and reached over for the gas can. I thought that would be it, but then Conley screamed, "Jim's on the island! He's out of his mind!"

We looked over, and sure enough, we could see someone sitting on the scum-covered rocks. Jim. Shirltless, wearing big Oakley sunglasses and track pants and those athletic sandals with the knobby soles that I cannot stand.

"What the fuck is he doing?" Baker asked, looking at the rings of boulders that I knew Barrett Archardt had used to bolster the shoreline of his island and protect it from erosion. But I didn't mention this trivia to her. She sounded very angry.

"I'll go get him, Baker," Taber said. "Just let me finish the gas thing."

"No, I need to talk to him," Baker said. And she jumped out and waded toward the rocks through a bunch of dead cattails.

"Tell him if he gets busted, I'm going to kill him," Conley yelled at Baker, who didn't turn around. "This was all his idea."

Baker continued grimly up the rocks. I just sat there silently watching her like a dipshit. What else was I going to do? Talk sports with Taber?

"Baker! Baby! You're here! Your hair is sparkling!" Jim shouted.

He kissed her then and babbled a bunch of other crap I couldn't hear. I considered my options. Start up the motor and leave? Jump overboard and swim home? But then I couldn't resist eavesdropping on her yelling at him. Stuff like, "You're having people over tonight?" and "Your ears are totally infected? Why the hell did you pierce them, anyway?"

Jim tried to paw her some more, but she wasn't having it. We all watched as she bitched at him to climb down and slosh through the water. Then, horrifyingly, she led him to my boat.

"Who the fuck's this dude?" Jim said. He sounded all breezy and entitled, like he wasn't soaking wet and wearing track pants, and his girlfriend wasn't holding his stupid little athletic sandals for him.

"It's Evan," she said. "You met him last night!"

"Good to meet you, dude." Jim smiled. With his freaky bleached teeth, he looked like a drunk toothpaste commercial.

Baker was buckling his life jacket for him like he was an infant, when suddenly he pitched his head over the side and barfed. A big gnarly awful barf with all these terrible choking noises. Finally, he took off his sunglasses and sat up, wiping his mouth.

Baker said, "Jesus, Jim! What the hell? And what's with your eyes? You're pupils are fucking huge!"

Jim put his cheesy sunglasses back on, and then I figured it out.

Jim waved Baker away from him while Conley and Taber watched from the pontoon rail.

"I told you, it's normal, Con," Jim yelled to Conley. "I'm surprised you haven't yakked yours up yet."

"I don't want to barf!" Conley screamed. "I hate barfing!"

"Don't barf on my pontoon." Taber's huge body dwarfed Conley's skinny one in concern. Conley shushed him. Baker unmoored us from the sign while I pulled up the anchor, and then she yelled to Conley and Taber that we'd meet them at Jim's.

We docked, and Jim staggered toward his cabin, which was dark but humming with party noise. Baker watched him go but didn't move. I sat there for a minute, wondering what her deal was, until she said, "Just head back to your house, Evan. I'm sorry. He's just . . . I don't know. He's gone a little overboard; he's been repressed for so long."

She didn't have to tell me twice. I got us out of there, and a minute later, she was mooring the boat to my dock.

"You better keep an eye on him," I said as we walked down the dock. "Mushrooms make you do some weird shit."

"What?"

It had been so obvious to me that I couldn't believe she didn't know, but I guess she *was* a fairly normal girl. Drinking is one thing, but doing drugs still is a big deal for some people, especially for Virginal Student Council types.

"Well, it could be acid," I said. "But usually you puke up the 'shrooms at some point. Plus his eyes. That's what made me think of it."

She stopped. The lights were off in our cabin; had my father gone back to bed?

"Is that why he went all nuts climbing up Story Island?"

"Maybe he thought it would look cool. Natural surroundings are much easier to take sometimes."

"Conley must have done them too. I don't think Taber did, though, do you? Since he was the one driving the pontoon."

I didn't know how anyone could say the word "pontoon" without laughing, especially so serious about it like she was.

"I can't believe they did this," she said, walking toward her cabin, her legs dripping water. She was shivering now, and the sun was all the way down. "Without even telling me. My fucking boyfriend tripping while wearing track pants. *Track pants!* He looks like he's in the Russian mafia. I don't believe in wearing track pants unless you are in an actual athletic situation, just so you know. And Taber goes along with it, like a damn dog! And me, too . . . Fuck! Why the hell did I wear white?" She had tripped on a branch and stumbled. Her shirt had gotten all stained and wet.

So I could see your bikini through your shirt, I thought, being a complete dirtbag. I smiled then too, proud that I didn't own one single pair of track pants. And I had run track, even. But the cut on the corner of my mouth cracked and started bleeding and without thinking I lifted up my T-shirt to dab the blood.

"Hey, are you okay?" she asked. "Evan?"

I turned away from her, then, toward my cabin. But she rushed beside me.

"Evan? What happened?"

She tipped her head to one side, staring at the scab on my nose. My elf ears too. God. I wished I could wear a fucking ski mask in public.

"Were you in a fight or something?" she asked.

"I wiped out on my bike," I lied.

"Bicycle or motorcycle?"

"Bicycle," I said. Though I didn't own a bicycle. Couldn't remember when I'd last ridden one, either.

She didn't look like she believed me, but she said, "My mom's boyfriend makes this salve that'll help that cut. I'll give you some if you want."

I shrugged. "It'll be fine if I don't smile."

I remembered, again, clearly as if it were on a video screen in front of us, the feeling of Tate's fist when it broke my nose. That nasty crunch sound so loud in my brain that I wondered if Baker could hear it too. That same sound kept me awake at night.

"Don't be a dork," she said. "Not smiling is fucking horrible." She poked me in the shoulder, like I was being a brat. But then she smiled and I could see she didn't think I was really a dork but just sort of funny, and even though she was griping about how she looked, she was super pretty again to me. I felt kind of drunk and dumb for some reason.

"It's okay," I said.

"Why are natural surroundings easier to take when you do mushrooms?" Back to her own concerns. Good. I didn't need her asking me any more questions about all my broken parts.

I explained about my one and only mushroom trip, in San Diego with Mandy and the movie theater bathroom.

"But isn't that dangerous? An old creepy island? And the sun going down?"

"Well, there's that house out there," I said. "My uncle went in it once."

"The Archardt House?" she asked, and I wondered crazily if she'd read *Under the Waves* too. Maybe it was required reading in Marchant Falls public schools?

"It was a long time ago," I said. "Maybe it's not there anymore."

"I thought that was just an urban myth," she said. "Though I read that Barrett Archardt owned the island, before it turned into a bird sanctuary."

Then she looked kind of embarrassed. Like she'd said something dumb.

"Where did you read about it?" I asked. Maybe, like bibles in hotels, every Pearl Lake cabin came with a complimentary copy of *Under the Waves*.

"I kind of . . . oh, don't laugh," she said.

"What?"

"I work at the Kent County Historical Society," she said. "I file things and work with the curator. Last summer I did an electronic conversion of letters from the Archardts. And I read them too. I'm kind of a history nerd."

Then my father opened the front door.

"Evan? Baker? Everything okay with your friends?"

Instantly, Baker slipped from her history nerd mode back into her chirpy student council mode. "Yeah, it's all taken care of, Mr. Carter!" she said, all cheerful. "Thank you so much for letting Evan take me out there."

"You going to the party now, Evan?"

I looked at Baker, and she looked like she wanted me to come, so I just lied. Told her I would. My dad looked pleased and slipped back inside.

"I need to shower and change my shirt quick," I said.

"Me too." She laughed at how dirty she was. Desperate to get away from her, I told her I'd meet her at Jim's and then went into the house. Where my dad was putting on his shoes and smoothing his non-hair.

"I'm going over to the Tonneson's to play some poker," he said.

"Cool," I said. My father would probably kill them all in poker, since he could count cards and do all sorts of unfair calculations. I never played poker with him for this reason.

"I kind of overdid it last night, so I won't be late," he said. "But you go and enjoy yourself."

"All right."

"They seem like nice kids, don't they?"

"Yeah, they're nice," I said, kicking off my flip-flops. I took off my shirt, which was bloody and gross, and my father flinched away from me, as if seeing my scar hurt him—the exact effect I was hoping for.

"I'm gonna just hop in the shower," I said.

"Sounds good." His eyes widened, like he couldn't believe Dr. Penny had already fixed my shower aversion. Acting as natural as I could, I went into the bathroom and turned on the shower. I watched a big black spider silently struggle as it washed down the drain, and then I sat on the toilet and watched the steam billow around the shower curtain for I don't know how long. I sat there until I couldn't stand how much energy I was wasting, and when I came out, my father was gone.

***

It was way after midnight, about a week later. I waited until I heard the logoff ding from my dad's laptop and the snoring that followed, then tossed my shave kit in a towel and slipped out to our dock. The blinding porch light from Baker's cabin was off and everything was dark and quiet. Safe enough.

The June water wasn't much warmer than it had been in April and May, but it *was* warmer. I'd been doing this long enough to notice the change, however small. I stripped and jumped into the water.

I swam out and back twice to the diving platform floating between Tom's and Baker's shorelines, touching the ladder like a goal, a compulsive thing I did each time to warm myself up. Plus the laps helped wear me out. I always slept great on bath nights.

I shaved in the dark, feeling bad about the chemicals in the shave cream, as usual. Would they make frogs turn hermaphroditic? What would E. Church Westmore say if he could see me? I shaved quickly because I hated thinking about those things and, in doing so, nicked the cut on the corner of my mouth.

Again. That was almost another part of the ritual too.

Then I washed with a bar of soap, rubbing it everywhere, including over my head. My hair was so short now I didn't bother with shampoo. To rinse, I swam to the diving platform once more, then pulled myself onto the dock and wrapped my towel around me. I sat for a while with my feet dangling in the water. This was my habit, every other night. When Baker had said she'd seen me, I started doing it much later. The bugs were less thick after midnight, actually, which was confirmed by E. Church Westmore in his chapter on mosquitoes.

"Evan?"

I jumped and my shave kit almost fell into the water. I stood up, checked the towel around me.

"I didn't mean to scare you," Baker said. "What are you doing out here?"

"Uh . . ."

"Do you always take baths in the lake?"

"Uh . . ."

She stood in a bathrobe at the end of the dock, wearing big unlaced brown boots. I hadn't seen her since that night I'd skipped Jim's party, and it occurred to me, again, how cute she was.

"I'm sorry," she said, stepping closer. My entire body popped up in goose bumps, and the scar on my chest felt as obvious as the yellow line on a highway.

"What are you doing out here?" I finally managed to say.

"I couldn't sleep," she said. "Is that why you're out here?"

No, I'm out here because I was beaten nearly to death in a gang shower at a redneck boarding school in North Carolina, I thought. *And I can't face using a shower in a bathroom without a lock on the door. Maybe not even then. I'm lucky I can take a shit in there.*

But I just told her that I couldn't sleep, either. That I swam to relax.

"Cold water doesn't sound too relaxing." She folded her arms over her chest in a way that made me realize she wasn't wearing a bra.

"You would think that," I said, a little peeved at her bossy tone. "But actually, it has the opposite effect. Cold temperatures make the body shut systems down."

I sounded like a dick. And a nerd. A dickish, defensive nerd.

"So," she said. "How've you been?"

"Okay. How about you?"

"Totally crappy. I think I'm depressed again. I get this way sometimes. It's just because of graduation and everything. I'm not good with change, I guess."

This all rushed out of her like she'd been waiting for someone to ask. Girls are like that sometimes. Asking you something they just want to be asked themselves. I knew this, but I never remembered it at key moments, of course.

"Uh, I'm ... sorry?" I said.

"Jesus," she said. "You've got goose bumps everywhere. Come inside—I'll make us a fire."

"Uh ..."

Was Baker hitting on me?

"My mom's at a craft fair with Keir. Don't worry."

"Uh ..."

"That way you can put your clothes back on and warm up a little," she added.

No. Not hitting on me. Thank god.

I followed her inside, and she showed me the bathroom,

which had a lock and was not nearly as gross as ours. Probably because it was all girls and that one gay-seeming guy living here. Plus there was a huge tub and shower and girly products all over the sink counter, including the cocoa butter lotion that she smelled like. I put on my boxers and T-shirt, which wasn't my idea of being dressed, of course, but it wasn't like I had a choice. Then I sat on her sofa with my hands over my thighs so that I wouldn't flash her my junk through the slot of my boxers, and she made a quick fire, which impressed me, because I hadn't met a girl who could build a fire before. Which of course I did not say.

Then she was quiet. She slipped off her boots and curled up in the chair across from me. She looked at the fire, and I looked around the cabin. It was nicer than ours, much cleaner, except the table was full of beer cans and a half-full bottle of Cherry Lick, the drink of choice for girls, Tom had explained when I asked him one day. Cherry Lick tasted sweet at first but went down like cough medicine. Tom said he couldn't stand the stuff, but Kelly loved it.

"That scar on your stomach is really big," Baker said.

"Yeah," I said. And then, so she couldn't push for more details, I asked, "When was graduation?"

"A few days after Memorial Day. I thought it would be such a relief, but now it's like I've got nothing to do. And Jim's all about making up for lost time, and it's getting a little old, you know?"

That sounded like Jim was bugging her to have sex with him. Though I wondered then if maybe she wasn't a virgin, after all. I mean, she seemed pretty chill just sitting here with me in her bathrobe.

"What have you been doing lately?" she asked. "You're never around."

Fuck. I'd been hoping she'd just keep talking. Some girls just go on and on, not realizing you're silent.

I shrugged. I didn't know why she cared. I didn't know what I was doing here, either. Though the fire felt good. Almost too hot. Like it was going to burn off my leg hair.

"My mom told me about your mom," she said.

I must have looked panicked. Because I *was* panicked. Fucking Adrian Carter! Why did he choose to become so forthcoming NOW?

"It's okay," she said. "They probably bonded over it. My mom's a widow too. Though they were separated when my dad died."

"Oh," I said. "When did . . . *that* . . . *happen*?" I was clearly becoming one of those squeamish idiots who can't say "dead" or "died."

"When I was five," Baker said. "He was in Texas for work—he did electrical engineering—and a car hit him while he was walking through a crosswalk."

"Jesus."

"Yeah. He was in a coma for three months. Down in Texas. I had to stay with my grandparents the whole time, which was okay—this cabin is where they retired before they died. I thought it was a vacation. But then he never came home."

"I'm sorry." I sounded like a goddamn funeral director.

"It's okay," she said. "It's not like I'm in *therapy* over it."

Right. *Therapy*. Anything but *that*. Therapy was obviously drastic shit for people with elf ears and Auschwitz hair.

"What happened with your mom?" she asked.

This was the question I'd been dreading since she brought the topic up, so I said the line I'd rehearsed in my head: "When I was eleven, I went to Scout camp, and she had an accident. She was taking out the recycling behind our apartment and there was a puddle of oil someone dumped back there and she slipped and hit her head. She was in a coma too, just a couple of days, though. She was dead by the time the camp director drove me back."

Dead. God. Such an ugly word to apply to your mother. My mother was a nice lady. Nice in such a way it was hard to think of her without my throat getting all tight and the rest of me getting Almost-Weepy. She was also very pretty. I'm told I look like her, but it's kind of hard to see a boy in the face of a pretty woman. Plus, she's all serene and relaxed in her pictures, and I go around in life pretty much twitching like a goddamn hummingbird.

"That's awful," Baker said.

"Yeah."

Now I really wanted to go home. I thought, almost porno-graphically, of E. Church Westmore's mind-numbing words.

"You want to smoke a bowl?" she asked.

Jesus. I'd have never guessed she'd suggest *that* next.

"Okay," I said, never more eager to smoke weed in my life.

Baker pulled out a Hello Kitty pencil case and unloaded a baggie of shake, a blue metal pipe, and a lighter onto the coffee table. She packed the bowl competently, like it wasn't her first time, and I tried not to act like blown away while we passed it back and forth. She didn't even crack a window, and I asked if I should, to air things out.

"You think my mom's gonna say anything?"

"Is she a big pothead?" I exhaled and leaned back on the sofa. Suddenly I felt so sleepy. And good.

"Not like the Tonnesons, but she smokes from time to time. It's not like she's irresponsible about it. She just thinks I don't know."

"What about that guy she's with? That gay guy?"

"Keir's not gay! Oh my god! You sound like Jim and Taber!"

I laughed. "I don't care if he's gay, but he dresses weird, you know?"

"Keir's just way into yoga," she said. "He's a hippie. He keeps bees and raises sheep. He's a hobby farmer, you know?"

"I've never met a farmer," I admitted.

"Have you ever eaten sheep's milk cheese?"

"No."

Fast forward to Baker spreading all this food out on the table off the kitchen. Cheese and bread and salami and potato chips and Hershey's kisses and licorice and a huge jug of this weird nutritional kind of strawberry milk. And Baker and me eating it all. This wasn't just weird because it was the middle of the night and I was in my underwear. For one thing, I never indulged in munchies in front of other people. Usually if I smoked weed, I was with some pothead chick and my focus wasn't food. For another, I'd never seen a girl eat like Baker. Girls tend to act like they survive on air. You only see them eating really wholesome stuff, like apples. Or super-seductive foods they can lick, like lollipops or ice-cream cones. But they never act like pigs like guys do, eating multiple bowls of cereal or an entire pizza, at least not without barfing it up. I'd known some of those barf-it-up girls, and they were the worst. So crazy. So clingy. The first to get deleted from my phone.

Baker ate with her hands, telling me to try a bite of this or that. Talked with her mouth full. Acted as if she didn't have a strawberry milk mustache and crumbs all over her bathrobe and one-half of her boob sort of hanging out. For being so normal-looking, Baker was one weird chick. Not a girl you'd picture to go with a football guy, though she looked the part, I guess, though she wasn't blond. But maybe Jim thought she was awesome. Because even high out of my skull, I could see that she was. Pretty awesome. And not just her body.

As if thinking summoned him, Jim appeared. His hair all messy, in his boxer briefs and no shirt. Looking like an underwear ad. Though he had a little more hair than your average underwear ad.

"What the fuck are you doing?" Jim asked.

If it was possible to run straight into the lake and drown myself, I would have. I was that shit scared. But being high made me fully immobile.

Baker said, all snotty: "Evan came over to hang out, and we're eating. I couldn't sleep, and I was bored. Not *all* of us pass out first thing."

"I didn't pass out. I fell asleep watching that movie."

"*A Clockwork Orange*," Baker said, even more snotty. "Right, so enjoyable for me." She turned to me. "Did you know that, Evan? That after getting down, all girls love to cuddle in bed with their boyfriend and watch freaks in nut cups sing show tunes while beating the hell out of old men with canes? It's what we all dream about when we're little girls."

Jim looked super pissed, but Baker looked all stubborn, like she wouldn't take it back. They went back to staring at each other silently and uncomfortably, while I stared at the table feeling flooded with information in that way that sometimes happens when you're high and everything is bombarding your brain. Finally, after I managed to sort out all the data—this could have been an hour or thirty seconds, there was no telling—I came away with three things. One, Jim wasn't going to kill me. Two, Baker Trieste was clearly not a virgin. Three, what the fuck was it with jock guys and *A Clockwork Orange*?

"So, what's going on, Evan?" Jim asked. Like he hadn't just been called out for being a loser in the sack. Like we did this all the time. Had midnight snacks in our underwear with his girlfriend's tit hanging out.

"Evan here was taking a bath in the lake," Baker said. "He's like survivor man."

"Were you with Conley? Skinny-dipping?"

"No." Baker was clearly happy to be my spokeswoman.

"That's lame of Conley," Jim said, yawning, putting his arm around Baker's chair. "So pussy. Who hasn't skinny-dipped with other people?"

Me, for one. But I wasn't going to mention it, since Jim and Baker started bickering about everyone's Last Chance Summer plans and I couldn't keep all the names straight. Smoking pot makes it harder for me to talk than normal—and thinking analytically? Forget it.

They were still arguing when we moved to the living room, Jim and me to the sofa, and Baker to her chair. Jim wrapped himself in a fuzzy knit blanket, which was funny, given how huge he was, but fine with me, because he sort of hogged the sofa and I wasn't a big fan of having another guy's naked skin that close to mine.

Their argument stopped, finally, because Jim got up and

went back to the bedroom. I thought Baker would follow him, but she stared into the fire.

"What's your Last Chance thing?" I asked.

"Huh?"

"You never said what you wanted to do this summer." I tried not to stutter.

"Oh, yeah," she said. "That's because no one wants to do it with me."

"Oh."

"It's not sexual, if that's what you're thinking."

"What is it, then?"

"I want to go to Story Island," she said. "I want to go inside the Archardt House. For real."

I was quiet. A little surprised that she'd want to do that. Since it hadn't been exactly fun scraping Jim's ass off the rocks that one night and she didn't strike me as a survivor-man chick who relished getting dirty and wet. But then neither did I, and I bathed in a cold lake regularly.

"But I can't do it, anyway," she said. "It's illegal."

"So is doing mushrooms and skinny-dipping."

"Story Island is a bird sanctuary," she said. "The DNR would notice if people pulled up in a boat and started exploring."

"Well, go at night, then," I said.

She laughed and said it might be easier if she swam ashore like a Navy Seal. Then I suggested a U-boat landing at dawn and she said, no, a helicopter dropping her off with a knife in her teeth was better yet and then I was laughing in that unnatural way that happens when you're high and can't tell how long time is lasting and whether what you're laughing about is really what you're laughing about, but you don't care. The definition of Not Thinking About It.

I woke up the next morning wrapped in my own fuzzy knit blanket—Baker must have put it on me, but she was nowhere to be seen. The room was cold, the fire was dead, and the kitchen table was perfectly cleared of food and cans and the bottle of Cherry Lick. Everything had been wiped down of crumbs. I slipped out of there, then. As if the whole night had never happened.

Dear Collette,

I should write about normal things. Like how I applied for a job at a grocery store and got my first car and that kind of shit.

But I'm not normal. Lucky you, the focus of all my imaginary therapy! You get to hear about what a fucking freak I am. Of course, Dr. Penny knows about you because my dad told her everything. So the point of this letter is to clearly identify my responsibility in what happened, but not to assign blame. Dr. Penny's big on defining responsibility. I smile at her and say I get it, but I don't, really. I know that I deserved everything I got. But you didn't deserve anything that happened. So I don't know what to say about that. Or how to fix it.

Probably you've noticed, but guys are fucking dirtbags. Me included. Well, I was. Sex is completely off my mind these days but before? You have no idea. Even now, out here in middle-of-nowhere Minnesota, I still see girls and strategize who'd make a good target, how I'd get laid, etc. I don't act on it, but I never really stop seeing it. I've been avoiding people as much as I can, but out here on this lake, people are always coming over and just walking in. It's okay if it's this one guy, Tom, who's pretty cool. We go fishing, because even though fishing is boring, it's kind of nice to have something to do. But this one girl, who has a boyfriend, is always coming over to our cabin, and I've taken to telling my dad I have headaches so he'll just tell her I'm sick or whatever. But I see her, with her friends, jumping off the diving platform in the lake, and I stare like a horndog at them and feel like I'm sick in a way that I'll never recover from.

Don't think about it too much—that's Dr. Penny's catchphrase. I don't understand it. I've never heard an adult tell me to think less about things—people always want you to think MORE.

It's not like what happened was because I didn't think about anything too much. I thought a lot—about the wrong things. When I could get you alone. How far you'd let me go. So I wasn't thoughtless at all. I figured I'd get what I wanted, and then we'd move, to some new city, some new beige condo, some new school where I didn't know anyone, and it'd start all over again. I didn't think about how small Remington Chase was, how I wasn't anonymous. But I see now that it was just a matter of time. That makes it sound like destiny, what happened to you and me. It can't be, though. Destiny sounds too goopy and romantic for such a horrible thing. But it happened and there's nothing I can do about it. Is this what Dr. Penny means? Don't think about it too much? Or accepting responsibility, but not blame? I can't tell the difference between those two words. So I just nod until the hour is over. And go home and ignore people and lie in bed all night without sleeping.

This is the worst letter in the world. Fuck it.

CHAPTER FIVE

I got hired as produce stocker at Cub Foods. It was a good job because I wore jeans and an apron and it didn't matter if I took a shower because I got dirtier than hell and nobody else I worked with seemed any cleaner than me. At least I brushed my teeth, unlike the other stocker, Terry Gribbener, and didn't walk around with a flap of chew under my lip, like Layne Beauchant, who was my supervisor and who pronounced his last name in a completely un-Frenchy way. Layne was only a few years older than me but already had a kid.

"What's your kid's name, Layne?" I asked while we were restocking bananas.

"Don't put those there. Them are organic. Look at the sticker. They're different colors."

"Okay."

"His name's Harry," Layne said. "And don't even look at me, because it was my girlfriend that picked it out. She calls him Harrison, but I hate that. It's just so faggy-sounding. I call him Harry. And you do too if you ever meet him. His mother needs to get it through her head that my boy's not getting his ass beat every second he walks out for recess. *Harrison.*"

"Why didn't you pick a name you both liked?"

"'Cause I was in the county workhouse and couldn't get out in time for the birth."

"Oh," I said. And shut the hell up. I watched Layne's tattooed knuckles (*KICK* on the right, *ASS!* on the left) point out where the rest of the bananas should go, and then he sauntered to the back room to get more, his wallet on a chain making his jeans sag.

※ ※ ※

When my shift ended, I drove home. It had been raining when I'd gone into work, but now was clearing off, and the sky was a weird sick-looking bright blue with the sun beating down hard but with a long line of clouds in the distance. I was starving, tired, and sweaty, and happy to see my dad had bought a bunch of stuff to make sandwiches. My father has never looked at food as anything besides fuel, so when he did set foot in a grocery store, he just bought a ton of stuff to put on loaves of French bread. He had left everything out on the counter for me. Meat and lettuce and tomatoes and hot peppers in the jar and three different kinds of cheese. I made two sandwiches and plopped down across from him at the table.

"I'm going for a swim," I said, when I finished.

"Taking your shave kit?"

I stopped, pushed in my chair. Did he know about my fake showers and late-night baths in the lake, after all?

"No, I think I'll let it get scruffly," I said. "The ladies like that."

"The ones I meet never do," he said, but he sounded light. Maybe because he never met any ladies? Apart from the ones on Pearl Lake.

"How're things with Dr. Penny?" he asked, as I set my plate in the sink.

"Fine."

"You like her?"

"She's okay."

***

When I got to my dock, I saw Baker out on the diving platform with Jim and Conley. Baker wore her striped bikini and her legs dangled into the water and Jim was beside her, shirtless. Conley lounged on her back behind them.

I waved—what else was I going to do?—and Baker waved back. Then Jim turned and stared at me. But didn't wave. He tilted his head and said something to Baker, and I felt like a dumbass and turned away. Hating that I had to take off my shirt in front of them.

I'd come up from underwater when Baker hollered, "Evan! Come here!" Unable to figure a way out of the situation, I swam to the diving platform.

When I pulled myself up the ladder, I could smell weed. Conley offered a joint to me, but I was all wet so I shook my head and sat down. I tried not to stare, but Baker looked pretty damn good in a bikini. Her bikini was the kind with the little knots tied at the hips—the kind where all you can think about is *untying*. Or at least they used to make me think that. Now I was like a fucking frozen eunuch.

"Where've you been, Evan?" Baker asked.

"Working," I said, looking up at a fat dark cloud that had just blocked the sun. The wall of approaching clouds bothered me. I wondered how long I'd have to stay to seem normal.

"Where do you work?" Conley asked.

I told her, and she nodded from behind her sunglasses, like being a shift worker at Cub Foods was about what she'd expect from someone like me.

"Bath time comes early today?" Baker asked.

"There's a reason they tell you to wash your vegetables before you eat them. And that reason is me and Layne Beauchant and Terry Gribbener."

Both Conley and Baker laughed, but Jim said, "Terry Gribbener? You work with that fucking loadie?"

"How do you know him?" Baker asked Jim.

"He used to go out with my sister," Jim said.

"What happened there?" Conley asked, passing Jim the joint.

"What do you think happened?" Jim asked, after he exhaled a bunch of smoke. "*She* went to college; *he's* working at Cub Foods."

My chest got all tight. I couldn't help but be offended. Not that I hoped to make a career at Cub Foods myself, but the fact that Jim could be that obvious of a prick flared through me. But then Baker chucked me a towel and told me to dry off my hands so I could smoke with them. I watched her light the joint, her boobs all awesome under the triangles of her bikini, and hoped this was the same pot from the night I'd first smoked with her. The kind that made me sleepy and lazy and would erase this for-no-reason panic feeling I was getting every time I looked at the sky.

I took a big hit off the joint and handed it to Conley, who passed it to Jim, who put it out and tucked it in the Hello Kitty pencil case that was sitting on a little inflatable thing, which they must have used to transport the towel and everything else.

"Taber's parents are out of town 'cause his grandma died," Jim said. "I told him we should get a keg."

"I don't think Taber's up for a party right now," Conley said.

"Taber's kind of a little bitch about stuff sometimes," Jim said, his hand running down Baker's bare back.

"God, Jim!" Baker said. "His grandmother just died! He might not want a house full of drunk people right now."

"It was just his *grandmother*," Jim said. "She was, like, ninety-nine years old. He's acting all sensitive, like it was his *mother* or something."

Baker glanced at me, all nervous. For a second, I regretted our dead parents talk. Most people didn't know shit about me, and moments like these were the exact reason they didn't.

"If you can't be sensitive about death, what *can* you be sensitive about?" Conley said, like some philosopher wearing sunglasses.

Jim stared at Conley, then Baker, looking completely hacked off.

"I don't know what it is with you girls lately," Jim said, sounding like a little bitch himself. "Conley's either talking about her ugly swimsuit or you're all mopey about school being over. There's fuckall I can say without you two jumping down my throat."

"You think my bikini's ugly?" Conley shouted, sitting up.

"No, god," Jim shouted back. "I couldn't give a shit!"

"Jim, come on . . ." Baker started.

"Evan, you heard him!" Conley shouted. "I mean, who *says* that to someone?"

I looked away from everyone, away from the wall of approaching clouds and the shouting. This right here was reason #674 that most of the time I Didn't Say Anything.

"How'd you get that scar, dude?" Jim asked.

"Bike accident," Baker said for me.

"Bullshit," Jim said. "That looks like you got in a fucking knife fight, dude."

Christ, I hated the way Jim said "dude."

I shrugged, and said, "Yeah, so what if it was?"

"You told me it was a bike accident," Baker said.

I shrugged. "I didn't want you guys making a big deal about my cancer."

"You have *cancer*?" Conley asked.

"The tumor was the size of a grapefruit," I said. Christ. Whatever weed this was, it was working.

"He's just making shit up, Conley," Baker said, catching on.

"My dad's an oncologist," Conley said. "Seriously, what kind of cancer was it?"

"I didn't have cancer," I said.

Baker kicked water at me. "Evan, god, just tell us what it was! You make it sound so mysterious. It's probably something totally basic."

Jim, shaking his head like he thought I was mental, started to roll another joint.

"I don't want anymore," Baker sighed, looking down at her toenails.

"Conley?" Jim asked, gesturing with the rolling papers.

"Sure," she said. "Why not?"

"Cancer Boy?"

There was that same flare in my chest again. Why'd this football-playing shitheel get a girl like Baker—who was smart as hell and had an awesome rack and gave him a pass to be with other chicks on top of it? In no universe was this fair or sensible. But given the fact that I was terrible at thinking of good insults to say on the spot, and the weed was good, I just nodded. I'd passed the joint to Conley when Baker suddenly stood up, adjusted her bikini sort of roughly, and dove into the water, splashing Jim, and swimming back to shore without another word.

Dear Collette,

Since Dr. Penny doesn't bother explaining to me the finer points of psychology and just has me do this stupid letter-writing thing, which makes me feel like a stalker and also miss you, if it's possible to miss you, since we didn't even know each other that well, and the thing I miss the most about you was watching you do the long jump. And also your boobs. That second thing I would never say to you—or anyone else—in a letter or in person. But this won't get sent, so what the hell, right?

Therefore, today's bullshit topic: What have I learned from someone else lately?

What I have learned from someone else lately is that you have to remember your anniversary with your girlfriend or else your life is miserable. I learned this from a guy named Tom, who I would call a friend, since we hang out a lot, but a couple of the times were accidental, so maybe we're just acquaintances. I don't know the rules.

So, the anniversary part. This is the date from which a couple has been together from some significant start point. This start point depends on the girl. Like, she could decide it was the first time you talked. Or the first time you kissed. Or the first time you hung out or went on a date. Which Tom doesn't have a clear memory of, or he'd have remembered, I suppose.

(For us, would it have been the first time you talked to me? But that was about Farrah. Which, by the way, I always wonder why they didn't take anything out on Farrah? Wasn't it all about Farrah and

Tate, in the first place? Or was it about you and Patrick? Or would it have been that first time when we skipped chapel? Maybe we don't rate an anniversary, because we were a secret. Not that big of a secret, obviously, since someone must have seen us in the courtyard and told Patrick and Tate. Sorry I even brought this up.)

Anyway. So Tom is hiding out in my room, and his girlfriend Kelly actually comes over to my house. I don't answer the door, since Tom doesn't want me to, because he says I'm a bad liar, which maybe is a good thing to have someone notice about you? Again, I don't know anything about anything. I need a goddamn life handbook or something. Tom explains how Kelly gave him this scrapbook of pictures and he's done nothing. Not even one of those awful roses from the gas station. Don't feel bad that I never gave you anything, by the way. I've never bought a girl anything. I'm kind of a dick on paper, as you might have picked up. Which might be why Dr. Penny makes me write this shit.

I wish I could say that there was a good resolution to this story, except there wasn't. Tom hung around my house and watched baseball on TV and bitched about Kelly a lot, which is probably not the best thing to do for your anniversary. He left pretty late and told me he'd come by in the morning to go fishing. I hate fishing, but I've been going with him, because though he is a crappy boyfriend, Tom is all right. So that's what I learned.

More later, Evan

CHAPTER SIX

On the day of the Tonneson's Midsummer Party, Tom and I went fishing to escape the preparations and to avoid Kelly, who was still pissed that he'd forgotten their "anniversary." Tom showed me the scrapbook Kelly gave him, which I had trouble even holding, because it reeked like perfume, was full of pictures of them kissing, and was the pinkest thing I'd ever touched in my life. Not having a mother doesn't expose you to many items in shades of pastels. Plus I wondered who the hell they made take all those pictures of them while they were kissing.

Midsummer was also my eighteenth birthday. My dad never did much for my birthday besides take me out to eat and give me some cash, so I was used to not making a big deal about it. But while we'd been at Cub Foods buying stuff for Mrs. Tonneson, I'd kind of let it slip that it was my birthday to Tom, which I regretted, since the Midsummer Party looked like it was going to be excruciating enough with all the glitter and costuming and, unlike Baker's barbecue, I had no way of avoiding it. Tom and I had been hanging out regularly due to his fight with Kelly over the anniversary, and there was no way I could duck out without him noticing. Which made me feel a little uncomfortable at first, because I wasn't used to being actual friends with anyone.

"I wish I was eighteen," Tom said, after we had been sitting in his boat for a while. "I'd take you to the dirty bookstore down on Shawton Street. But my birthday's not for two weeks."

Tom was grouchy, which wasn't normal. He was usually pretty content in general, and fishing made him happier still. He didn't mind that I never brought my own reel, that I just sat there reading E. Church Westmore's book and eating all Tom's sunflower seeds while he listened to baseball games on his little radio. We were such a portrait of boyish goodness out on his boat fishing that I felt like we were in a TV movie on one of those wholesome family channels that shows reruns of *Little House on the Prairie*.

"You've lived all over the place, right, Evan?" Tom asked. "Met a lot of chicks?"

"I guess," I said.

"You ever go out with an Everything-But Girl?"

"A what?" I asked.

"See, Kelly's got this pact with her big sister. A virginity pact. Their mother got knocked up at like age sixteen or something. Had her sister and then Kelly real quick and never married the dad. I don't even know if they have the same dad, actually. Anyway, then her mom found Jesus and that changed everything and now the older sister goes to some religious college in Missouri and has convinced Kelly that she can't have sex until she's married. They made this pact; they even have matching necklaces for it."

"Necklaces? For not having sex? Seriously?"

He nodded and spit a bunch of sunflower seed shells over the side of the boat.

"Hey, man. Kelly's great. But that's sounds awful."

"That's where the Everything But comes in. Because . . . there's technicalities. So, maybe she won't have regular sex. But that doesn't stop her from blow jobs."

"You're kidding."

"Nope," he said. "But it's like a trap. Like the free buffet at a casino. Everything's open season, except that one key area."

"So . . . Jesus doesn't mind blow jobs?"

"I guess not." Tom grinned a little, despite himself.

"What does Jesus think about oral on her? And . . . ?"

"He seems cool with all the rest of that too," he said, his face getting red.

"I take back what I said before. That doesn't sound too bad."

"No, it's worse. All I can think about is that one damn thing I'm not allowed to do. It's ridiculous."

It *was* ridiculous. Tom, with his baseball pennants and his pickup truck and his sunflower seeds, engaging in acts that were sexual crimes in some states. But I also wondered why he couldn't write Kelly a dumb poem or buy her something that would make her feel better about the anniversary. I know I'd have done it for the remote possibility of a blow job. At least Dirtbag Evan would have. Who knew what the hell I'd do now. Probably nothing. Probably hide in my bedroom and read about the mating habits of loons.

"Can't you make her a CD?" I suggested. "Bring her flowers?"

"She hates all the music I like, and flowers aren't *personal* enough," he said. "I mean, unless I sent with them a long-ass letter about how great she was. And I can't write for shit. Especially not *letters*. Who writes letters anymore?"

I put a big handful of seeds in my mouth and started chewing through them.

"You're in luck, man," I said. "This is truly your lucky day."

***

Later that night, I was playing Frisbee with Tom and Stoner Guy (actual name, Jesse) when Kelly came over, all lovey acting. Tom had given her the letter I had written (recopied in his handwriting, of course, with a few roses from the gas station too), and she was holding it all and crying and acting so goopy that Tom hustled her away as if she was contagious. But then Jesse took me behind the compost bin and we smoked a joint together. He had lost his pipe and apologized for the joint, but I didn't care. I told him about the pipes in my cabin, and we made plans to smoke the rest of his bag out of those another time.

"How old are you, Evan?"

"Eighteen," I said. Hoping he didn't know about my birthday.

"Damn," he said. "I'm the only junior here. You going this fall to Marchant Falls?"

"No," I said, not wanting to tell him that I was technically a junior too but planning to get a GED or homeschool myself online or anything else possible besides walking into some new hellhole again. "We're just here for the summer."

"Are my eyes red?" Jesse asked. "My girlfriend gets pissed when I smoke."

"No, you're okay," I said, not wanting to get too close to him. Though Jesse seemed pretty harmless, I wasn't used to this friend thing yet.

We walked back to the party, which I had been avoiding with the Frisbee, as there was actual dancing on the deck, which was decorated insanely with all this gauzy stuff and Christmas lights and little hanging lanterns. Plus my father was swinging around Brenda and Mrs. Tonneson and a bunch of other middle-aged ladies in a way that made me want to die. Everyone seemed pretty wasted and way too happy for adults, but this was fairly normal for the east side of Pearl Lake. Everyone out here seemed to drink and play cards and board games almost every night, and my father was one of the group as if he'd done it his whole life.

A bunch of kids were gathered around the fire pit, and Jesse and I sat down with them. Baker was there, with Improbably Tan Redhead, and Tom and Kelly were smashed together on a lounge chair, Kelly still oozing all over Tom. Baker poured Jesse and me some fairy punch from a pitcher, which she had spiked with rum. Kelly whined again for Cherry Lick—she didn't like rum. I gulped a bunch, though—it was actually pretty good—because between Tom and Kelly and Jesse getting all touchy with the Tan Redhead, I didn't know where to look.

"You're not wearing your crowns!" Tan Redhead said. "Jesse!"

"What did I tell you about that?" Baker scolded. Tan Redhead produced two boy-fairy crowns for us, which we put on obediently, as Baker had said earlier that people who acted too cool for costumes and theme parties were lame and lacked self-confidence.

"Where's Conley?" Kelly asked.

"She went to Jim's," Tom said.

"But he's in town tonight with Taber," Baker said. "Jim hates the Midsummer Party."

"How can you hate Midsummer?" Kelly screeched. "It's so beautiful!"

I was feeling pretty sloshy right then, which was good, what with all these people and rules about crowns. Baker kept refilling my fairy punch cup, though, and I just slouched lower in my lawn chair until I didn't have a clear view of my father twirling around Brenda Trieste, who was wearing this weird dress that looked made out of glitter-soaked rags. I looked at Jesse, who was adjusting his fairy crown like it itched and then Tan Redhead kissed him, and Baker said, "Jesus, enough with the public displays of affection!"

"It's Midsummer! What do you expect!" Kelly hollered.

"You know how I feel about that," Baker said, settling beside me in her lawn chair. She looked a little drunk herself, but nowhere near as drunk as I felt. And unlike me, Baker looked good. I wore a shitty T-shirt and shorts, with the same hoodie I always put on when it got cold and buggy at night, while Baker, dusted with the glitter she'd been decorating with all day, wore this tight shirt that was covered in stars and a little denim skirt that made me wonder how she could sit down without her ass falling through the straps of the lawn chair. Her legs were very long and tan, and I wished she wasn't sitting by me. And that she didn't have a boyfriend. It made me want to inch my chair away from her, how good she smelled and how cute she was and how her hair tickled my elbow in the breeze.

The conversation turned to Jesse and Tan Redhead. Baker was lecturing them because Tan Redhead had asked out Jesse, who was younger, and Baker wasn't having it because she said guys should do the asking out, not girls. Jesse sat there silent and looking thankful to be stoned.

"Wait," I said. "Why does he have to ask again? What's the problem with her doing it?"

"If you're a girl, you shouldn't have to chase people," Baker said. "Women have enough problems in life, without having to add that to their burdens. Men benefit from the whole patriarchal construct. They get paid a dollar to my seventy cents. So they can nut up and do the asking out."

"Jesse's so shy," Tan Redhead said. "He wouldn't ever approach me. Because I'm *older*."

"It shouldn't matter," Baker said, holding up the fairy punch pitcher to Tan Redhead, who shook her head, saying she had to work in the morning.

I wanted to argue with Baker, but I was too high to form a sentence. Then she got up and went into the Tonneson's cabin, kind of huffy, like we were all ignorant sexist pricks or whatever.

"She's just pissed about Jim," Kelly said. "He's such a dick about Midsummer."

"She should dump his ass," Tan Redhead bitched.

"Why?" Jesse said.

"Well, why not?" Tan Redhead said. "When people are assholes, you don't reward them by being their girlfriend."

"Maybe she likes him," Jesse continued. "He *is* the quarterback."

"You're just saying that because he's Jim Sweet," Tan

Redhead further bitched to Jesse. "And he's the quarterback and you're a year younger and think he's *god.*"

"I don't think he's *god,*" Jesse corrected. "I just recognize that Jim Sweet outweighs me in every possible sense. Weight, muscle mass, coolness, sports records, number of chicks he's done it with . . ." Everyone laughed and Jesse continued. "The fact that he doesn't drive his dead grandmother's Buick . . ."

Tan Redhead yelled something about saving money for a better car instead of spending it all on weed, finishing with, "If you did that, then you'd be as cool as Jim Sweet."

"Wait," I said, finally able to be coherent. "His name is Jim Sweet? JIM SWEET? *Really?* That's his whole name? Someone named a baby *Jim Fucking Sweet?*"

Jesse and I started laughing and the cut on my mouth ripped open again, and Tan Redhead freaked out, but I just wiped the blood on my shorts and kept laughing. Kelly rolled her eyes at us like she was disgusted by our immaturity and Tom smiled, but he wasn't stoned, so I knew he didn't get it. But I didn't care, because I was laughing and Jesse was laughing and I was having fun even though my father was slow dancing with Mrs. Tonneson. I could hear loons crying in the distance, and it was beautiful.

***

I was all cotton-mouthed and had to piss, so I went into the Tonneson's cabin to gulp some water and nod at the adults who were drinking wine in the kitchen while eating cupcakes. But the Tonneson's bathroom was occupied, so I went out toward the compost bin/pot patch and unzipped to piss. Which turned out to be a terrible choice, because I could hear people whispering—it was faint, given my left ear was still fucked—a girl's voice saying, *Someone's coming, would you stop it, already?* Which made me freeze. Had I just walked in on Everything But featuring Tom and Kelly?

Then Jim Sweet—JIM SWEET!—emerged from the other side of the pallet fence, pushing past me in the dark. I zipped quickly but then—surprise! Next came Conley, the strap of her tank top fallen over, her blonde hair a mess. Her eyes went wide when she saw me, and she staggered back.

"It's not what you think," she snapped.

So I turned and ran out of there, faster than I had in weeks, back to my dock, where I proceeded to hock up a bunch of spit and bleed some more from my mouth and laugh and cry and who the fuck knows what else. Then I collapsed against the wood dock and watched the sky spin full of stars.

Happy Birthday to Me.

Dear Collette,

Have you ever stayed up all night at a party? I'd never done that until my eighteenth birthday.

This year, after Jesse and Tom tossed me into the lake and we all went swimming out to the diving platform, Baker gave me a towel and Kelly taught me this card game called Presidents and Assholes, which I couldn't figure out, so I kept losing and drinking more. Then Baker made me do shots with her, which involved me barfing off the Tonneson's dock while she patted my back and hollered, "Time to rally, Evan!" After Kelly and Tom slipped off to do Everything But* behind the compost bin, Tan Redhead drove us into town at three in the morning, and we ate pancakes at Denny's. Probably the best pancakes I've ever eaten. Baker smoked a joint with Jesse and me after that by the Dumpster behind Denny's. Then we almost got busted when one of the Denny's line cooks came out for a smoke break, but luckily it was none other than Layne Beauchant, my supervisor from Cub Foods. Baker freaked and clutched my arm until I shook hands with Layne and he laughed and took a hit off Jesse's joint and said he was surprised that I "partied" because I didn't seem like the type. He asked me what the hell we had on our heads and then Jesse couldn't stop laughing, because we were wearing Midsummer fairy crowns, though some of the tin foil was peeling off. I couldn't begin to explain, so I asked him how many damn jobs he had, and Layne said that having a kid wasn't cheap. On the way home Baker and I sat in the backseat, *smushed together a little, which made me nervous, but she was talking loudly about how you should never go out with people that have the same hair color because it's obviously a genetic thing and on and on, a whole layer of arguments and rules that outraged Tan Redhead and that I couldn't follow because pot makes me stupider, not smarter. Plus I have black hair and Baker's is brown, the same color as her insanely named cheating boyfriend Jim Sweet, so her policy was void when it came to us. (There is no "us," of course, because she is normal and I'm a lunatic. Anyway.)*

Matched sets are a bad idea, Baker said. Tan Redhead said that was bullshit; should she break up with Jesse if they were both redheads? And that Tom and Kelly were both blond, but Kelly dyed her hair, so what about that? To which Baker started talking about innate traits and evolution and, finally, I just interrupted her by saying, "You have an assload of rules, you know that?" Which made everyone laugh and then Baker pulled away from where her leg was touching mine and got all snobby and said I barely knew her. I apologized and said I was super baked. Then Jesse put the radio on some Mexican station, which played a bunch of music with flutes and guitars that was pretty relaxing, and by the time we got back to Pearl Lake, the sun was coming up and I was feeling good. Still a little high, but not sloshy like before. And then we sat on Baker's dock and she got us coffee and when she gave me a cup, I felt like she had forgiven me for saying the rule thing and the four of us watched the sun rise and it was fucking beautiful.

I slept until three in the afternoon the next day. Then woke up and wrote this.

Later, Evan

*Everything But Have Sex. Which means no penis/vagina intercourse but all other options are okay. There are girls who do this. It's apparently a religious thing. I can't decide if it's genius or evil. Tom thinks it's evil, for the record.

CHAPTER SEVEN

Probably you shouldn't make promises when you're drunk. Or plan things, either. Because that's how Baker and I ended up on Story Island a week later.

Tom had overheard us talking about it at Midsummer, how Baker wanted to go there because summer was wasting away, but she didn't want to go alone, because what if she fell in a hole and died or something. Though my drunk ass told her I'd come with her, I pointed out that it wasn't exactly stealthy to moor a boat to a No Trespassing sign by a protected bird habitat. But Tom reasoned that he could drop us off, go fishing, come back in a few hours, and no one would know. It was a fairly big island, after all.

So, after wading through the weedy water, helping each other up the boulders, pushing aside slippery scum and extending hands to each other until we reached the top, we were on Story Island. I wore shorts and an unstained T-shirt and running shoes and had loaded my backpack with food, water, and bug spray (and *Under the Waves*, because what if we got stuck there? That book was like my security blanket). Baker was beside me, her hair in two ponytails down her shoulders, with her own backpack full of who-knows-what, in a pair of very short shorts and tall rubber boots and her bikini top under a Marchant Falls Track T-shirt, which was a little see-through, but I was too distracted to check because of the fuckloads of bugs and the overgrown, mushy ground that made me wonder if Soren's claim about quicksand wasn't bullshit. E. Church Westmore hadn't said anything about quicksand. I wished I'd looked it up beforehand, but Baker had come over earlier than I expected, banging on the door and chatting with my father as if they'd known each other forever.

"What's your best track event?" I asked, as we headed into the brush. Though I was a little freaked, I decided I should go first, being the man and all.

"The 1500," she said.

I thought to ask her time on that but didn't want to one-up her with mine. Plus, what if hers was better? I was taller than her by a lot, but still. I hadn't told her I ran track—had I? I didn't think I had. Pot made it harder to talk for me than usual, but Baker could be pretty pushy with her questions.

"But my favorite's the long jump," she added.

Of course it is, I thought. Imagining those ponytails flying behind her as she whooshed through the air and wondering why I'd agreed to do this. While Baker made me laugh, she also made me nervous, especially when she started in on her rules, which she was doing as we pushed through pricker bushes and clouds of gnats.

"People shouldn't sleep with their significant others'

friends," she said.

I guessed this was about to be a rant against Jim and Conley. A discussion I wanted nothing to do with. "Oh, should there be a *rule* about that or something?" I said, all smarmy.

"Yes," she said. "A clear one too. Because it's terrible. Even if the whole secretive thing's hot; it's not worth it."

She was completely wrong about that, but whatever. I wasn't up for an argument.

"Yeah," I said, swatting at a horsefly.

"Don't sound so convinced, Evan!"

"Well, what do you want me to say?" I asked.

"Anything!" she yelled back. "It's common courtesy to reply when someone speaks to you!"

Fucking unbelievable. Because I doubted she wanted to know my opinion on this. Which was that I never cared if girls I got down with had a boyfriend. I'd never even bothered to ask. It didn't bother me in the slightest, who was fucking who, as long as I was involved in some of the fucking, really. It was pretty insane, how long I'd skated by without that kind of information mattering.

"All right," I said, exhaling for a long time. "It's probably not the best idea, getting down with your friend's chick. But people get too crazy about sex stuff in the first place. I mean, it's not like you're getting married in high school. This isn't Kentucky, right? Shit happens sometimes."

"Wow, Evan," she said. "That's the most I've heard you say in one breath."

"Well, you asked," I said.

"Don't be so touchy . . ." she said. "Oh my god, look!"

I pushed aside a twisted branch, and there in front of us was the biggest ruin of a house I had ever seen in my life.

As we walked around the Archardt House, Baker did all this oh-my-god!-ing. I couldn't blame her. The place was amazing, beyond gothic. Slate black roof and dark brick and a round, pointy turret to one side and a sunken gate all around it. Windows everywhere, stained glass and ornately shaped, all reflecting back the wild green surrounding us.

"Can you believe this? Holy fuck!" she said. "An intact piece of history—here on a bird sanctuary! Aren't you glad we did this?" Her eyes were wide and hopeful, a really pretty blue.

I was glad, yeah. But I was annoyed with her. And I couldn't stop staring at her. Her boobs popping up under her T-shirt. Those crazy-hot ponytails of hers that I just felt like grabbing. I felt like an animal alone on this island with her. Plus I hadn't taken a bath because my father and Brenda Trieste were out on our deck playing Parcheesi until three in the morning. With all the sweating I'd just done to get to the Archardt House, I probably reeked worse than ever.

Still, when Baker climbed over a pile of bricks by the broken main gate, I followed her. Maybe I was nutless, but I didn't need to advertise it.

At the giant front door, a thick rusty chain looped through the door handles and was secured by a broken padlock. It looked like something you'd need a tetanus shot to touch, but Baker just threaded it out of the door handles and dropped it on the stone steps in a shower of rust flakes. Then she tried the door, but it wouldn't budge. Which wasn't surprising—the door was huge, like in a movie where the heroes storming the castle have to bash it in with a giant tree. Probably the latches were rusted or the wood water-warped. Or maybe it was just locked, the owner having taken the key long ago. Maybe it was one of those skeleton keys, lost in some antique shop in the middle of Vermont. The idea of which I kind of loved but figured Baker would hate.

"Let me try," I said. I pushed against the door while pressing into the handle, and it busted open.

"What the . . . ?" she said.

I shrugged, like I did things like that all the time and moved aside so she could go first.

"I hate it when guys do that," Baker said, stepping into the Archardt House.

"Do what? Display their awesome masculine strength?" I asked, like a cocky bastard. "Or insist on 'ladies first?'"

But she didn't answer. Because we were inside the Archardt House and it was amazing.

"Amazing" wasn't quite right, though. Because it was a wreck. Dull with dust. Rusty and musty and sad. I could hear something flutter above us, as if the place was full of mice and owls and bats.

But the amazing part was the structure itself. The house was enormous. We were standing at the bottom of the biggest staircase I'd ever seen. White marble steps with an ebony banister and newel posts with carvings of bows and arrows. Not ergonomic or child-safe but still beautiful. A gloomy chandelier hung above us, rattling slightly as if there were birds roosting in it. Empty gaslights lined the walls.

Baker and I stood there, our backs to each other, staring, as dusty yellow light seeped in through the high windows.

"I wouldn't try those stairs," I said.

"Aren't you dying to see what's up there?"

"I'm completely creeped the fuck out, to be honest," I said, looking down at the rotted, dark carpet, beneath which squiggles of moss grew between flagstones. Baker pushed away from me, then, and sighed contentedly, as if she couldn't take in enough of the place. There was an old mirror, discolored and dark, above a small table. I saw my reflection—scraped-bald head, pointy elf ears, bumpy nose—and the house behind me, darker, dirtier, dustier. The walls were empty, the windows curtainless. Baker's rubber boots crunch-squeaked on the stone floor, and I followed her into a larger room off the entryway.

It was flooded with light from a giant picture window that looked over a weedy patio of broken flagstones and crumbling pillars. There were two rotted-out camelback sofas, bits of fabric barely holding the structures together. A fireplace that was twice as tall as me, with a cluster of fireplace tools and a heap of ashes in the hearth—I wondered if those could be carbon dated, and we could get the true time of the last fire in this house. I thought of saying as much, but then wondered if that wasn't right and Baker would laugh at me.

The sitting room also had a large black grand piano, with a candlestick holder on it, the kind you see people carrying around in scary movies. The piano bench was upholstered in faded-to-gray black velvet. I ran my hand along the dust on the piano in a long streak.

"I wonder what's in here," she said, stepping toward a doorway.

"Baker, wait!"

She smiled. "Are you scared, Evan?"

"It wasn't clear from the 'completely creeped the fuck out' comment?"

She laughed and I followed her again through another hallway until we were in an enormous kitchen. A wide prep island topped with a slab of white marble had a rack of copper pots hanging above it. There was a huge old-fashioned furnace oven and reddish slate floor tiles, porous and stained. The sinks were enormous enough to lie down and bathe in.

"Gross." She pointed to a dead mouse in a drain.

"Aren't you going to take pictures?" I asked. "Not of the mouse, I mean."

"Yeah, I will. I want to see everything first, though."

We continued exploring. Baker especially liked the pantry and the laundry room and the summer kitchen building out back—she talked at length about the servants that would be needed, how they'd can tomatoes and make jam in the summer kitchen instead of heating up the main kitchen in hot weather. I liked listening to her nerd out about this, because it gave me a reason to look at her that wasn't pervy and meant she wasn't lecturing about rules or patriarchy or how she would like to pin all of womankind's woes right on the head of my penis.

"Let's go upstairs." Words Dirtbag Evan would have loved for any girl to say, in any other parallel place and time that was not an old dump of a house on a mosquito-ridden lake island. I told her I'd pass.

"I'll go first if you want," she bargained. "I weigh less, so the stairs should support me."

"Thanks a lot." I acted wounded. "You have no idea how hard I work to get this skinny."

She laughed. "How could you get any *skinnier*? Go eat something. I'll holler if I need anything."

I told her I'd watch her go up the stairs to make sure she

made it, and then I did, trying not to look at her ass but doing it anyway. Acting like staring at her wasn't pervy but constituted a kind of safety issue, which it was, but not more than 20 percent of it was true concern. The other 80 percent was me contemplating why American society allowed women to wear certain things without it being illegal and how great that was and how life would be in one of those Muslim nations where women were required to live out their days underneath the clothing equivalent of a tablecloth and even with *non-monogramy*, did Jim Sweet know what a huge dumbass he was?

I went outside and ate a sandwich and drank some water and tried to read some E. Church Westmore, but the sun was too bright and I couldn't focus, so I walked around the house. I could hear birds chirping and bugs humming. It felt good to move around, even though my shoes were getting muddy. I wasn't going to be on an indoor track anytime soon, though I probably should take a run and see where I was at. I thought about asking Baker to come pace with me but then worried she'd ask why I was so out of shape. Or that she'd wipe the floor with my ass and I'd feel like a complete loser next to her boyfriend the quarterback. Or ex-boyfriend. Whatever the fuck—their non-monogramous thing made me nervous. I never brought up Jim Sweet and Conley to her, and not just because his name made me giggle like a four-year-old. I told myself that Baker probably thought about it enough already.

Behind the Archardt House was a big oak tree surrounded by patches of moss. I sat down beneath it, scraping mud out of the treads of my shoes with a twig. It was shady and cool, and I was worn out. Being around Baker—being around anyone, actually—made me buzz with tension. The idea that she was near and available, but not in my face, was nice, though. Though we were trespassing, though she had a kind-of-boyfriend, I felt okay for the first time since we'd moved. Like I'd outrun something bad, and now I could relax. I took out old E. Church and stuffed my backpack under my head and started reading.

E. Church was discussing Pearl Lake's past as a logging operations route, due to its connection with the Beauchant River, and that the deepest parts of the lake on the north side had many logs that had sunk to the bottom before they could be transported downstream. These logs hadn't rotted because the depth was too cold for the microorganisms that do such work. I thought about all those thwarted logs, stacking uselessly at the bottom of the lake, untouched by any sawmill, left abandoned and to themselves.

Safe.

From inside the house, I could hear Baker yelling, "Evan, you're totally missing out. Come back. I've got to show you this shit! Evan!"

I just smiled. And for a moment Jim Sweet and his fucking fists and his oversized wingman were as far from me and Baker Trieste as . . .

I must have drifted off, because I woke up startled, hearing voices. I looked at the tree wavering green leaves above my head and didn't know where I was for a minute. I'd been dreaming about the cupcake shop in Tacoma. Collette had walked in, carrying one of my Uncle Soren's hand-carved pipes. She said she was disappointed, because she never received one letter from me after all this time. Her face was bruised and a smeary tear dripping with eyeliner crawled down her freckled cheek and I was trying to tell her how sorry I was, but I couldn't speak. It was as if my voice box had been removed.

My face was wet with tears. Jesus, I was crazy. I quick wiped all the weepiness away with my T-shirt. The good feeling I had before falling asleep was gone, and now I just felt stupid and worried that Baker would find me bawling in the dirt.

Then I noticed some words carved on the tree above my head. Squinting, I twisted my head to make sense of them: *Soren & Melina.*

"Evan! There you are," Baker shouted.

I sat up then, my head knocking into the tree trunk.

"Sorry. I kind of dozed off."

I stood up and rubbed my head and Baker started jabbering about the upstairs and all the photos she'd taken and that Tom had texted he was on his way, but she was so happy because this was awesome and I was awesome for coming with her and we should come back again tomorrow!

Then she hugged me and her hair was soft under my chin and I tried to hug her back so she wouldn't feel how tense I was, but before I could formulate how to do that, she disentangled from me and we started walking while she continued describing the upstairs.

"There are seven bedrooms total," she said. "One is a nursery; you should have seen the cradle. It was beautiful. The dresser's full of baby clothes and blankets—a whole handmade layette. I have no idea how they've stayed preserved, but the roof of the house is intact, and there weren't any broken windows up there, which I think is strange, don't you?"

I nodded, but she barely noticed. She rambled on about the master bedroom and the fireplace and the bow-and-arrow carvings in ebony wood, and it would've been boring, if she weren't so cute and excited about it.

"And, oh, I almost forgot," she added. "There's a library on the main floor. On the other side of the staircase? I thought it was a coat closet, but they didn't use closets in that time period and it's just a really dark hallway. I didn't get a chance to look at all the titles. Do you have any water? I'm super thirsty."

I handed her my water bottle, and she chugged it. We were almost to Tom's drop-off point. The relaxed feeling I'd had before started coming back. But only a little. Because the thought of *Soren & Melina* made my stomach drop. I looked at my watch.

"Is that an Ironman? Are you a runner?" She grabbed my wrist to check out my watch.

"Yeah." I wished she'd stop touching me.

"Evan, why are you always so silent and mysterious?"

"I'm not mysterious. I'm just . . . economical."

She laughed. "So, what? You run long distance? Marathons?"

"I used to do track," I said.

"What events?"

"The mile."

"Really? What was your best time?"

"I can't remember," I said.

"Bullshit."

She kept bugging me to tell her, and I wouldn't, so we stood there getting aggravated by each other for a while.

"What do you mean the mile *was* your best?" she asked. "Don't you still do it?"

"Not currently." I felt edgy. Feeling like it was weird how we didn't know each other that well, but she was hugging me and getting all personal and I was exhausted from avoiding her questions. And now I had a question of my own, carved on a tree on an island in the middle of Pearl Lake.

"How old are you, anyway, Evan?"

"Eighteen. It was my birthday last week."

"*What?*" she said, in a delighted-but-outraged way that told me that, should she have any rules about birthdays, I would soon be learning them.

"Don't tell me you're one of those people who's all blasé about their birthday. I *hate* that. I mean, really, it's insulting, because like we wouldn't do something special for you! Why didn't you say anything?"

"Because I'm not six years old?"

"We could have made you a cake at least."

"Who's we?" I asked. "You and Jim Fucking Sweet?"

Her eyes darkened, and she turned away.

I knew I'd been a prick, so I didn't say anything more. I knew I should apologize, but I didn't really want to know what the deal was with her and Jim, anyway. I didn't want to hear about their non-monogramy, and sure as hell didn't want to get caught in the middle, taking sides or judging or whatever. The whole thing was crazy and too fucking familiar. So we didn't say one more thing to each other, not even when Tom pulled up, not a word the entire time, even when we reached the shore.

Dear Collette,

    I liked running. Not because I'm super healthy or competitive. It just seemed like a good thing to do. Like, physically. Like I knew I could outrun a killer or whatever. Or that my body would work the way I wanted it to work. I don't know. I didn't think about it a lot. I do now, but only because my body's all fucked up and I can't just do whatever I feel like doing anymore.

    Anyway, watching you long jump used to totally turn me on. Which is gross to say, but it was a beautiful thing. Really, I'm not kidding. I don't know how you did that. Or how anyone does that. I didn't used to think of myself as such a fearful fucker, but I think I am. Have always been one.

    Another thing I should have asked you about. How do you make yourself just jump like that? Run like hell and then lift off? I should have asked you, but I didn't.

Later, Evan

CHAPTER EIGHT

"You have plans for the holiday weekend?" Dr. Penny asked.

I shrugged. I was tense as hell. The Soren-and-Melina carving was driving me nuts, and here Dr. Penny was small talking again, which she did sometimes, though I didn't get why. Maybe to teach me how to be a better conversationalist? Therapy was fucked up.

I could see why she asked, as it was Friday, July 3. Generally, my dad and I weren't really the holiday type, but I didn't know what was standard on the east side, as Baker wasn't talking to me and Tom had been working overtime for his mom on building her summer theater sets. Jesse had texted me about hanging out, but we hadn't managed to connect. Clearly I was a dope about having friends.

Meanwhile, my father had lost his mind. When he wasn't hanging out with the free-love crowd on the lake, playing poker, and making chili—I had no idea he could cook—he was napping on the sofa or playing my video games, the game cases scattered all over the floor. It was like living with a roommate, not a father, and I wondered if he ever planned to get back to normal again.

Dr. Penny was saying, "You've made some friends, though, yes?"

I nodded.

"Not just girls, either, your father says."

"You talk to my father?"

"We talk on the phone once a week."

Suddenly, I wondered if she knew how much I'd lied to her. All my nodding at her made me feel like a supreme bastard. Dr. Penny never asked to see my letters to Collette; she never asked anything of me, really, except that I show up once a week and listen to her spout catchphrases. *Accept responsibility, not blame. Listen to your body's messages. Welcome all feelings. Don't think about it too much. Inhabit the fear.*

"He says you've been showering too. That's good to hear."

Now I really felt shitty. Did my dad think I was cured? Was that why he was finally relaxing? Drinking and playing *Call of Duty?* I was such a dick.

So I explained, uncomfortably, how I'd been bathing in the lake. Faking my dad out. How I couldn't bring myself to shower.

"If there was a lock on the bathroom door, maybe I could. But I just can't," I said.

I thought she'd be mad, but she was okay. I still got a lecture on *inhabiting the fear*, though. How I *inflated my anxiety* when I gave into it, how *avoidance empowered fear.* I tried not to nod like before, though it was hard to look her in the eye, knowing that she and my father had weekly calls about my craziness.

"Keep trying with the shower," she said. "You might have to go slow. But it'll come."

***

After my appointment, Jesse texted me, so I picked him up. Thinking he might want to smoke out, I'd stashed one of my Uncle Soren's pipes in the glove box. Having guy friends made me feel like everything I did was somewhat corny in its thoughtfulness, but Dr. Penny laughed when I suggested as much. She said that I was merely being kind and that was what you did with friends, even if you were a guy. *Friends support each other*, she said, before she had told me to have a good weekend. Which Jesse and I were kicking off early. Because whenever I thought of *Soren & Melina*, I pretty much wanted to puke. It wasn't that I was super in love with my father to begin with, given his weird avoidance and everything. But the idea that I was anything like him in the dick department, that my mom was just another dumb chick charmed into shit—by HIM, of all people—was disgusting. And really sad too. For all three of us, if I really thought about it.

We got stoned and went to Dairy Queen, where we sat outside, me eating a Buster Bar and Jesse, a Butterfinger Blizzard. While we ate, I stared at the blonde chick at the counter of the Dairy Queen (profile: long hair, black nail polish, decent face, zero boobs) and Conley the Cheating Blond popped into my head.

"What's the deal with Conley?" I blurted out.

"Huh?" Jesse asked between bites. With the long red plastic spoon in his mouth, he was basically making love to his Blizzard. His eyes were even closed.

Seeing that made me laugh my ass off. God, I could finally see why people turned into potheads, just for the laughing alone.

When we finally stopped laughing, my stomach hurt and I was sweating like crazy.

"You know, the whole screwing around with Jim," I said.

"What?" Jesse asked. "Conley and Jim?"

I explained what I'd seen at Midsummer. Jesse's red eyes widened.

"Conley's her best friend," Jesse said. "Baker'd shit if that happened."

"But didn't she say they could see other people?"

Jesse laughed. "That's such bullshit. You'd have to be insane to believe a chick who told you that."

Hadn't she basically been talking about Jim and Conley that day on the island, about getting down with your significant others' friends? Maybe she was just bluffing with all her pronouncements about seeing other people, though. *Nonmonogramy* did sound too good to be true.

"I'll ask." He pulled up another blob of Blizzard while somehow dialing his phone. Asking seemed like a terrible idea, but you know, pot and lowered inhibitions.

While Jesse had a broken-off conversation with the Tan Redhead, I thought about Jim and Baker. They were leaving for different colleges, but maybe they were one of those couples that kept constantly breaking up and getting back together for the excitement and drama. Though Baker didn't seem like one of those girls. Except for her swearing and drinking and weed-smoking, she didn't fit my preferred profile. She was someone that I would have never picked to like.

Not that it mattered. Baker hadn't come over in a while, and I wouldn't have cared, much, except for that easy feeling that day on Story Island and how she had said she wanted to go again. I wondered if she'd gone without me.

While Jesse pushed through a stupid conversation with Tan Redhead, Tom called me and said we should come get him; he was at the high school and sick of making theater sets. Jesse wrangled out of his conversation somehow, and we went to get Tom, who jumped in my car and reached across from the back to tune in a baseball game, which he listened to intently as if the announcer was giving step-by-step instructions on how to save someone's life, but before I could drive off, Jesse's phone rang. The Tan Redhead again. He stepped out of the car to get bitched at in privacy.

"What's Kelly up to?" I asked Tom, during a commercial.

"She's in Wisconsin for a family reunion. But she's banned from the lake for a while. Her mom busted her after the Midsummer Party."

"For drinking?"

"Mmm hmm," he said. "And for a big old hickey behind her ear."

"What?"

Tom looked embarrassed. "Well, if she hadn't put her hair up for church, no one would have noticed."

I laughed. I'd never given anyone a hickey, never received one, either. I was kind of proud of this fact.

"So what happens on the fourth of July around here?" I asked.

"Oh, there's fireworks and stuff out on the lake. No party or anything. Not too much patriotism on the east side."

"Nothing's going on tonight?"

"Nope," Tom said. "Not unless we make it happen."

After Jesse finished getting yelled at, we bought some shitty fireworks and then went to Mackinanny's to get hamburgers and so Jesse could buy more weed from the dishwasher. Then the three of us drove out to the Starlight Drive-In to see a movie. We all smoked out and then played Frisbee until the sun went down and the movie started.

This would have been a nonevent, except for the fact that I normally had no friends and never did anything that didn't involve some girl I was trying to get down with. But while enjoyable and probably something that would make Dr. Penny proud, that wasn't the only significant thing of the night. Because between features, while I was taking a piss in the nasty bathroom behind the concession stand, three girls came by and started talking to Jesse and Tom.

They were a little sleazy-looking but still cute, nothing you'd be hesitant to touch. Long hair, all done up differently, all wearing shorts and tight shirts and everything was tan and made-up and smelled like cake frosting. The blond with the nose piercing kept talking just to me, which made Tom and Jesse snicker, and at first, it was hard to talk to her, but it came back to me. It'd been so long since I'd kicked anyone any game, and this girl looked up for it. She tilted her head when she looked at me, and I could smell Cherry Lick on her breath, which wasn't an asset or anything, but fit my old profile. And felt pretty awesome, honestly.

We sat on the back bumper of my car talking, until her friends got bored with Tom and Jesse's loyal-to-their-girls ways and decided to go. But the blond waved them off. She said her name was Lana and she asked me if I wanted to drink with her and I said yes and chucked Tom my car keys and followed her in the dark across the gravel parking lot, the lights of the movie flickering around us. I could hear Jesse and Tom laughing about me and loadie chicks. *"Should I call Taber?"* Tom hollered.

I didn't take her up on the drinking (Cherry Lick mixed with Sprite, *ugh*), but just grabbed her and we started making out behind this beaten-down shed beyond the gravel lot of the drive-in. She tasted like she was a smoker, and of course, there was the Cherry Lick thing, which wasn't great, but it felt good to touch a girl again. Especially one who let me do whatever I wanted, no objections. I had never done it with anyone standing up, and it seemed like that might soon change. I didn't have any condoms on me, but Lana looked like the type to carry her own.

Then the worst thing happened. My worst fear, the one I refused to inhabit. The one I'd managed to forget about for a while at a drive-in theater in bumfuck Minnesota.

"Lana!" a male voice growled, and she sprang away from me screaming.

"Who the fuck is this asshole?" the voice said. I was blinded by the lights from the theater screen and couldn't see shit.

Lana turned to me, like she was struggling to remember my name.

"Evan, right?" she said. "Please, Layne, don't hit him. Please."

"Layne Beauchant?" I asked.

"Evan Carter?" Layne said, stepping closer until I could see his face.

"Is this your girlfriend?" I said, my voice cracking. "Because, I had no idea, man . . ."

"No, this ain't my girlfriend," Layne said. "Jacinta's in the car with Harry. Lana's my sister."

"Half sister," Lana said, all crabby.

Beyond the somewhat-batshit fact that Layne had taken his son to see the R-rated car-crash/fuck-fest we'd just watched was the much more terrifying fact that I'd been making out with his half sister. Which was better than doing it with his baby momma. But not by much.

"Jesus, I thought you were Randy Garrington," Layne said to me. Then he turned to Lana. "He's back in town, you know."

"Like I'd even talk to that fucker! God, Layne!" Lana said, wrapping her arms around herself. I'd kind of undone her shirt, and she hadn't bothered to button it back up, which I thought was weird. Did she think we'd chat with her half brother and then just dive back into getting down?

"Randy's fuckin' crazy," Layne told her. "You stay away from him. Both of you."

"Is he here right now?" I asked.

"I don't know," Layne said. "But Randy's been obsessed with Lana since he went to jail, so hanging around her isn't a bright idea. At least not in public," he added, chuckling.

"Oh, fuck off, Layne," Lana said.

"What did he go to jail for?" I asked.

"He tried to steal a car," Lana said, sounding bored.

"And aggravated assault," Layne added. "Don't fuckin' forget that. I'm serious, Lana! Evan here works with me, and you're not going to get another guy's ass kicked because you're being stupid."

That pretty much was my signal to bail. Lana looked pouty. I told Layne I'd see him at work and then sprinted back to Jesse and Tom. Where I caught a bunch of shit for having lip gloss all over my T-shirt and a hickey on my collarbone—so much for my pride about hickeys. I didn't realize Lana had done that, but again, I hadn't really been thinking. Wasn't that the draw of girls, though? Of sex, in general? So you could stop thinking for one goddamn minute?

***

When I got home, my dad was asleep on the couch. I woke him to say I was home, and he got up and staggered to his bedroom. I wondered how much of his insane behavior lately wasn't just another method of getting into Brenda Trieste's pants. God, it was beyond disgusting, imagining him with his old man body and bald head, putting on the moves to get down like that. The whole thing just made me want to punch him. Plus those names on the tree! I couldn't think about that without my guts seizing up. Still keyed up from the drive-in drama, I got a towel and my shave kit and ran down to the lake.

The water felt good, washing off the Cherry Lick and ciga-rette smell. But the high from Lana was gone, and now I just felt like shit. Like all my instincts were pervy and creepy. Like it made sense to get my spleen pried out and my left ear de-stroyed and my wrist sprained and my nose and ribs broken. The damn cut on my mouth hadn't busted open thankfully, but it stung from whatever chemical was in Lana's lip gloss. And I was a dick who deserved all of it.

I swam out and back to the diving platform. Decid-ed I should start running again. It was too bad I didn't like basketball or football, something teaching me how to take a hit. I thought of what it'd be like to get punched by Layne's tattooed knuckles. *KICK ASS!* was pretty much right.

I soaped up and then floated around to rinse while fireworks randomly popped off, Roman candles flitzing up in the air and then sparkling onto the water. I wished I could watch this kind of thing every night of the week. Maybe I'd sleep better.

I was standing at the dock about to push out of the water when I heard her.

"Evan?"

"You're fucking kidding," I muttered, sinking back into the water.

Baker. In her bathrobe and those brown boots. Again.

"Can't you just add 'Evan's nightly bath' to the list of east side traditions and leave me to it?"

"You don't own this lake." She sounded snippy but slipped off her boots. "Don't look."

"Whatever," I said. But I didn't look. Held my breath, kept my palms flat on the dock. Wondered if there should be some special, overly long German word for this feeling I was having, this intense mixture of turned-on irritation.

"What's that?" She bent over and poked my collarbone. I kept my eyes shut, though I could smell her. Cocoa butter. I thought she was talking about the circle necklace my mother had given me, but no. She'd spotted Lana's hickey in the light streaming from her screen porch. The one mark on me that I'd never managed to get before this evening. Great.

I wanted to die, but then I heard a splash and turned to see her treading water, her wet hair like little black whips down her shoulders.

"You know?" I said, all pissy. "You *do* have a dock of your own."

"You know?" She mimicked my pissy tone. "*You've* been a dick. From a manners standpoint, you should be apologizing instead of being so goddamn hostile."

I didn't know what to say to that, so I swam out deeper.

"I wish you'd told me," she said, her voice still annoyed. "Instead of having to find out secondhand."

I thought I knew what she was talking about. But I was currently naked in a lake in the middle of the night with a cute girl who was also naked and I wasn't sure how to act. There wasn't a handbook I could just look this up in, unfortunately. Though Baker Trieste probably could have written one.

"Jim and Conley," she said. "Thanks a lot for telling me."

Damn, she was pissed.

"I think it's some drug thing," she said. "Maybe they bonded over their hallucinogenic night together. Which sounds dumb, since what do I know about mushrooms? But then again, Conley and Jim *do* live on the same street back in Marchant Falls. Could it be just a convenience thing?"

Maybe, but what did I know? Plus this didn't explain why she was skinny-dipping in the lake with me, unless I was just a tool she'd use to feel better. Which made me think of all the girls I'd known, nationwide, that I'd used similarly. Christ. Add some self-loathing to that overly long German word.

"I thought you weren't having rules anymore," I said. "*Non-monogramy.*"

"Non-mono*gamy*, god!" she said. "Can no one pronounce

that word? Is it *that* hard?"

"Whatever," I said. "I thought it was open for you guys to see other people."

"But not Conley! Not my best friend!"

"But did you say who was okay and who wasn't? You can't really expect him to know what the rules are if you don't tell him first."

I couldn't believe I was taking up Jim's side. Jim was sort of a tool, but Dirtbag Evan could relate. *Non-monogramy* was her idea, and she hadn't been clear about it. That wasn't Jim's fault.

"I think Jim's doing all this because of Taber."

"What?"

She looked at me like I was dense.

"Yesterday, Jim was at Taber's and he saw this photo of me sitting on Taber's lap. It was from when Jim was at football camp last summer. So Jim freaks out and tells me I'm a whore for cheating with his best friend."

"Just because of a picture?" I asked. "Why would . . ."

"Why would Jim get mad about me being with his best friend, if he's already cheating with *my* best friend, you mean?"

"Yeah," I said.

"It's kind of a long story," she said. "Jim and I weren't even going out when that picture was taken. That was in August. Jim didn't ask me out until September. Conley, Taber, Jim, and me—the four of us hung out on the lake all last summer. Sitting on the diving platform, waterskiing, drinking, going out to eat. All that shit. Then Jim leaves for his stupid football camp and Conley gets grounded and so it's me and Taber, on our own for two weeks."

I nodded, not really knowing what she was getting at.

"So I slept with Taber, okay! It was my first time!" she said in a loud, harassed rush, as if I had beaten it out of her like a cop with a phone book.

Well. *That* I didn't see coming. Baker with Taber, the four-ton noseguard? *Jesus.*

"It was kind of a weird accident," she continued, less loud now. "We were watching a movie at his house in town while his family was out here at the lake. For two weeks, we'd done everything else you can do in Marchant Falls. There was nothing else left, you know?"

I nodded as if I understood. But I didn't care, because now I was panicking about where the hell Jim Sweet was. Since I was cornered naked with his also-naked, kind-of girlfriend and backstroking across the lake didn't seem like much of an escape plan.

But Baker obliviously jabbered about Taber. How he bought her Dairy Queen. How they played tennis and went bowling. I was getting a little nauseated, when she paused and looked back to shore, as if someone was coming.

Was it Jim? Jesus Christ I needed to get out of here!

"So that night?" she continued. "When the movie ended? We were sitting on his bed, and he just kissed me. And the next thing I knew, we were doing it and . . ."

She stopped. Which was understandable. But I was glad she was done describing the fuck out of it. My head was busy with exit strategies that didn't involve my male frontal nudity.

"It was pretty awkward," she continued. "But also very cool. I mean, he's this huge guy, you know? And because he plays football, you might think he's super rough. But he was a virgin too. And the whole time he touched me, he was so gentle. And shy. It was like he was almost worried, like he thought he would break me or . . ."

"Well, no kidding," I interrupted, because I couldn't help it anymore. "Taber's *huge*. He probably *could have* broken you."

I wondered if I'd been an asshole to say that, but she went on.

"So then Jim came home and Conley got ungrounded. For a while, it was kind of awesome. Romantic and tragic."

"So, you're non-monogramous because you're secretly in love with Taber?" I blurted out, because I was anxious for her to get on with it. Girls have this way of telling stories where you think they've come to the point, but then the whole thing shifts and then they're explaining their eating disorder or some other thing you don't see coming. Reason #476 to never have a girlfriend.

"No! I mean, Christ. I don't know! The first time you have sex with someone it's not necessarily wonderful in terms of performance. But that doesn't mean anything, right?"

Sure it does, I thought. *It means don't have sex with* her *again*.

"I guess before that night, I hadn't really considered Taber, you know?" she said. "Until those two weeks, I assumed a lot about him. Around Jim, Taber's always quiet. Jim sort of dominates everything. So after we did it, Taber went back to being quiet. And then Jim asked me out. Which was stupid—why did I say yes to Jim? Probably because I was mad at Taber. Why was he such a pussy about it?"

"Maybe it wasn't him," I suggested. "Maybe Taber knew Jim liked you and felt guilty or something."

"Maybe" She swam toward me. I could hear loons calling across the water, and a Roman candle flew up and sent spools of reflected light in spirals on the water around her shoulders and everything, Baker, too, was so beautiful that I felt dizzy. Almost-Weepy. Dr. Penny had been on me lately about medication for my anxious brain; I wondered if it would kill my chronic crybaby tendency too.

Hey, Dr. Penny? I imagined myself asking. *What about a pill for when you're naked with this cute chick in a lake in the middle of the night after you got caught making out with your boss's half sister and the cute girl's telling you all this shit about some dude she slept with and also she's gorgeous, but you can't imagine touching her because you're afraid of everything and everybody . . .*

"Anyway, Conley's a cunt and I'm just . . . I'm a complete wreck, I guess."

In addition to feeling certain my insanity was now probably visible to Baker, I was reeling how she could look so pretty while calling someone the c-word.

"Jesus, Evan, are you even listening?"

"I should have told you about Jim," I stuttered. "I'm sorry. I didn't get it, I guess. I thought that was how you wanted it with him."

"Well, *no*. But it's okay." She swam past me toward the dock. "I forgive you. Friends?"

I nodded and looked away when she got out of the water. Waited the appropriate time for her to put on her bathrobe and step into her boots.

But when she said good night, I stopped her.

"You want to go to Story Island tomorrow?"

"Sure. Get Tom and come by for breakfast in the morning."

I flopped back into the water, watched her go. Exhausted by the whole thing. How would I ever get clean again?

Dear Collette,

Is half of the shit guys do to impress chicks entirely lost on you? I think you don't even notice all the crap that we do.

For example, I suspect you don't know this, but no guy wants a girl who is bigger than he is. This is not a fatness thing. Most guys want a girl who looks like a woman, with tits and ass and stuff. But, also, he wants to be as big as her, so side-by-side things look proportional. He doesn't want to look like a little scrawny weasel with a caved-in hairless chest and stuff.

Not that I want a lot of hair on my chest, really. But just that I don't want it to look like the chick I'm with is babysitting me.

Also, you know that strutting thing guys do? With their chests all puffed out and their arms hanging from their sides in an affected way, like they're carrying invisible beach balls? Like their biceps are just TOO HUGE for their body and they can't walk normally from all the bulk? Tell me this doesn't turn you on. Tell me this is something you laugh at. Because I HATE that strutting douche shit. And sometimes I think guys don't do that for chicks, anyways. I think they do it for other guys, just to demonstrate their toughness and muscularity. Which makes me want to punch something.

Also, do you really give a shit about our muscles? Or our cars? I think you only care about hair. I swear, chicks used to talk about my hair all the time. Which made me feel gayer than anything else. I mean, literally gay. Like, if a girl liked my hair so much, it must mean I was cultivating some hairstyle thing. Really I just never wanted to get it cut. It was laziness, not style.

Later, Evan

CHAPTER NINE

The next day, after scarfing down waffles with sweetened ricotta from Keir's farm—everyone complimented him on it, but all I could wonder was how Brenda could sleep with a guy who wore a shark's tooth necklace with the world's tightest purple muscle shirt—Tom dropped Baker and me at Story Island, saying he'd be back around noon.

Baker didn't say much the entire walk to the Archardt House, which sucked, because it meant I had nothing to think about except for how I shouldn't stare at her ass. That and how I wanted to hide from her the whole reason for my coming back to the island in the first place. *Soren & Melina.*

We went into the Archardt House, just like before, me pushing open the door for her, though this time she didn't bitch about it and I didn't lord it over her. She was excited to show me the library, and it was very cool. Every wall was crammed with books, and there was a long ladder that rolled along a track. Plus a couple of rotted-out leather chairs and a desk that probably weighed as a much as a tank.

"I think it's my favorite room so far."

"That's because you haven't been upstairs," she said. Was she being flirty? I didn't get her. Still, because I was a damn dog, I watched her go upstairs, just like before, except this time it was 100 percent pervy. Then I hauled ass back to the oak tree.

I hadn't imagined it. *Soren & Melina.* The letters were blocky and masculine, but it wasn't like you could exactly write in cursive with a knife.

I walked until I came to the summer kitchen. We'd only looked in it briefly, so I stepped inside, and a bird skittered out over my head, which made me almost shit myself. The summer kitchen was full of dead leaves and old nests and had a musky, nasty scent. There were chipped enamel countertops and an old black stove. The place looked like a perfect location for kids to get wasted or make out. Baker called that kind of thing a historical desecration. She said it was bad enough we were damaging the integrity of the Archardt House by coming in without permission and proper equipment.

The cupboards were full of broken mason jars, but there was one in the corner that wouldn't budge. I knocked it with my fist until it swung open. On the top shelf was a glass peanut butter jar full of dead bugs, fishing lures, and lead weights. Beside it, an old BB gun. On the bottom shelf was a ragged, blue cloth-covered book, big as a notebook and bound with a faded leather strap that looked like a man's belt.

I unstrapped the belt and opened the book. The cover page had a circle drawn in pencil and inside it, also written in pencil, was this:

Soren,
I have always loved how you love your home.
This is your book to show me how much.
Love,
Melina

The book was all drawings and charts and lists. A diagram of a raven's wing, sketches of beaver dams. Lists of fish caught, the dates and times and coordinates in the lake, weights and lengths. Bullhead, northern pike, walleye, bass. Feathers and flowers and leaves pressed into the pages. It was kind of beautiful, actually.

I knew just a little about my Uncle Soren. He'd been an outdoorsman and a marine. He didn't have a permanent address. And he didn't get along with my dad. That he was an artist on top of all that was unexpected. He couldn't have been more different than my father.

Soren's book pushed through the seasons as if they weren't months apart but days. Winter ice fishing. Summer storms. And drawings. Dragonflies, geese migrating, a hand-built canoe, boats turned over on the shore, leaves changing colors.

I heard Baker calling my name. I latched the belt back over the book, shoved it in my backpack and stepped out of the summer kitchen.

"Evan? What are you doing?"

"Just looking around," I said.

"Tom just texted me. There's a thunderstorm coming, so he's on his way."

She looked at me suspiciously, like I'd been jacking off or

something in the summer kitchen. We started back toward the drop-off point, and to avoid any more questions, I asked her how long she'd known Kelly.

"Since seventh grade, why?"

"What's this whole Everything-But thing?"

"Oh, poor Tom," Baker laughed. "It's pretty hilarious."

"It's not hilarious. It's completely insane."

"That too. Kelly's building the sex thing up way too much. She's going to be so disappointed when it finally happens."

I nodded. It wasn't that I didn't understand Kelly's moral flexibility, of her bargaining shit down with Jesus. I thought it was somewhat decent of her to give Tom *something* to work with. But I also agreed with Baker. Like penis-vagina sex would really change anything about their relationship and their behavior. Such a simple thing, really, compared to all the unholy activities they did in an effort to maneuver around it.

"You have to tell me now," she said. "Because I told you. And I've never told anyone about that before. Not even Conley knows."

"What are you talking about?"

"About Taber and me," she said, like I was brain-damaged. "You have to tell me your First-Time story."

"You're kidding, right?"

"I'm assuming you've had a first time?"

"Jesus! Give me a little credit!"

"How can I? You never talk about yourself at all."

"Why do you want to know?"

"Because it's interesting," she said. "And it's only fair. I told you mine."

"I never asked to hear yours."

"True. But it was nice to finally tell someone."

"Technically, you told Jim before you told me."

"I never told Jim shit," she said, angry.

"Maybe you should. Since you're non-monogramous and all."

"Don't be a dick," she said. "Come on! Just tell me! You know I won't say anything."

"Fine," I said. "But no interrupting. No questions or commentary, either."

"Why can't I ask questions?"

"Because it'll drag the whole thing out longer."

"Okay, fine. But how old were you the first time?"

"Fifteen," I said, without thinking.

"Jesus! That's super young."

"That sounded like commentary," I said.

She apologized all over the place, but the whole thing bugged me. Not just because there was no way I'd ever tell her the true First-Time story. There were plenty of other crap sex stories I could pass off as the First—there was no shortage of awkward situations I'd put myself in since Tacoma. But mostly because it depressed me, this guy I used to be. Dirtbag Evan Carter, who lived for that whole game. Profiling, checking every girl out. Who could meet a loadie chick at the drive-in and get her shirt off in less than twenty minutes.

But the guy I was now? *That* guy considered it a breakthrough that he'd actually yanked it for the first time a few nights ago. A breakthrough worthy of reporting to Dr. Penny—if I ever told her anything that actually mattered. For a girl, Baker was strangely normal about sex; she had no idea how fucked up I was about this and a million other things.

"It was in San Diego," I said, sighing. "My first job at a mall. I took tickets for the merry-go-round in the food court. The Merry-Go-Round Master, people called it. So, I met this girl. Her name was Mandy. And she asked me . . ."

"What'd she look like?"

"Interrupting!"

"You have to give me something to imagine, Evan."

"Why do you need to imagine this at all?" I yelled and she shut up. "Mandy was cute, I guess," I allowed. "A little taller than me, though. She was older than me too. She asked me to front her a couple of bucks because she had to buy tampons and she wasn't getting paid until the next day and she'd just got her period and none of her coworkers had anything . . ."

"Where did she work?"

"American Eagle. And shut up."

"Sorry!"

"I didn't have any cash, but I had a credit card my dad gave me for groceries," I said. "Because my dad always made me buy groceries. Though we mostly ate takeout. Anyway, that's off-topic . . . So we went into CVS and got the damn tampons. And then . . ."

"*You did it for your first time with someone who had her period?*" Baker screeched.

"No! Jesus!" I said. "I didn't call her for like two weeks. It was gone by then. At least I think it was."

"Pretty dickish not to call someone for two weeks, Evan."

"That's because I *was* kind of dickish, Baker."

"Not so dickish that you wouldn't buy tampons for a girl you'd just met."

"It's not like she asked me to *insert* the damn thing."

"Well, you haven't gotten to *that* part of the story yet."

"Hilarious," I said. "I'm so glad I told you that."

"It *is* kind of weird that she asked a guy to help her with such a girly problem."

"Mandy was a weird chick," I said. "I suppose she didn't think I was too threatening. Me being the Merry-Go-Round Master and everything."

"I can't believe that's a real job! Was it . . ."

"Interrupting!"

She shut up then. We stood at Tom's drop-off point, which made me hit the gas on this whole dumb story.

"When I called her, she said we should see a movie and I asked if she wanted to smoke out first. But Mandy said she had some magic mushrooms. So we ate the 'shrooms in her car and she talked me through it and, yes, I barfed them up in the parking lot. 'Shrooms taste disgusting, by the way. She gave me some gum to get the taste out; she said she loved chewing gum when she tripped. Then we went to the theater—this was at the same mall where we worked—and saw a kid's movie, I think. Maybe *Toy Story*? I can't remember. So anyhow. I'll skip describing the whole drug thing because it won't make any sense and who really gives a shit, you know?"

"People's drug stories are never as interesting as they think."

She was technically interrupting, but since she agreed with me on the point, I let it ride. "Right, so you know the part about the men's room and the black-and-white tile, so I'll skip that too," I said. "Mandy obviously couldn't drive, so she called this guy to get us, which freaked me out, because I thought she liked me, but the guy just dropped us at Mandy's house. She actually lived not too far from my house, which was bizarre, considering how randomly we met. I didn't know this at the time, on account of my pinwheel eyes and everything. But I figured it out later.

"No one was at her house, except for her tiny little dog who was bugging the shit out of me. Biting my shoelaces. Mandy kept laughing, but it drove me nuts. I hate little tiny dogs, by the way. You could say it's one of my rules. All dogs must be bigger than a goddamn lunch box, maybe. How's that?"

Baker laughed and I couldn't help but feel a little better about telling her this. Even though it wasn't the true First Time one.

"To get away from the damn dog, we went down into the basement," I continued. "The entire basement was her bedroom. Like, she had a bed and a desk and a television and everything. Even a washer and dryer."

"Did you do it on the washer?" Baker asked, all excited.

"I wish it were that cool," I admitted. "But no. We laid on her bed, doing our druggy thing. Listened to music. Talked in that stupid spacey way. I'd never done 'shrooms before, and Mandy was a good person to do them with, because she seemed to know what should happen. And I guess she thought sex should happen because she just rolled over on me, and since I was out of my mind, I let her. So. We did it and in the morning I walked home and slept for eighteen hours and my father thought I had the goddamn flu and I let him think that. There. The End."

Baker, surprisingly, didn't talk for a minute.

"Feel more complete as a person for knowing that?" I asked, gulping a bunch of water.

"Didn't you guys use birth control?"

"Well, yeah," I said, a little surprised at the question. "I had condoms."

"Well, how did you get the condom on? If you were so wasted?"

I thought back to that night at the cupcake shop. The Cupcake Lady unwrapping it, rolling it onto me. I had sat there like a complete moron while she did everything, like a baby getting his diaper changed. *God.* Where the fuck was Tom?

"Jesus, Baker. It's a condom, not a graphing calculator. It's not *that* difficult to figure out."

She laughed. "And did you like it? The sex, I mean, not the condom."

"Well, it *happened*, didn't it? I must have liked something about it."

"How do you know you actually *did it*, then?"

Now *I* laughed. "Baker, I don't think a guy can be so high he doesn't realize *that* is happening to him."

But she said, "That kind of sucks, though. That you weren't really *there* for the whole thing."

Jesus, Baker was naïve. Didn't she realize that if guys were really "there" during sex, they'd probably come before the girl's pants came off? There was no "being in the moment" for me, not with sex. Not after the Cupcake Lady. Not if I didn't want to feel like a complete idiot. (And even then, a lot of times afterwards, I *did* feel like a complete idiot. Hence, the ritual phone number deletion.) For me, sex was a matter of thinking about everything else unsexy in the entire world in order to keep it from ending too soon. Were all girls this clueless? It seemed so luxurious, being a girl. Just getting to lie there, completely unconcerned about how the whole thing depended on the behavior of your dick.

"At least I wasn't as caught off guard the next time I did it," I said.

"You and Mandy did it again?"

"No. I never talked to her after that."

"You mean you've done it with more than . . ."

"Hey!" I shouted. "You asked for the First Time story. Not the Every Time After That story. So, that's all you get. Be sure to have your friends be specific about what level of absorbency they prefer when they ask me for tampons. Is that Tom's boat? Yes. Thank fucking god."

"You know, Evan? You really are hilarious when you start to tell a story. You really need to talk more."

I wasn't sure if she was serious or not. But I held out my hand to help her climb down the rocks.

Dear Collette,

One of the last things we talked about (to the extent that we talked about anything) was condoms. Like, you said to buy some and I said I had some already. But what you didn't know is that I had some there in my track bag right at the moment. I always had condoms. I mean, even now I have them. Though they're pretty dusty under my bed at this point.

ANYWAY. I was sort of a freak about carrying condoms. Usually chicks make you jump through hoops before getting down, like first kissing, then boobs, then down the pants, etc. But it took just one instance where things went straight to fucking and that made me a believer. Lucky the chick had condoms that time. But every time since, I've had them in my wallet. I know that's supposed to be bad for the latex, but I think that's only if you leave them in there for a hundred years in the heat of the desert or whatever.

So, now you'll imagine me like some soldier of fortune, with condoms like ammo wrapped around my chest. But I believe strongly in condoms. They avert babies and disease. They make you seem responsible, not slutty. They make the girl relax too, because you're taking care of the risky part. Like you're a professional. Roll it on, squeeze the tip, turn back to her, ready, set go. Like I'd just done a little disappearing act on myself and became something confident and wonderful. You can't see through my latex disguise! You will love this so let's get down! You don't want to know how many times this worked in my favor.

God I feel like a fucking asshole sometimes. All the time, really.

CHAPTER TEN

My father was bugging the fuck out of me.

It wasn't just the hanging around with Brenda and the Tonnesons, acting like he was this charming, talkative person who lived for whiskey sours and endless hands of Spite and Malice on the deck. Which was phony enough. But then he'd be the same as he always was toward me. Silent. Nodding. Giving me like two sentences of information per day. His son—the person he actually lived with. It was like he finally figured out how to be normal with other humans but didn't think I deserved the same treatment. As if the fact that he'd sent me to therapy, that I'd almost died, and everything with Collette—meant that I was some psycho foaming at the mouth that you had to treat with caution.

Not that I knew what I wanted him to do or say to me. All his rambling the first few weeks we'd been here hadn't been any better. Made me worried he'd just start bawling again, thinking about my mom.

At least at Pearl Lake, there was always something going on. When I wasn't at work, there was always someone hanging around the lake.

Mostly, I hung out with Tom. Tom was very easy to be around, like he'd taken his personality from a template marked "Boy" and just followed it to the letter. Not that he was boring as a result. His hippie parents probably wondered why he didn't like community theater and eating lentils, I'm sure. But Tom resisted all of his parents' weirdness.

In addition to fishing and baseball, Tom also talked a lot about cars, since he worked at a car wash. He was going to some college in Iowa I'd never heard of—the same place as Kelly—and he had no underlying angst aside from the fact that he was a virgin and his girlfriend wouldn't give it up. But he didn't complain about that much, either. He liked Kelly, you could tell, even when she squeaked cutesy crap all over him. Even when she dyed her hair from Charcoal Briquette to White Blond (which was a huge improvement).

So when Tom left for a weeklong baseball tournament, and Jim texted me to come over to his cabin and hang out, though I hadn't ever hung out with just Jim and Taber before, I took one look at my father socking away beer and kettle corn while playing poker with Brenda and Mr. Tonneson and the choice was clear.

***

Taber and Jim were eating a bucket of chicken and watching TV. Jim had this giant black dog that was slobbering and begging for the chicken and Taber would go to give the dog some and Jim kept freaking out: "Don't give her table scraps! She's enough of a fatass as it is!"

"Dude, you're such a cock to your dog," Taber kept saying.

Jim offered me some chicken, but I shook my head. Pulled out my pipe and a bag of weed I'd bought from the dishwasher kid at Mackinanny's a week earlier and offered it up.

"Can't," Jim said. "I'm driving tonight. We've got plans. There's a party we need to attend."

So Taber and me smoked out while Jim took a million years in the shower. Probably bleaching his fucking teeth too.

Meanwhile, Taber had turned on a movie, Jim's favorite, *A Clockwork Orange.* I'd never really seen the whole thing, but it inevitably showed up in the background at some point at every school I'd attended. Wherever guys congregated and were comfortable enough to scratch their balls, this fucking movie was sure to follow. Anyway, I recognized the awful old '70s colors instantly. It reminded me of a children's educational show but all demented and gross.

"You have to see this one part," Taber said. "He's chasing around this old lady with, like, this giant statue of a dick." He was forwarding scenes and couldn't get the remote to work right.

I wasn't too high but was high enough to feel a little shitty. Watching this movie wasn't helping. It reminded me of Remington Chase, for one thing. Plus everyone was so ugly and awful-looking. At least in modern movies, chicks look decent. Even naked, the chicks in *A Clockwork Orange* skeeved me out. And I really didn't need to see the main character walking around his apartment in his underwear (scratching his balls, of course)—even at fast-forward speed.

Finally, Jim got out of the shower—still shirtless, smelling like body spray, and—yep—scratching his balls. He said we needed to go. All bossy, like we'd been the ones holding shit up.

"Hang on, I'm getting to this one part," Taber said.

"Baker hates this movie so bad." Jim sat down and put on his shoes. "You even quote it and she starts yelling."

"Where *is* Baker?" I asked.

"Doing something with her friends."

"Here it is!" Taber said. We all sat there for a minute and then on the screen there was this lady in a horrible orange jumpsuit and everything was like space-age furniture and one of the guys in white wearing the nut cups was singing "Singing in the Rain" as he kicked the shit out of this old guy. Then the nut cup guy cut out holes of the woman's orange jumpsuit so her tits hung out and then basically made his friends hold the old guy down, forcing him to watch while he jumped on his wife.

"Hey, should we go . . . ?" I asked. Because right then, I wanted to throw up everywhere. Splatter barf all over the bucket of chicken on the coffee table that Jim's dog kept sniffling around. I kept seeing Collette and her face screaming in a way I'd never seen it, would never see it, and her crying, and it felt like it was me being held down to watch her, not the old man in the movie.

"Wait, this isn't the right part . . ." Taber fiddled with the remote again. In my experience, this was easier with YouTube, where apparently thousands of guys like Taber and Jim had lovingly curated and tagged the most ultraviolent bits for all our viddying pleasure. But I wasn't about to tell Taber this—at least not without throwing up on his shoes.

I got up and went to the bathroom. Which wasn't any better. It was all steamy from Jim's shower, plus I could have sworn he used the same body spray as The Rammer. I regretted smoking out. Coming over here. All of it.

Then Jim yelled, "Come on, Evan, we're going!"

Jim drove us in this tiny little woman car. A hatchback of some kind that he said was Taber's mother's. Tom would have known the make. Taber could barely cram his body in it, and I had to sit behind Jim, because Taber's seat was so far back.

"I found us a loadie party, dude," Jim said. "Guy who sold me the mushrooms told me about it. So you and Taber can get lucky."

I tried to imagine me getting some game. Even though I still felt like shit.

"I won't even get drunk, so you don't have to worry about getting home," Jim continued. "Unless you go back to *her* trailer. Then you're on your own." He laughed.

"Fuck you," Taber said. Like he was sensitive about his loadie chick's feelings in advance.

"I'll steer them toward you guys," Jim continued. "I mean, they probably aren't used to anyone who has all his teeth."

That was true, if Terry Gribbener, my Cub Foods coworker, was any indication. The few teeth Terry had were a slimy yellow, and his breath was worse. So probably Jim's blinding-white dentures would be especially dazzling.

"We going to the south side?" I asked.

"No, a trailer park in town," Jim said. "Riverbend *Estates*," he added.

"Stop at a gas station," I said.

"What for?"

"I need a couple of supplies if we're going to make this happen."

Plus, I needed to get my head right. If there were hot chicks at this loadie party, maybe that would be all I'd need. Maybe Lana'd be there, even.

Taber stopped at a Spur, and I ran in and got a couple packs of Marlboro Lights, some gum, two lighters, and a three-pack of condoms. Back in the car, I divided it all between me and Taber. Jim couldn't believe it, and I didn't know if it would work because I never scammed girls in a group before, but I thought it couldn't hurt.

Fast forward to being at a shitty trailer park party, where it was all grass stamped down to dirt and crappy laundry lines and a rusted-out carousel at a playground area holding a keg wrapped in a black trash bag full of ice. Jim kept approaching little groups of chicks with his big fat smile and corny-ass lines that somehow made them open up and talk to us. Which was helpful, because me and Taber got completely shitfaced, me kind of rushing Taber to drink more and more with me, in order to shake my shitty feelings.

Which was fine—the dose of *Clockwork Orange*'s greatest hits seemed less gross the drunker I got, though reality started to resemble the scene where Alex gets down with those two chicks he meets in some fucked-up mall (though that scene was for shit, because the director ran it in quadruple speed, as if he knew it would be less enjoyable that way). The main thing I remember is what happened with these two girls, one in a red dress and one in a turquoise tank top. The red dress girl smoked all my cigarettes like some kind of nicotine pig and wouldn't stop hollering at me in this scratchy man's voice. She had big tits, but beyond that she was annoying and gross. Turquoise Tank Top was at least cute and normal about being flirty, and soon she and Taber disappeared.

I was out of cigarettes and feeling awful, but Red Dress chick wouldn't quit dogging me. Finally, I went behind some bushes and made myself barf just to feel better. Jim found me and asked where Taber was.

We didn't have to wait long to find out. A few minutes later, while I was shoving three sticks of gum in my mouth to kill the barf taste, Turquoise Tank Top was back, giggling with her girlfriends.

Instantly, Jim and I ran back to the tiny car. Where Taber was passed out in the backseat, half-naked, still wearing the condom.

"Jesus!" Jim yelled, slapping Taber awake while I pretty much collapsed laughing.

"We gotta go home," Taber moaned. "Please. I don't want to see her ever again. Please. Once was enough." Taber struggled to clean himself off and piss in the bushes and then squished into the backseat again in misery while Jim started the car.

"Jesus, it reeks in here!" Jim bitched, cranking down his window. "Roll yours down too! That must have been some funky-ass chick!"

"Fuck you," Taber muttered.

"I feel like we should contact Ford about this," Jim said. "Tell them it's possible to get laid in the back of a Fiesta."

"Get those cigarettes outta here, will ya?" Taber groaned. "I don't want my mom to find them."

But as Jim started turning the car around, Turquoise Tank Top came running toward us, two other girls with her, including Red Dress Chick, and I yelled at Jim to drive, but he didn't get it at first. The girls shouted at us, and one of them bombed the soda cup full of Coke and Cherry Lick against the roof of Taber's mom's car, where it rained down into the open windows, and we peeled out of Riverbend Estates laughing like fucking idiots.

Dear Collette,

I've never gotten down with a chick when we were both all the way naked.

Shocking confession. Have you ever done that?

I always laugh when I watch a movie where people have sex and everyone's fully stripped down. Or the girl's stripping off her stuff all slow in front of the guy. As if there's time for that. As if you don't need to have your shoes on in case someone's stupid parents come home earlier than expected.

I learned the importance of the half-dressed bangage from this one chick I met at a house party. She made me hold onto her bra, so I left it on my wrist like a bracelet the whole time we got down. Sure enough, not five minutes after we finished, this drunk guy barged into the room and puked on the carpet. Good thing we were dressed and able to exit quickly, right?

I think if that were my Last Chance Thing, that would be it. To be all-the-way-naked with a girl, in a bed. A comfortable, real bed. And all the time in the world. No worries, everything safe. Nobody barging in barfing or interrupting or laughing or busting us or anything. We could see everything of each other, and I wouldn't freak out about it, because I'd have time and she'd be understanding and everything would be good and slow and nice and fine and I wouldn't care if she liked me because I'd like her, like a normal person for once, and not be all sorry for her and manwhorey about it.

Maybe you have to be married to get down like that? I can't imagine being someone's boyfriend, much less husband.

Later, Evan

CHAPTER ELEVEN

Since Taber, Jim, and I had to clean out the Cherry Lick and cigarettes and the condom box and everything else from Taber's mom's car at a self-service car wash at two in the morning, I woke up pretty late the next day, on the couch at Jim's cabin— his parents nowhere around and not giving a shit what he did, apparently. Beside me was Jim's dog that wouldn't stop licking me. Covered in dog hair and Cherry Lick and feeling like a pile of ass, I walked home. Before the loadie party, I hadn't had time between work and appointments with Dr. Penny to bathe. And now everyone was out on the Tonneson's deck, eating and playing cards, Baker included, so I could hardly use my usual mode of getting clean.

I went into the bathroom for my daily shower staredown. The bathroom door was lightweight; it made a fluttery sound when you shut it, like it was made out of cardboard, not wood. Completely shitty. If it were up to me, all bathroom doors would resemble those terrorist-proof reinforced steel cockpit doors on airplanes.

But shitty door or not, I still reeked like the bags of onions Layne and I unloaded the day before, with Cherry Lick and cigarettes on top of that. So I decided to turn on the shower. Just turn it on. To get used to the sound. Dr. Penny said you had to go slow. That avoidance made it worse.

Listening to the sound of the water rushing on tile made me feel like I was back at Remington Chase. Which was crazy—YOU ARE SAFE, I yelled at myself in my head. Then I could hear Collette, crying, which made no sense, since that happened much later. How much later? I never asked the true timeline of that night. If Dr. Penny thought I should know the specifics of how everything went, she probably would've made me write magical letters to the Charlotte police department.

I shut the shower off. I was sweating. The steam fogged the mirror, and I yanked open the flimsy-ass door and was about to flop back onto the couch and sulk when I saw Tom loping across the yard with Kelly and got an idea. Watching Tom help Kelly into the boat, I ran outside before he could start the motor.

I mean, a door needing a lock—how hard could it be? I could do calculus and chemistry when I paid attention. I had taken industrial arts. There had to be instructions online.

"You got a drill I could borrow?" I asked Tom, all casual.

"Sure," he said. "It's in the shed with all the summer Shake-speare shit."

***

If you ever want to quickly feel like a giant dumbfuck, just go into a hardware store and stare at a display of doors for a while. Still, forty minutes and forty bucks later, I drove home, feeling better. Closer to not smelling like girly booze and sacks of yellow onions.

The gathering at the Tonneson's was still going, so I took the long way around to the shed for the drill. Then I slipped back the same way. Sneaking around was necessary, because I'd gotten used to life on the east side, everyone in your business. Mrs. Tonneson borrowing someone's back massager and talking loudly about it out on her deck. Baker cutting Tom's hair on her screen porch. Brenda dragging her laptop over to my dad every time the screen froze. I knew way too much about these people. Their hemorrhoids, their carpal tunnel, their grandmothers with dementia.

Fast forward to complete fuckery. I followed the instructions on the dead-bolt package—really, I did. But I wasn't five minutes into drilling holes when I completely cocked up the entire thing. None of the holes were aligned and the doorknob rattled around like it might fall out and the drill pretty much cracked the flimsy-ass door in half. I wanted to tear the whole thing off the hinges like the Hulk.

"What're you doing?"

My dad. In the kitchen. With Brenda. They were holding a bunch of dirty dishes.

"I was putting a lock on the door . . ."

"It's completely destroyed," my father murmured. I heard Brenda say, "I'll get Keir."

"What were you thinking?" my dad asked, his forehead wrinkling. I stared at the floor. Keir and Brenda returned, and Keir puzzled over the giant crack running down the center of the door.

"Did you get locked in or something?" Keir asked.

"He was installing a dead bolt," my father said.

"What's going on?" It was Baker, holding a big drippy chocolate cake on a plate. Apparently, it was dessert at the Carters now and the whole east side was pouring into our house to witness my idiocy firsthand.

"Evan was trying to fix the bathroom door," Brenda murmured. That was generous of her.

"You need an entirely new door, Adrian," Keir said, wiping his hands on his muscle shirt.

My father sighed. Stared at me like he wanted to call Dr. Penny. I wiped sawdust off my hands.

"Sorry," I said.

"A pocket door might work better," Keir added, examining the wall. "Take up less space."

"Why do you need a lock when only two people live here, Evan?" Baker asked, getting out a stack of plates from the cupboard. "Or do you bust in on him when he takes too long to do his hair, Mr. Carter?" Everyone laughed.

"Privacy is very important," Mrs. Tonneson said. "Especially when you're the age Evan is . . ."

Jesus. She made it sound like I was inspecting my first dick hairs.

"I usually knock," my dad qualified. "If the door's closed, anyway."

"Maybe it's Adrian who needs privacy," Brenda said, laughing.

"Guys like their solitude in the bathroom," Mr. Tonneson said. "We go to the can to get away from it all."

"Gross," Baker said.

I felt like killing myself, Baker imagining me taking a

dump while reading the sports page.

Tom and Kelly came in, then. "What's going on?" Tom said.

"Did someone try to break into your bathroom?" Kelly asked.

"Whoa, Evan, did you do that with a drill?" Tom asked, lifting up his baseball cap in surprise.

"Remind me not to ask him to work on the Shakespeare sets," Mrs. Tonneson murmured.

"Who wants cake?" Baker asked.

***

A few hours later, Keir and my dad dismantled the door, and unable to look anyone in the eye, I went to town to get my paycheck and ended up grilling out in Layne Beauchant's back-yard, drinking a Miller High Life and watching his little boy Harry toddle around naked in his plastic kiddie pool. After my day of shame with the bathroom door, this bottle of beer tasted pretty damn good. Jacinta—Layne's girlfriend—was grilling hamburgers and sweet corn while telling me about how a co-worker of hers got in a fistfight at the vending machine in the break room and the cops came. Jacinta worked in an office, so that was high drama.

Layne came outside and kissed Jacinta on the neck. He took off his boots and dirty socks and pulled up a chair beside me, putting his feet into Harry's pool and cringing.

"Damn, that water's cold!" he shouted.

"Don't swear in front of your son!" Jacinta pointed her spatula at him.

When we sat down to eat at the picnic table, Harry wasn't

having it. He cried when his dad made him put back on his Spider-Man underpants ("Big boys don't eat dinner naked," Jacinta said) and didn't want to sit on his plastic booster seat (jacked from Layne's job at Denny's, no doubt). Harry cried until Jacinta sweet-talked him with some corn on the cob, which he ate while smiling at me with his little kid teeth. Harry was blond like his father, but had his mother's features, which was a good thing. Layne wasn't ugly, but he had a really threatening look about him that said in every possible way that he wasn't anyone to mess with. Jacinta was pretty foxy, though she looked tired. She yawned while she put ketchup on her hamburger bun.

"Your mom came in again to the store today with Harry," Layne said to Jacinta. "She was talking about getting that dumb Elmo cake for the party."

"Elmo!" Harry said.

"Hmm," Jacinta said, cutting up Harry's hamburger with her fork. "The last I talked to her, we were going to just do cupcakes. They're easier for kids. And no plates."

"Cupcay!" Harry said. "Elmo cupcay!"

"Why can't you like Cookie Monster, little man?" Layne asked his son.

"Elmo!"

"Christ," Layne muttered. "Elmo is such a goddamn douche."

"Quit swearing, will you? He can like Elmo all he wants, Layne. It's not *your* birthday party, is it? *You* have Cookie Monster on *your* cake."

"Maybe I will," Layne said, all grumpy but grinning.

"Lana called me," Jacinta said to Layne. "Asking me for Evan's number."

Oh, god, I thought.

"She fucking around again with Randy Garrington?" Layne asked.

"Don't say 'fuck' in front of your son," Jacinta said.

"Well, is she?"

"How should I know?" Jacinta said. "All she said was could I get Evan's number."

Harry reached for my corn, and I handed it to him. I've never been a big fan of sweet corn.

"Harry, sit down and eat already," Layne said, his mouth full of hamburger. Then he muttered, "Lana should leave Evan alone."

"Why?" Jacinta asked. "Do you have a girlfriend, Evan?"

Though she was a girl and said she was my friend, Baker was far from the standard definition of a girlfriend. Even if I believed in *non-monogramy*, even if Jim suddenly disappeared from the planet, I could never kick Baker game like I would any other girl. And not just because she had a sort-of boyfriend who could crush me into powder. Baker was too smart, would see through my bullshit. Which explained why I ended up with dumb chicks like Lana. Maybe I wasn't built to have a girl-friend.

"No girlfriend," I said.

"Well, you must think Lana's cute," Jacinta said. "Since you hooked up at the drive-in."

"Jesus, is this the smallest town ever?" I asked.

"Pretty much," Layne said. "Get used to it."

"Lana's all right," I said.

"Then what's the big problem?" Jacinta asked.

Layne launched into his opinion that Randy Garrington

was a crazy psycho and that Lana didn't have any sense when it came to guys and that I was a good kid and Lana should just finish her vet tech training and get a damn job so that when someone knocked her up she'd at least have a way to make a living.

"God, Layne. That's your sister you're talking about!"

"Half sister," Layne corrected, tipping back his beer.

"Knocking girls up isn't really my thing," I said.

"Give me your phone, Evan," Jacinta said. "I'll put her number in for you."

"What? No, you can't do that," Layne said, smacking my hand back.

Harry started to cry, and while Layne reassured him that I was okay and no one was fighting, Jacinta looked at me like, *as soon as Layne leaves I'll give you the number.*

After dinner, Layne and Jacinta flipped a coin over putting Harry to bed or cleaning up and Jacinta won and left Layne and me to deal with the dishes and dump out the pool. Their house was tiny and the lawn needed mowing and pinned up on the laundry line were a bunch of girl clothes and little boy T-shirts and there was a sandbox full of rusty Tonka trucks, but I didn't care because no one had ever invited me over to eat with their family like that, much less my supervisor at my job. It felt awesome, actually. A really adult thing to do.

Layne scrubbed the grill with a metal brush while I sat at the picnic table peeling the label off my beer bottle. After a while, he said, "Fine, I'll give you Lana's number. But on two conditions."

"Okay."

"First, you can never be with her in public. As long as

Randy Garrington's around town, anyway. You have to be like, here, in my basement with the door locked. Under the cover of darkness. With no other people around."

"Are you serious?"

"Randy Garrington's crazy," Layne said. "Stupid fucker even tried to mess with my older brother Tim once. And Tim's been in prison. Trust me, Evan. You don't want to deal with Randy. The guy's a fucking psycho."

This gave me a chill. And it was July-hot out.

"Okay," I gulped. "What's the other thing?"

"You tell me what went on with you before you moved here. Why you don't have a spleen, for instance. Who broke your nose? And that cut on your lip that never heals up."

I never expected Layne, of all people, to ask me outright about any of that. I figured he'd consider my busted-up features as just another day in the life of your average badass like himself.

"How do you know about my spleen?"

"You wrote it on your medical form for work," he said. "I actually read that shit, you know. I *am* in charge of you. And while it don't seem like you're insane like Randy, Lana *is* my sister."

Half sister, I thought, automatically.

"It's a long story."

"I'm not going anywhere."

It took a while to explain it all, but he didn't interrupt. Layne listened across the table, smoking a cigarette, quiet and serious with his Don't-Fuck-With-Me expression, which made me relax. Made me think that he'd heard stories like mine before. Though, more likely, he'd been the one delivering the ass-kicking.

When I finished, Layne raked his hair out of his eyes and sighed.

"Christ," he said. "So what's gonna happen to them?"

"I don't know. The court date's next June, if you can believe that."

"What happened to the girl?"

"She moved back to Boston," I said, my voice cracking a little, because the part about Collette was always the worst. "She was in the emergency room the same night as me. The cops told my dad that she probably won't be able to have kids. Two guys at once—there was a lot of internal damage."

"Christ," Layne said again.

We sat for a bit listening to crickets and the sound of his next door neighbor's music thumping.

"Give me your phone," Layne said. "But I'm adding one more condition."

"What's that?" I asked.

"You come over to my brother's tow shop this weekend," he said. "Tim's got a heavy bag down there. Me and him can at least teach you how to punch."

Dear Collette,

I'm sorry I'm sorry I'm sorry I'm sorry I'm sorry I'm sorry I'm sorry I'm sorry I'm sorry

I'm such a cock

I completely suck

CHAPTER TWELVE

A week later, Layne and I went to Tim's tow shop. Tim was on the phone when he came to the door, so he motioned us inside. We passed a tool bench and a Jeep with a smashed-in bumper in the repair well until we were in the back, where there was a foldout couch, a desk with an ancient computer, and a little refrigerator, where Layne got us each a can of beer.

The whole place smelled like oil and gas and dirt. A box fan in the window made a *Sports Illustrated* swimsuit calendar flutter against the wall. Layne pulled out some hand wraps from a metal utility locker and started talking about them while he wrapped up my wrists and palms. I tried to listen, but I was distracted by Tim on the phone over in the repair well. He was talking in that specific way that told me it was a girl on the line. I couldn't quite accept the fact that Layne's tattooed, ex-con brother might have a softer side, so I was eavesdropping like crazy.

"I'll come pick you up," Tim was saying. "Yeah? I like the sound of that. What? You tell that cocksucker he can talk to me about it . . . Oh, you think? Well, put on the coffee, girl, 'cause I can go all night . . ."

God. Even Tim's cheesy girl conversations sounded badass.

I noticed then what I was wearing: flip-flops and a T-shirt that said *Hey Cupcake!* in swirly pink lettering, from the cupcake shop in Tacoma.

Tim came in, grinning, saying he'd been wanting to meet me, which again, seemed corny to me in its kindness, despite Dr. Penny always telling me that's how friendships work and to get over it already.

Tim was taller and bigger than Layne, with more arm tattoos. He did the same kind of wallet-on-a-chain with jeans thing, but his T-shirt was tighter across the chest because of all his muscles and he was more handsome than Layne, though he still looked tougher than hell.

Tim hung up the heavy bag from a chain—he flipped it around like it wasn't filled with a hundred pounds of sand or the crushed skulls of the Beauchant brothers' enemies or whatever fills heavy bags.

"All right, make a fist," Layne said. "Keep your thumb out, never inside."

"I like it bent up a little," Tim said. "Feels better that way."

Like he was a connoisseur of violence. Which I guessed he must be.

"You want to connect with the index and middle fingers," Layne continued. "The other two fingers aren't as strong and break easier."

"Your fingers break? From hitting someone?"

"If you're hitting hard enough, sure," Layne said. "Usually your hands get all cut to shit too. But a few cracked knuckles or a broken finger is better than a busted nose, right?"

"You've got to hit them right, though," Tim said. "Because then it's over faster."

"So don't draw out the ass-kicking, then," I said, kind of joking.

"The sooner it's over, the better," Tim said. "That's the point. You don't go around *attacking* people, fighting dirty like that asshole Randy Garrington. Remember that time he went for my nuts after he brought Lana home drunk?" he asked Layne.

Layne looked pissy and said, "Evan, go ahead and fight dirty with that fucker. Stomp on his nuts—you won't hear me complaining."

Tim shook his head, like he thought Layne was a barbarian.

"Okay, so remember," Tim said. "A street fight isn't a movie, where the guys stand there forever taking a million hits. And it isn't like boxing—boxers train so they'll last longer in the ring. Normal people go straight down on the first hit. You break someone's nose? There's blood everywhere, their whole face swells up so they can't see shit, and it's over. So bank on getting one lucky punch done right and then running like hell. Can you run fast, Evan?"

I nodded.

"Good," Tim said. "Hit him and get the fuck out of there."

"The nose is a good target, right in the center, hurts like a bitch," Layne said, and the ridged bump on my own nose tingled at the thought. "A lot softer than the jaw too. Though most people can't take a hit in the jaw, either. But start with the nose. You remember how much that shit hurt, and you think about wanting to deliver that to someone else."

Of all of it, I could remember the moment my nose broke most. But very little else after that. Which was probably a good thing, overall, because thinking about being destroyed while naked in a shower did zero for my confidence, especially since I was applying for my man card while wearing flip-flops and a cupcake T-shirt.

We started out with me hitting Tim's open palms, Layne coaching behind me, which made me feel like a little kid learning to piss in the potty. Especially when they would say stuff like, *good, good, that's nice, that right hand's good, huh?*

Then we did the heavy bag, which was horrible and hard. Layne said I needed gloves, but Tim said I wasn't training for a welterweight matchup and needed to get a sense of my hands. I felt ridiculous while they argued, and then Layne's phone rang, so he ducked out to talk while Tim lectured me on the importance of stance. He reminded me of Dr. Penny, except with totally different catchphrases: *"The power comes from your body, not your fist"* and *"It's not the size of the dog in the fight, but the size of the fight in the dog."*

"Use everything you got from your feet up, and you'll lay the other guy out flat," Tim said. "Keep hitting, beyond the point of impact. Don't stop once you make contact. Push all the way through to the other side. You do that and it's over before it starts. Guaranteed."

I nodded, feeling less stupid, because Tim was smiling-yet-serious and I could tell he didn't think I was completely hopeless.

"Let's get some water and see where the fuck Layne is," Tim said.

I gulped water like I'd been in the desert. My arms were burning.

"I gotta pick up some Tylenol," Layne said. "Harry's got a fever. You're doing good, Evan."

"Yeah, he's picking it up quick," Tim added.

"Don't you have to be somewhere?" I asked Tim.

"Not until nine," Tim said, with a grin that made me instantly jealous of the fact that he had a chick waiting for him.

***

We kept on with the heavy bag. Tim's phone rang again, but I didn't eavesdrop this time. I just imagined Tate Kerrigan's square face and Patrick Ramsey's hammy one and thought, *One lucky punch.*

"Pull back fast," Tim said. "Out and back. Assume the first punch didn't work and you have to do another one. That's how boxers work, at least. But your right's pretty strong. That's your advantage."

I hit a few more to the bag, and Tim said, "You better stop, or you'll be sore tomorrow. You can unwrap them wraps by yourself?"

"Uh-huh," I said. Tim pulled out a wad of keys and started fiddling one off the ring.

"Here," he said. "For if you want to come and hit if I'm not around. I'll pull down the garage door, but this one locks up the side one when you go."

He was grinning as he walked out, and I didn't know why until I got to my car and standing there, swinging her purse on her shoulder, was Lana.

Dear Collette,

It turns out fighting is about thoughtless efficiency and speed. I know this now because Layne and his brother Tim are teaching me to box, which is very embarrassing to be taught, Collette—even though I'm told one of my hands is "good."

I shouldn't be surprised that being ready to throw-down without getting tangled in questions and decisions—in thinking—is a key skill in fighting. If there's one thing I used to know, it's how to be ready without a second thought. I used to be a fucking expert in not thinking.

A good fight, so I'm told, has just one punch. I think the same's true of getting down. The more I learn about fighting from Tim and Layne, the more I realize I already knew.

I am an expert in being a slutty fucker. I should have my own advice column. Who needs college?

Later, Evan

CHAPTER THIRTEEN

After I started boxing regularly out at the tow shop, I slept like a fucking rock. So I went as often as I could. The morning after a particularly long session with the heavy bag (and Lana showing up as I finished), my father and I were both crunching through cereal in silence. Typical morning. But then he went and said something completely atypical.

"You need some new clothes."

"What?"

"Every time I see you, you've got an old crappy T-shirt on," he said. "I make decent money. Just because you don't have a mother to tend to this kind of thing doesn't mean you have to go around looking like a hobo all the time."

"Like a *hobo*?"

"It's not just you. Brenda's been on me about how I wear the same thing every day. She thinks a little color wouldn't hurt."

"Dad?"

"I'm saying let's go buy some new clothes, Evan."

"Brenda's gay boyfriend coming with us?"

My father laughed. I shivered with a kind of happiness, hearing him laugh. He did it more and more lately. Though usually never with me. I usually heard it coming through the window of my room as he sat out on our deck with Brenda drinking whiskey sours and playing Tripoli or cribbage.

So he drove us in his Mercedes—an odd car for two badly dressed guys, no doubt—to what amounted to the main shopping center in Marchant Falls: a Sears surrounded by a strip mall. It made me feel sad for Marchant Falls, compared to other places we'd lived. But also a little protective. So what if Marchant Falls was tiny and unhip? I'd rather go fishing with Tom or eat chili dogs at the Dairy Queen with Jesse or knock around Story Island with Baker, and if it meant there was no Macy's or Cheesecake Factory, then so be it.

"Are you almost out of gas?" I asked, as we pulled into the parking lot.

"No, the gauge is broken."

That was weird. My father tended to be anal about things being broken.

"Aren't you going to fix it?"

"Probably not. The nearest Mercedes dealership is sixty miles away. I should get rid of this car. I think it makes me look like a prick."

I had never considered this, but Marchant Falls was the first place we'd lived where the car stood out.

Despite becoming a man of the people as far as his car was concerned, my father didn't seem wild about shopping at Sears, so we started with the strip mall. Right away he found a pair of blue flip-flops in a giant bin sitting outside of a dollar store.

While he went to buy them, I went to the nearest men's clothing store. I was staring at dress shirts when he came into the store, wearing the blue flip-flops.

"Where are your other shoes?"

"In the trunk."

"What the hell is on your toenails?"

My father smiled down at his feet.

"Nice, huh? You really missed out last night over at Brenda's."

"Whiskey sours aren't my thing, Dad."

"Last night was sangria," he corrected. "Also, Bailey's milk shakes. It was a kind of girls' night. Quite a sociological experience. Your mother wasn't so rigidly feminine, of course, so my background knowledge isn't extensive. But Baker was having a crisis so there were certain female rituals to be observed."

"What happened to Baker?" I tried not to sound as alarmed as I felt.

"She was looking for you, to start with," my father said, sorting through a rack of shirts.

"What did you tell her?"

"I said you were out. Probably with some girl, knowing you."

"You didn't really say that, did you?"

"I did," my father said, and I could tell he was smiling, even though his back was to me. "I think I'll try this red one."

I didn't get why he didn't just try on the damn thing over his current shirt; that was how I always did it. Of course, since the uniforms at Remington Chase, it had been a long time since I'd deliberately gone out to buy any kind of clothing at all.

"Baker asked me if you had a girlfriend," he called from the dressing room. "I told her it was usually plural, but I currently didn't know. She didn't believe it when I said most of the numbers in your phone are girls. I told her that you didn't tend to keep those numbers long, though."

This was a little surprising. Given that he seemed to know nothing about me except that I was fucked-up. But like his calls with Dr. Penny, he was showing a definite sneaky side. Like he could only be interested in me when I wasn't looking.

I was hovering between wanting to punch him and loving that he knew anything about me when he opened the dressing room door.

"What do you think? Is red a good color for me?"

"I don't know. How can you tell?"

"No idea." He stared at himself in the mirror, the stubble on his head golden in the harsh dressing room light.

"Well, it matches your toenails." The saleslady behind us snickered.

"I look like my father," he said, sighing. "But he had all his hair. And never wore red."

My dad took his red shirt to the counter, and I added a couple of T-shirts in boring colors—grey, black, white—and he shook his head.

"No color? No style, Evan? Really?"

"What the hell did those women do to you last night?" I asked. "Cut your balls off after they painted your toenails?"

He laughed again, and I couldn't help smiling too.

"You have to understand," he said, as he handed the cashier his credit card. "It was a female crisis of tremendous proportions. Baker's boyfriend came over, and there was a big throw-down of some sort."

"'Throw-down'?" I asked. "Like, he was violent?" My hand curled up into a fist reflexively. Thumb out. I was a little surprised at how quickly I'd absorbed the Beauchant brothers' lessons.

"Oh, no," he said. "They just had a loud argument in the yard."

"So, what did Brenda do?"

"Hell if I know," he said. "From what I could make of it, it sounded like they shouted at each other and finally the guy just left. Something about her best friend cheating? That part was sort of unclear to me."

"I think it's unclear to Baker too."

"By the time I went over there, it was over," he said, as we exited the store. "Peggy was blending up Bailey's milk shakes. I hadn't had Baileys in years. Your mother used to like it with coffee. They were good, though Peggy thought they clashed with sangria."

"Who's Peggy?"

"How long have we been living here, Evan? You know Peggy! Tom's mother?"

I kind of wanted to punch him again. Like he was in the habit of knowing people's names! I couldn't help it if I was bad with names. I never had good reason to remember them. Which was mostly his fault, to be technical.

"Then Baker took out this device used to sand off calluses from your feet," he continued. "For some reason women endeavor to make their feet as defenseless as a newborn's. Brenda wanted to use it on me, but the damn thing looked like a vibrator. The polish is where I drew the line."

"Dad!" I looked to see if anyone was behind us.

The next store was all perfume, and strangely, my father wanted to go in.

"What are you doing?" I asked.

"Do you have somewhere else to be, Evan?"

"No."

"Then relax already."

The perfume store was staffed by two cute girls who I might have thought appealing, had I not been with my toenail-polished father at the time. But he had no embarrassment whatsoever, accepting the samples one girl gave him and listening patiently while the other told him about the deals of the day, then thanking them both politely like they'd just handed him the Nobel Prize instead of samples and a coupon. It kind of cracked me up, but the place gave me a headache, so I dragged him out the door.

"What the hell made you want to go in there?"

"Those girls were cute, didn't you think?"

"Dad!"

"It's not like I've got work to occupy my mind, Evan. Why not get your thrills where you can find them?"

Because that's how you lose a spleen, Dad. If you recall. Again, I wanted to punch him.

"Those girls were my age. And perfume shops aren't exactly thrilling."

"Brenda would never wear any of that crap," he said. "She prefers essential oils. She says they integrate better than synthetics with the skin's chemistry."

"How would you know *that*, Dad?" I asked, a little shocked. "You paying attention to Brenda's *skin* these days?"

He reddened all the way up to his shaved skull. I was happy

to have popped him in a sore spot for once.

"What's going on with you and Brenda?"

"Nothing, Evan," he said, in a voice that was familiar. Economical. Inviting no more discussion.

The last stop in the strip was a sporting goods store and my nonathletic father acted like the whole thing was another sociological experiment so he enthusiastically followed me in.

"So what happened with Baker and her boyfriend?" I asked.

"You mean the unfortunately named Jim Sweet? Good god. His mother must have hated him."

"Jim's not all that bad. Though his name sucks."

My father laughed and continued. "Mostly it sounded like they both regretted their behavior. I don't know. Much time was spent explaining to Baker how she was going to college and things would change anyway. That if she valued loyalty, she should insist on it in the future. Then we ate a bunch of ice cream."

I doubted loyalty was important when you were non-monogramous. But it didn't seem like Baker understood that concept any better than Jim Sweet could pronounce it.

"Then what happened?"

"More beautification activities. And a debate about whether Baker should just ask you out. Of course, I said that would probably make your summer."

I spun around from the wall of running shoes I was looking at.

"*You. Did. Not.*"

"Of course not. I may have only had one girlfriend my entire life, but I'm not that stupid."

"Mom was the only girl you ever went out with?"

"Being into math isn't exactly an aphrodisiac, Evan."

True enough. Neither was baldness. I kind of felt sorry for him, then. For missing out on so much. Although, at least he had his spleen still. Though it was possible Soren might have had a go at him at one point. I couldn't imagine my dad in a fight.

"Baker doesn't believe in girls asking guys out, anyway."

"Well, I don't see how that makes sense. She practically grew up in The House That Feminism Built."

"She didn't explain all her weird rules?"

"Bailey's milk shakes don't make people terribly articulate."

He picked up a horrible sandal that had so much Velcro on it that I grabbed it out of his hand and forcibly set it down.

"Those are awful, and if you buy them, you will look like an old man," I said. "And do me a favor and stop going over there drinking if you can't keep your mouth shut about my sex life."

"I didn't realize we were discussing your sex life," he said, very entertained. "Does Baker factor into your sex life?"

"As much as Brenda factors into yours."

My father turned away. Like he was suddenly very interested in basketball jerseys. Take that, nosy fucker, I thought.

I found some clothes at the sports store. Things with actual colors, even. My father looked at the baseball bats and soccer cleats and hockey sticks like things in some kind of museum or zoo set up for his amusement. Sports had never interested him before, but now he was asking me all sorts of questions about things he assumed I knew about, being that I wasn't allergic to physical competition.

"I don't know shit about football, Dad," I said, when he asked about the helmets. "I'm not really one for team sports."

"At least you like athletics in some fashion," he said. "I should buy some running shoes. Maybe I should start running with you? You still run, right?"

"I'm kind of getting into boxing, lately," I said.

While he tried on running shoes, I explained about Layne and Tim and the heavy bag at the tow shop. (Everything except how Lana and I sometimes did it on the foldout sofa, of course.)

"I would love to see that," my dad said.

I thought of my nerdy math and computer genius father with the Beauchant brothers—Tim's prison tattoos and Layne's mouth full of chew—and the whole thing made me want to die a little.

***

We went to Mackinanny's for lunch, and by then, though I was feeling okay, I was also tense. Aware that we hadn't done anything like this in . . . ever. Obviously, we had gone to stores and restaurants and everything. But it was different that day. Not that he was telling me all his feelings or asking me to explain all my secret desires, either, but we were hanging out as if we did it all the time, as if it was normal for us to shoot the shit and laugh at each other's jokes. To steal french fries off the other's plate. For him to ask the waitress, without even blinking, to bring two glasses with the pitcher of beer.

As we sat there with our guts stuffed, me finishing off the pitcher of beer, he asked, "You boxing for any particular reason?"

There. That was why I was tense. I'd been waiting for him to bring up something like that. Say that he was worried. Or that we'd be moving.

But what could I say? *Dad, I'm learning to box so I can fuck my boss's half sister?* Which wasn't really true, though it wasn't all false, either.

"I told Layne what happened in North Carolina," I said, trying to act casual. "He asked about it because of my medical form at work. It was kind of his idea."

"It's a good idea," he said, sipping his beer. "I wish . . . I guess I've always been pretty passive in my approach to conflict."

"The Beauchant brothers know their way around a street fight."

"Really?"

"You can't meet them for one of your sociological experiments."

"My father used to beat us," he said.

I set my glass down with a loud thump. "What? Grandpa Carter?"

"Random and for no reason." He was solemn, staring at the greasy paper in the onion ring basket we'd demolished earlier. "He was a volatile, angry son of a bitch. You never knew what might provoke him. Soren and me. Our mother too. She tried to get between us, protect us, but that usually made it worse."

"I didn't know that." I suddenly felt a little shitty for thinking this whole day was about me. That everything was about me, actually.

"I didn't see a reason to tell you," he said. "He died before you were born, anyway. The only reason I bring it up now is that when he was sixteen, Soren fought back. Our father, the bastard, never expected it. Because Soren was calculated. Had waited and planned. Figured he had nature on his side, of course. It was all another cycle for him. He was growing, our father declining. So, one day, when something set him off, Soren hit him back. Put your grandfather in the hospital."

"Whoa. That's crazy."

"You're absolutely right," my father said. "Crazy. And effective. My father didn't stop hitting us, but he definitely thought twice about it when Soren was around."

I didn't know what to say. It was like looking at a new person. A person who annoyed me and never said anything most of the time but who let women paint his toenails and bought clothes in colors and bent the rules so I could drink beer with him. Who grew up in violence, was saved by his brother. And then stole that brother's girl, the only girl he'd ever had, and then she died. You'd think knowing such information would make me more sympathetic to him, more understanding of how he'd come to be the way he was. But as we drove home and I tried to reimagine him, a younger man, not bald, not nerdy, someone picked by my beautiful mother, and instead of some lightning bolt of clarity, the whole thing just gave me a splitting headache.

Dear Collette,

I'm supposed to imagine giving up my coping mechanisms and what would happen if I did. I don't have to write this in a letter, but I'm used to doing that. Plus, I don't want you to think that I am neglecting you.

I don't really think I have coping mechanisms or that they are bad or that they need to be given up. So, I take baths in the lake. Because showers bother me. Especially ones in bathrooms without locks on the doors. Dr. Penny thinks I need to come to terms with this because you cannot bathe in a Minnesota lake during winter. But I told her we would probably be gone somewhere else by then, anyway, and it wouldn't be her problem anymore, to which she said, Yes, Evan, but it would still be your problem.

I try to shower. Every morning. Just the noise of the water beating on the tile scares the shit out of me. And don't even ask about putting a lock on the door. Let's just say I had to pay my dad back to replace the entire door, and the replacement didn't have a lock, either.

Then there's my haircutting. I keep my hair cut really short, since it freaks me out to think it could be used against me, like it was that night in Connison. Did you know that this is why Alexander the Great prohibited beards for his soldiers, thus ushering in the modern concept of the clean-shaven, jarhead marine? Facial hair could be pulled or grabbed, making it a point of vulnerability. Which I tried to explain to Dr. Penny, but she wasn't having it.

They shaved my head in the hospital, to deal with some of the contusions and stitches. And I liked it. Because it's like being in disguise. So I still cut it. Every morning. Sometimes I cut it again at night. It's kind of uneven, and little spots are always growing out.

If I quit cutting it, I would have approximately five minutes back each day. Which doesn't seem like a lot. I could yank it a couple more times a week, which is not something I need to be doing more of, trust me. Or run a couple more miles. Though I run about ten miles a week, so that's not really necessary, either.

The thing is, with longer hair, my elf ears wouldn't be noticeable. And I wouldn't look like a cancer patient. I realize I don't look good. The demented-peach-fuzz pointy-ears look is pretty much the opposite of badass. But even if I grew my hair out again, I will never look or be as badass as my friend Layne or his brother, Tim. (You know, the ones who are teaching me to box.) Tim and Layne were probably taught to uppercut and jab in nursery school, while I was learning that Hands Are Not for Hitting. You should see the Beauchant brothers. They would have never let anyone touch you.

Later, Evan

CHAPTER FOURTEEN

A week later, Tom and Kelly dropped Baker and me off at Story Island. Kelly, pointing out all the No Trespassing signs, was confused, but Tom told her he would take her to Northwood for lunch if she didn't bug him about it. Northwood was the fancy steak place that my father had shown me our first weeks in Pearl Lake. As they boated away, we could hear Kelly asking Tom if she should go back and change her outfit.

"Poor Tom," Baker said, as we started toward the Archardt House.

"He signs up for it," I said. Having sex with Lana made me less sympathetic, I guess. I felt guilty about Lana some-times—how we never kissed or went anywhere, how blatant-ly it was about getting down and nothing else—but at least I didn't feel like chewing the plaster off the walls as much anymore.

"Don't get me wrong, I love Kelly," Baker said. "But I think she assumes Tom's just going to put up with her shit forever."

"Well, he might. Maybe they'll get married."

"Ugh, that's so gross," Baker said.

"I know. But it at least lets me imagine a happy ending for Tom."

"Oh, he gets plenty of those," Baker said. "Kelly basically blow jobs her way out of any argument."

"Jesus. I can't even imagine."

"Oh, what*ever*. You're a *guy*. I bet you can *easily* imagine."

"All right, fine. But not with Kelly, at least. I mean, what's with her hair?"

"The blond's way better, though," Baker said. "Before it was like she char-grilled it."

I laughed. Though I was hardly one to criticize people's hair.

"I wish I didn't have to leave for college right now," Baker said. "The Archardt House is so strange. I could write a kick-ass paper about it if I was still in school."

"Dork," I said.

"Oh, shut up. Don't you think it's weird how well-preserved the house is, though? You'd think there'd be more broken windows. And upstairs, there's places where I swear the plaster's been repaired."

"Maybe the DNR looks after it."

"But technically the DNR's job is natural resources, of which the house is not one," she said. "I mean, why else do you think that we haven't been caught out here yet? The wildlife people have enough crap to do. Are you even listening?"

"Not really," I said.

"Dick," she said, and girl punched me.

Baker and I had been coming to Story Island more

regularly in the last few weeks. But we never really planned out our trips there. Sometimes we hiked around. Sometimes we just snooped through the house, me usually in the library, because I got a kick out of all those old books. But Baker got more personal, liked to dig through cabinets and drawers. Sometimes she'd have weird requests for me, like have me move furniture so she could inspect the wallpaper pattern or hold the measuring tape while she plotted out the dimensions of each room. I didn't really care what we did, actually. The whole island gave me a weird relaxing feeling that was so good it was almost embarrassing. Of course, if I had to pick my favorite room, it would have been the library. Which was weird, given that most books I had to read for school bored the shit out of me. But these old ones were cool. I even liked how they smelled. Kind of musty and burnt.

"I'll be upstairs," she said, as we stepped into the front entryway. "I want to take a few pictures of the lattice framework on the bed. And the columns on the patio are . . . Oh, shut up." She headed up the stairs. "I know I'm a geek."

After an hour of paging through books, I got sleepy. I stretched, listening for Baker's movements. We were so casual, acting like the Archardt House belonged to us. Like we were just going in and out each other's cabins like people on the east side did all summer long, and not trespassing illegally on a protected island.

I wandered to the piano room. That's what I called it; Baker called it the drawing room. She had a technical name for everything. Through the window, I could see her in the side yard, crouching down and taking pictures of weeds coming out of the crumbled flagstones. I looked at her for a minute: the muscles in her legs, her ponytails swinging around her shoulders, the way she focused on each shot.

She turned toward the window, and I stepped back, though I doubted she could see me through the grimy glass. I didn't want to bug her, so I went back to the library and sat on the giant tank of a desk and drank some water. Then, pausing to listen for Baker's footsteps, I took my Uncle Soren's blue cloth book from my backpack and started looking through it. Drawings of river otters and different varieties of pondweed. Instructions on weaving a seine to capture minnows for bait. An explanation of the purpose and use of a Secchi disk. A floor plan of the Archardt House, and what looked like dates and notes about it. Stuff like *Sealed hole in master bedroom* and *Replaced broken window in library.*

"Hey, dumbass."

I jumped, as if Soren himself had appeared. But it was Baker, sweaty from being outside. She pulled herself up on the desk beside me and gulped a bunch of water from my bottle. I leaned away, not wanting her sloppy drinking to get on the pages of the blue cloth book.

"What is that?" she asked.

"A book."

"No kidding." She edged closer to me. "Is that your man journal?"

"Yeah. It's my man journal where I press leaves and draw pictures and tell all my private thoughts."

"Really?"

"No."

"Someone's crabby today. Need your loadie girl to come give you more hickeys?"

She brought up my mystery loadie girl a lot, but I never admitted to anything, and her annoyance with me was kind of enjoyable, actually.

I shut the book and slid it into my pack.

"Why are you being so secretive? Did you find it here?"

"I found it in the summer kitchen," I said, sighing, because, of course, then she wanted to go to the summer kitchen and look around. Which I normally wouldn't have minded. But right now I wasn't up for it. I didn't want to have another meeting of the Dead Parents Club. And I didn't want her assuming the book belonged to local history, either.

"Are you mad at me or something, Evan?"

"No, I'm fine," I muttered. "Let's go."

Once in the summer kitchen, I pointed out where I'd found the book, and Baker began examining the corner cupboard. Gently laying the contents of the peanut butter jar on the floor. Running her fingertips over the fishing lures and lead weights. Holding up the BB gun to see if it would still shoot. I sat on the floor and opened the blue cloth book to a drawing of a loon's head, the red eye creepy but somehow beautiful too. Below it, a list of loon calls—the hoot, wail, tremolo, and yodel—and all their various meanings and uses.

Just as I started to wonder if my dorky fondness for E. Church Westmore was a sort of throwback gene from my uncle, I turned the page. And then I was caught again, my throat getting hot and tight, sure signs of being Almost-Weepy. It was a drawing of my mother. Her head tilted to one side, not facing front directly, like she was looking toward another point on the horizon. Obviously, she was much younger in the drawing, but I could still recognize her. Her hair black as the diagram of the raven's wing, black as mine. With a slight smile, and her name below the fading shadings of her neck: *Melina*. Written in fine, gentle script, as if the letters themselves were precious to him.

Beneath were these words:

Loons do not mate for life. This is wrong, and a persistent myth, though many would like it to be so. The importance of a nest site is the main factor of consequence in mating habits, and it is determined by the male. Fighting for a home is the province of the male alone. So it is the territory they protect and cherish above all, not a mate, not the young that they lose all too easily.

I stared at the drawing and the words, so dazed that I again didn't realize that Baker had sat down by me. I quickly turned the page back to the red-eyed loon.

"That's really beautiful," she said.

"It's my uncle's book," I said. "He's the one that came here first. On a dare, my dad said. Soren. My father's brother. They never speak. My dad doesn't know where he is, even. They haven't seen each other since my mom's funeral."

Quietly, we looked at the loon's red eye. I was still feeling Almost-Weepy. Probably closer to Actual-Weepy. With Baker sitting beside me. I felt like dying because I was going to cry in front of her. Over my mother. Over *loons*. It felt like another occasion for an overly long German word.

Then Baker turned the page to the drawing of my mother. Which made me suck in my breath even more.

"Is that her?" she asked.

"Yeah."

"What's she doing in your uncle's book?"

I didn't want to say what I suspected. That my father was as big a dick about women as his son, though his count was admittedly much lower than mine. But the same principle remained. That Adrian Carter had somehow, in his silent, math-geek way, managed to steal away my mother from Soren. Maybe in the same way he was dancing with Brenda and drinking whiskey sours and not caring if his gas gauge broke.

"I don't know," I said.

"Do you think they were together? Or was he just secretly in love with her?"

I shrugged, looking at the drawing. Maybe I was the least romantic guy on the planet, but I didn't think you made a drawing like that if you didn't feel something intense.

What happened next was horrible. Baker touched my mouth. My lips. With her fingers. Softly. Then she kissed me and I swear, I felt like I'd been shot. I shut my eyes and couldn't move.

After all the time we'd spent together, on Story Island, on the docks and the diving platform, that night in the lake skinny-dipping, on her screen porch or the Tonneson's deck, at the goddamn Dairy Queen with Tom and Kelly while she scarfed down a Peanut Buster Parfait (which she liked to call a Penis Buster Parfait, something that cracked her and Tom up, because it made Kelly shriek in embarrassment)—all the times I'd thought about her, naked or otherwise (okay, mostly naked) and how out of reach she was for me—I'd never considered she would do this. Because it was pointless, liking Baker. Because I was me and she was Baker and she was awesome and going to college, long jumping away from me and my stupid, tortured, late-night lake bathing, daily haircutting, scarred stomach and broken nose and elf ears and constant split-lip existence . . .

She pulled back, then. Before I could even open my mouth. Before I could even enjoy it. Our little moment of non-monogramy.

She said, "Your mouth is bleeding. I keep forgetting to get you that salve Keir makes."

"It's okay." I sounded like a sick twelve-year-old.

"Sorry, Evan." She stood.

"It's okay."

"I don't know why I did that. I'm with Jim. Even if . . . Well. Sorry."

I wanted to say that technically she could do whatever she wanted. But maybe things had changed since the big fight? Maybe they'd figured things out, ditched non-monogramy? I watched her silently collect up the bits from the peanut butter jar and the BB gun and put everything back into the cupboard. Then she started looking around the summer kitchen, like nothing had happened. So I did the same. Strapped the book shut with the belt and shoved it into my backpack. Stood up and tried to get a hold of myself.

She turned to me and checked her watch. "Tom should be here soon. Meet you at the drop-off point?"

I nodded. She had kissed me, and I sat there, frozen. She probably thought I was gay. Or lying about all my sex stories. Or maybe it was a pity kiss, because I was a sad orphan with a dead mother. Whatever it was, I wanted to die. Especially thinking about how she packed everything up afterwards, like the whole thing was too shameful for comment. Baker, who had a comment about everything.

Dear Collette,

Fear is our topic today. Dr. Penny says we cannot eradicate fear entirely, because it's a biological response designed to keep us safe. She says we can dial back our fears should they overtake our life, though. Learn to balance them, especially if they complicate our lives. Like cutting one's hair every morning. Like bathing in a lake instead of showering. Like sleeping with a girl you don't really like but not being able to stop. Like wanting to get your GED instead of attending your senior year. Though I don't understand why a GED is so crappy—isn't it the same thing as the damn diploma?

I'm supposed to take an incident where I was recently afraid. Examine that incident and then inhabit the way I felt, then pull back from the situation and rotate around it. Look at all the possible responses available; see all the other angles. Because that's the thing about fear. It's single-minded. It reduces your choices. And what's the point of being alive if you don't have choices?

But I can't talk about the incident where I was recently afraid with you. It involves another girl, and I'm afraid (ha-ha) that it might hurt your feelings to know about it, because, though it has been months since we were together and our relationship was pretty new, I still feel warm and kind toward you. And after what they did to you—my fault—all I want is to sit beside you in bed and smooth your hair. (I imagine this with both of us fully clothed, by the way. Totally legit, Collette.) So, I'd smooth your hair, like my mother used to when she was trying to get me to fall asleep and I was too hyper. I'd tell you that you're an amazing girl. I remember you in the Connison hallway, your legs in red socks, calling me a dummy and telling me to let you in my room so you wouldn't get caught. Helping yourself to the guy your friend liked. No fear in that, Collette.

That is the angle I like to inhabit the most. I'm too chickenshit to inhabit any angles where I could have changed what happened in that unmentionable situation. So I just think of you, pushing yourself into my life, and me opening the door and both of us inside, the door locked, safe. I inhabit that angle just fine.

Later, Evan

CHAPTER FIFTEEN

"My break's over in fifteen minutes," Lana said, hooking her fingers into my belt loops.

We were in the penned-in area enclosing the Dumpster and the recycling behind The Donut Co-op. There were people in this world who ate out of Dumpsters, and the owner of The Donut Co-op had spent extra money to enclose everything because he couldn't stomach the idea of such desperation.

Speaking of desperation, there I was, at 10:17 on a Friday morning, condoms in my pocket and my hands under Lana's Donut Co-op apron, pushing up her skirt. Far from the cover of darkness, breaking all of Layne's rules about his half sister. Because both of us were desperate. Me, because I couldn't stop thinking about Baker in the summer kitchen; Lana, because she had a big exam in her vet-tech class at the community college that afternoon. She called me on her way into her shift at The Donut Co-op saying she needed me to get her mind off it.

So, of course, I shot up from a dead sleep and rinsed off in the lake while the fog at sunrise was still burning off the water, then brushed my teeth and drove into Marchant Falls like a goddam firefighter headed to a four-alarm blaze.

Only to sit through The Donut Co-op's morning rush. While Lana satisfied the carb and caffeine demands for the entire population of Marchant Falls, I paged through my uncle's blue cloth book. I couldn't look beyond the drawing of my mother, though. I just went back to the beginning of the book, seeing what I'd already read. Safer there.

The sleaziness behind the Dumpster took longer than fifteen minutes, though. Which sucked, even if Lana seemed to enjoy herself. Maybe it was smelling a million dead donuts while bees buzzed around crushed pop cans. Maybe it was the way the sun dipped behind a slab of clouds, turning the bright morning grey and depressing. Maybe both, because even with those spectacular noises girls make when they allow you to touch them, I couldn't close the deal. Finally, Lana said she had to get back.

"Sorry," I muttered, chucking the condom into the Dumpster and zipping up. Lana giggled while she straightened her apron.

I felt like a complete loser. There's nothing like sex for knocking out *persistent, negative thoughts*—Dr. Penny's phrase for my anxious brain. And now even that relief was unavailable.

The sun blasted out again as the clouds passed over. I felt like doing something ridiculously showy for Lana, like buying her flowers, something gigantic like they put around the winning horse's neck at the Kentucky Derby. Lana just gave herself to me, and now it looked like even that wasn't enough. I didn't know if I should apologize or what. I couldn't think of anything to say. Though Lana didn't say much to me, usually, anyway. Beyond telling me where she'd meet me and whatever, she mostly just told me I was *good*. As in, after we'd finished doing it and I was coming back to life, she'd say, "Damn, Evan, you're *good*."

Probably a year ago, I would have been insanely proud of this compliment. No other girl had said anything like that to me before. But Lana saying it just made me feel shitty. Because fuck if I knew why what I was doing was *good* for Lana.

Before she went back inside, I kissed her good-bye. Something we never did, really. But I felt awful at that point. Lana stood there, a little shy—SHY! after fucking me behind a Dumpster!—tucking her hair behind her ears while I wished her luck on her test and kissed her again on the cheek. And she blushed—BLUSHED! after fucking me behind a Dumpster!—and went back inside The Donut Co-op.

Completely wrecked and depressed, I drove to Cub Foods because Friday was payday and I figured I'd pick up my check before heading home. But I wasn't thinking clearly, so I didn't consider that I'd see Layne—he's the one who gave me my check, obviously—and I felt like what I'd just done was written all over my face.

Luckily, Layne was distracted. It was Harry's third birthday party tomorrow and Jacinta's mother was out of town helping some relative and Layne and Jacinta had no idea how to make mini Elmos on five dozen cupcakes.

"Listen," I told him. "I used to work in a cupcake shop. Why don't I make the Elmo cupcakes? It's the least I can do."

Layne looked at me like I'd just announced I was gay and leaving for Hollywood to become a movie star.

"I'm serious," I said. "It's no big deal. We did special orders like that all the time."

"You sure, man?" he asked. "'Cause I can get a couple of those mixes in a box or something..."

"I got it, don't worry. What time is the party tomorrow?"

"Three o'clock."

"I'll take care of it," I said. "And call me if you want help cleaning or whatever."

I filled up a cart with everything I'd need for Harry's cupcakes. Butter and sugar and eggs and flour and food coloring and paper cups and chocolate and the whole nine. Fully from scratch—no bullshit mixes in a box for me.

※

I was feeling a little less shitty about the Dumpster dive with Lana and heading back to Pearl Lake with all the cupcake crap when my phone rang with an unknown number. Which never happened to me. I had maybe a dozen numbers in my phone and never gave out my own number if I could help it.

"Evan, it's Baker."

"Hey, what's up?" I tried to sound normal.

She said she was at the Historical Society and her car wouldn't start and could I come over?

Apparently, it was my day for good deeds. First, Lana, then Layne, then Baker, who was standing by her little green Honda looking stressed-yet-thankful when I showed up.

I tried to start her car (because it's what guys do, right?), but it was dead all right. Baker couldn't remember if she'd left a light on or what. Of course I didn't have jumper cables. But Baker was in a hurry to get back to the lake and said we could come out later and jump it.

"What's the big hurry?" I asked.

"Promise you won't call me a dork?"

"Promise."

"I ordered some genealogical data about the Archardts, and it came in today. I can't wait to read it."

"Dork."

"Dick," she said back. "So what are you doing today, besides rescuing girls?" She looked me over like she expected to find more hickeys.

"Rescuing girls?" I asked. "In a Subaru Outback? The vehicle of choice for lesbian Golden Retriever owners?"

"My mom's not a lesbian," she said. "And neither are you. Unless that's some other mysterious thing you're hiding about yourself."

"Today I'm making sixty Elmo cupcakes for a little boy's birthday party," I said. "He's turning three tomorrow."

She gave me the same look Layne had.

"I'm not kidding. It's my boss's son, and I'm helping them out. You can even come over and witness it if you don't believe me."

Baker grinned and I felt like maybe the weirdness from the summer kitchen had passed and we could get back to our regular setting of me just secretly liking her while dicking someone else and her just being supersmart and unavailable while smelling delicious.

She came over after I'd messed up the first round of cupcakes and sat at the counter eating some of the mistakes. At first she seemed like her regular self, happy and curious, but there was something off a little bit, something hesitant.

"What's the matter?" I finally asked. Because girls want you to ask. They don't want to be alone with their shitty feelings. Unlike me, who always got along famously in the company of my special crappy thoughts.

"It's Jim," she said. "He's been gone all week for this family reunion, but he's coming home tonight."

"So."

"So he won't stop texting me. He's all paranoid that I've cheated on him," she said. "Like last time he was gone."

"Have you?" I asked. Trying to act like what happened in the summer kitchen was too lame to count as cheating. Which it probably was.

"No," she said. "But he means like the time with Taber."

"But aren't you non-monogamous, now? Why should he care?"

"I guess," she said. "But it doesn't matter. Jim thinks I'll get back at him because of Conley. As if I've got time to sit around planning revenge! He doesn't get that it's enough of a job for me to hate Conley."

"You don't *have* to hate her. You could just change your rules a little."

She ignored that and said, "He came over a while back all drunk and pathetic and saying he was sorry. It was so out of character. I felt bad for him. It's like he doesn't get it."

I didn't really get it, either, to be honest. I just shrugged at her.

"You know what I wish?" she asked.

That more guys were exactly like me? I thought. *That I would lay you out on this counter and strip off your clothes?*

"What," I said, holding my breath while I ladled batter into paper cups.

"I wish my life could be normal again," she said. "This summer has been completely abnormal. Everything ending. Everything that could go wrong went wrong, you know? My best friend totally turning on me. Breaking up."

"You and Jim broke up?"

"We're leaving for college in like two weeks," she said. "So even if we're together *now*, we can't really be together, *then*. I thought maybe the whole see-other-people thing would make it easier, but that just made everything shittier. I should have just acted normal."

"I'm not sure anyone's normal." Dr. Penny was fond of mentioning this to me, actually.

"But I've never been one of those people who wanted to be different!" Baker insisted. "I like buying my clothes at the mall like everyone else. Doing my homework, being in sports. Just being *regular*. I think my dad was way more regular. Like me. I don't want to be like my mother. Wearing tie-dye at forty-eight and making no money teaching at a dinky college and acting like a hippie freak."

"Dating a gay guy who raises sheep while wearing women's yoga pants," I added because I couldn't help it.

She said, "Keir's not gay!" We debated Keir's sexuality for a while, which was a better topic than her dead-but-regular dad.

"Seriously," she said. "Do you even know what I mean? About being normal?"

"Yeah, sure."

"That's it?" she asked. "You're just going to say, 'yeah, sure,' to all that? You just happen to perfectly agree with me? And don't tell me you're being economical. We're having a conversation. It's one of my favorite things to do with you."

"Besides trespass on bird sanctuaries?"

"And skinny-dip in the lake."

My face got hot at that, so I rerouted to the question at hand.

"I've gone to six different schools since I was thirteen," I said. "I get wanting to be normal. Being the Fucking New Guy you don't need to manufacture additional weirdness. You know that you're like the first normal chick I've ever hung out with? I mostly stick with abnormal chicks. They don't usually have a problem with the Fucking New Guy."

"You mean with fucking the Fucking New Guy?"

"Exactly," I said. "I was a very slutty new guy."

She laughed.

"But really, you're not *that* normal. I mean, sure, you go out with a quarterback and are like student council president of the east side. But you also swear all the time. And drink and smoke weed. And the first time we met, I'd have guessed Kelly was the slut and you were the virgin."

She laughed. "God, Evan, you're such a dork about people sometimes! Like you can just tell what people are like by how they look!"

I could have argued about this all day with her, of course, but figured Baker would just think what she wanted, anyway.

"Whatever," I said. "Not that you're abnormal. Though the history thing is a little weird. But that's cool. People should like what they like, right? I mean, I'm sorry about Conley and Jim and your devirginizing and . . ."

"*Devirginizing?*"

"I'm just being a dick," I said. "I mean Taber. Your secret

muscular lover."

"You're not a dick. And Taber's not my secret lover."

"He was so gentle, even though he's a 250-pound noseguard . . .'" I said in my worst imitation of a girl voice.

"Dick." She threw a dish towel at me.

"There's been good stuff this summer," I said. "Abnormal or not. I liked hanging out with you, at least."

She didn't say anything, just kind of hunched up her shoulders and smiled. Then she came around to where I was mixing up frosting. She nudged me with her elbow and said she would help me make the cupcakes.

"Sixty cupcakes is a lot," I warned. "I'm out of practice, and I don't have the Cupcake Lady of Tacoma watching over me anymore."

"Who's the Cupcake Lady of Tacoma?"

"Long story."

"Be economical."

"You'll have to get me drunk first to hear about it," I said. "And I can't drink and make Elmo cupcakes. Sorry."

***

We spent the next few hours making cupcakes, though I had to bust out most of my skills from the cupcake shop for Baker's help to be worth it. She could barely crack an egg without disaster. I showed her how to sift powdered sugar, how to use a pastry bag. How to make Elmo's red, furry head, how to pour to the right spot so it wouldn't overflow or be too short. I ended up doing most of the work, but she found all the little details fascinating, though I couldn't resist mentioning that she was pretty inept for a girl named Baker.

"Baker's my mother's maiden name," she explained. "My dad was super Catholic and traditional; he wouldn't let my mom keep her last name when they got married. So she gave it to me, instead. Kind of ironic. I can't cook for shit, and my mom isn't much better."

"What's your middle name?"

"Margarete. My grandmother's name. What's yours?"

"McElhatton. I have no idea whose horrible name that is, though."

"You should ask your dad. Evan McElhatton Carter," she repeated. "That's a mouthful."

"So is Baker Margarete Trieste," I said back. "Your last name sounds like the word in Spanish. *Triste*. It means 'sad.'"

"Trieste is a city in Italy, though," she said. "Plus 'sad' doesn't really match my personality."

"More like mine," I said.

"That's just your mysterious bullshit economical front," she said, nudging me from the sink with her hip and rinsing her hands. "English surnames are typically occupational. Like, Baker? That was literal. Our people probably made bread for a living. Your people were cartwrights, most likely. That or they drove them."

"How do you just go around knowing shit like that?"

"I don't know," she said. "It's naturally interesting to me. I just pick things up. It's all there, if you know where to look. The old ways of doing things. You just have to stand still for a minute to see it."

We frosted half the cupcakes and had the rest cooling by late afternoon. I made us grilled cheese sandwiches and then, hot from hanging around the oven, we went swimming and laid out on the diving platform like corpses under the sticky sun, me with my wrist over my eyes, sneaking looks at her in her striped bikini with the little knots tied at her hips.

"I had sex with Jim two weeks after he asked me out," she said, rolling to her side to face me.

"What?"

"I would have done it earlier, but car sex grosses me out," she said. "Still, I initiated it."

"Uh . . . Okay?"

"Jim says I'm the most sexually aggressive chick he's ever met," she continued. "Which made me feel bad, at first. But what the hell was he complaining about? I just didn't see the point in waiting. I already knew what sex was like, you know?"

"Um, why are you telling me this?"

"Because it's another thing about me that's abnormal."

I laughed. "Having sex isn't *abnormal*. It's like the most normal thing you can do. Though maybe not with Jim. I mean, don't take this the wrong way, but his bleached teeth? Kind of freak me out."

"You should see his mother's teeth," she sighed. "They're obsessed with that in his family."

"You want abnormal?" I asked, rolling to my side. "This one girl I did it with? Stacy? And no, I don't know her last name. I didn't know Mandy's last name, either."

"Gross, Evan!"

"Stacy had this hang-up about being clean. Always took a shower just before I came over. Sometimes she wanted to even do it in the bathroom."

"You showered together?"

"No, she never told me *I* had to be clean, though I always

was, because she made me self-conscious. But *she* had to be, like, freshly scrubbed and shampooed in order to get down with me. And that's where we almost got caught too. In her goddamn bathroom."

"No!"

I explained about the heat rash I got from the greenhouse and her mother raiding the medicine chest.

"You realize that sex story has an actual *rash* in it, Evan."

"I'm not *proud* of it. Just trying to make you feel better."

"Thanks," she said. "But I don't have anything else to offer up in this department. Unless you want to know what Jim's sex face looks like."

"Ugh. Please, no."

"How about Taber's?"

"Stop."

"My sex stories are boring," she sighed. "No bathrooms or drugs or moms coming in or anything. I'm very good at being sneaky, I guess. Obviously you suck at that."

"It's not my fault we don't have privacy at this age."

"That's what I'm looking forward to about college," she sighed, turning on her back again.

"So you can get laid in peace?"

"Yes," she said, with zero hesitation. Was it possible for Baker to be any more awesome? No. No, it was not. "Also, so I won't have to feel bad about being dorky about academics," she continued. "Because everyone else will be smart there too. Plus I can get the hell out of Marchant Falls for once. Do something different. Those things too. Are you going to college, Evan?"

"I doubt it."

"Why?"

"The fact that I made cupcakes for this birthday party tomorrow is about as far ahead as I plan," I admitted.

"Have you always been like that?"

"Yeah."

"Will you stay in Marchant Falls for school?"

"I don't know. My dad's work kind of drags us all over."

"That sucks," she said. "I wish you could stay. Because you and your dad? It's like you've been on the east side forever. I can't imagine it out here without you."

That was probably the nicest thing anyone had said to me in . . . *ever*.

"You should stay, Evan," she repeated. "It's terrible that you'd get comfortable and then just leave."

"I guess."

She was quiet for a minute. I lifted my wrist from my eyes and saw she was staring at me.

"Your mouth," she said. "Does it still hurt?"

"Not really. Just keeps cracking open."

"Come on. I'm getting Keir's salve before I forget one more time. Come on, move your ass." She stood over me and kicked my leg with her bare foot. "I bet I can swim back faster than you."

"The hell you can," I said, pushing her in and then jumping in myself to chase her to the shore.

※ ※ ※

"Sit still," Baker said.

"This toilet is broken or something."

"Keir's in Big Sur on a yoga retreat," she said. "He'll fix it when he gets back."

"I could fix it, you know."

"Like you fixed your bathroom door? No thanks." We were in Baker's cabin, in the bathroom. Which had a lock and an amazingly huge bathtub, but the toilet lid was missing a bolt on the hinge and sliding all over the place. There was also the fact that Baker was standing in front of me with her boobs at eye level. I didn't know where to look.

"Keir makes this from honeycombs from his farm," Baker continued. She dabbed the salve on the corner of my mouth. It was the color of honey and felt like drippy, delicious-smelling glue.

"It's all organic," Baker added.

"Well, that's good. Since I'm probably going to end up ingesting most of it."

"*Ingesting*," she repeated. "Who even says that word? God, Evan. You're such a dork sometimes."

I could barely stand it. Feeling her touch me. Breathing in how she smelled.

"Okay, *there*," she said softly. "Let that set for a minute. Before you go and *ingest* it. Put some on every night before you go to bed too. You can keep the whole container."

I stood up, then, so I was standing like one inch from her. Way too close. But for some unknown reason, she didn't step away. She looked at the cut on my mouth, then into my eyes, her own eyes wide. And nervous.

I don't know what it was. Her nervous eyes or the August heat or that she was so close and smelled like my mother's cocoa butter lotion, but I just did it. Without thinking. Slipped my hands under those little knots at her hips and pulled her to me and kissed her. I didn't care if the salve was getting everywhere or that she might think my cut mouth was gross.

She pulled back right away.

"I shouldn't," she said.

"Right," I said. "Non-monogramy. I forgot."

She rolled her eyes and I thought she'd back off, call me a dick, and then we'd pretend it didn't happen. Again. We'd finish frosting the cupcakes; maybe she'd go home, go back to Jim, and I could go back to privately feeling like an elf-eared dumbshit. But we just stood there, staring at each other, my hands still on her hips, her hands still around my shoulders. Then she got this *oh-fuck-it* look on her face and lifted up on her tiptoes and we kissed again under the bright hum of the medicine chest light.

I hadn't ever imagined actually touching Baker. In my mind, I'd just *looked* at her. Never put myself into the scene, just pictured a naked Baker-shaped object, something to think about while yanking it. So while the real thing was obviously much better, it still felt a little strange. Her skin sun-warmed and sandy, her hair dripping lake water on my bare feet. Her boobs against me, so soft. Her nails scratching through the back of my neck. It all felt so good it made me dizzy. For once I was in a bathroom and my heart was pounding like crazy for a reason.

"You sure Jim's not back yet?" I said. Wanting to lock the door.

"We've got time," she said.

Then she pushed me down on the wobbly toilet and sat across my thighs, her legs wrapping around me. I was stunned by this—by her. This wasn't supposed to happen with someone like Baker, even if she was sexually aggressive, because she was someone I liked. To talk to, even. Someone I'd have to see every day. God, she was nothing like Lana.

It was shit manners thinking of Lana while touching Baker's boobs, but I couldn't help it. Baker was so different from Lana, and not just physically, either. She was so serious. No giggling. No letting me take charge of everything, like Lana did. Lana practically rolled on her back and waited to be petted, but Baker was very *busy*. Like she had priorities, things she just had to find out. Her hands were everywhere, doing all sorts of random but outstanding shit like tickling my nipples and running over the bumps of my spine.

"Evan, that scar is *so* not from a bike accident," she whispered into my ear, which was like hearing the ocean roar into my brain. "How did you really get it?"

"Long story," I whispered back.

"Be economical."

"I kind of ruptured my spleen," I said, my face at her sternum, while I untied her bikini top and chucked it on the floor. God, she had great boobs. They were just so . . . cute. Pretty. Awesome. *Jesus.*

"How do you *kind of* rupture your spleen?"

"Do you really need to know right *now*?" I asked. And we didn't talk anymore for a while. Just touching and breathing.

Then she said, "Where's your dad?"

"I don't know."

"My mom's in town," she said. "She could be back anytime."

"Okay."

"I don't have anything here we could use," she said. "I never . . . I wasn't the one who bought them."

I nodded. *BECAUSE WAS SHE TALKING ABOUT HAVING SEX?*

"So?" she asked.

"So what?" I asked back. Not sure if she was shutting this down or ratcheting it up.

"God, don't be dense!" she said. "Do you have any condoms?"

"Not on me right *now*," I said. "They're in my room."

"So . . . should we go to your house, then?"

"Do you want to?" I asked, my voice all scratchy.

"Yes."

She stood up and the sudden shift of weight nearly knocked me off the wobbly toilet seat, and she laughed and tied her bikini top back on. I felt a little sad to see her awesomeness covered up.

"Let's go," she said. "Don't forget this." She put the container of salve into my palm.

"The door should be open; I'm right behind you," I said, looking down at my fly, which was completely obscene. "Just give me a second . . ."

She laughed. "The shower runs ice-cold for the first few minutes, if you think that might help," she said. "And put some more salve on your mouth. I think I licked most of it off."

"Okay, yeah."

"I'll go first and make sure no one's around, just in case," she said. "You want a glass of water?"

I nodded and she slipped out to the kitchen. I shut the door and gave my dick its usual lecture. Running cold water on it seemed too harsh.

But I was taking forever to calm down. My heart was racing

like I'd just finished a mile sprint. And though I should have just followed her to my house, where the condoms were and the sex could happen, I realized it was pretty gross to get down with two different chicks in less than twelve hours. Bad manners, Baker might have said.

Trying not to think about it, I locked the door and turned on the shower. And then, I just took off my shorts and got in. The warm water felt like a heated massage. I looked at my lake-water-wrinkled feet on the white tile, then slowly closed the shower door on its track and just stood there, not even soaping up. Just stood there, thinking about how dumb this fear was. Wishing it would go away. I shut my eyes, breathed in and out. Thought of Baker's boobs. Of sex. Of anything else besides what I couldn't stop seeing and hearing. The shit of that night in Connison. The water raining over me, I willed all of it, the faces of Collette and Tate and The Rammer and the orange tile, to fade.

But when I turned the shower off, it was still there. Stronger. Full-color, top-volume panic, thick and heavy on my neck, like that lead vest they lay on your chest at the dentist to take pictures of your teeth. And getting out of the shower, though Baker's bathroom was nothing like the one at Connison, was even worse. Toweling off especially sucked. Standing there naked, I was full-on crying and surging with adrenaline. My mind was broken, like it couldn't understand that I wasn't at Remington Chase, that I was far from Tate Kerrigan and The Rammer and Collette. I couldn't get my swim trunks on fast enough, even though they were sandy and freezing cold.

There I was, crying, shivering, my fingertips cold and numb, with Baker waiting for me, expecting me to swagger into my house so we could fuck. The towel bunched in my fists, I looked at my feet, at the water dripping onto the bath mat. I was such a loser. Hot girl waiting for me—and not just any girl, a smart one, a nice one, someone I liked to hear speak, someone I wanted to keep knowing and not delete from my life—and there I was, crying in her bathroom. I wanted to scream at Dr. Penny: *You know why I don't inhabit the goddamn fear? Because it feels fucking horrible. Like everything I've ever done is wrong.*

But I wasn't doing anything wrong. I wasn't making Baker cheat on Jim. They were non-monogramous, right? I'd given her an out too—she just hadn't taken it. So I wasn't forcing her. She wasn't drunk. She'd made this decision, so I couldn't be guilty of anything. I was safe. Everyone was safe.

I AM SAFE. I AM SAFE. I AM SAFE.

After thinking *I AM SAFE* a million times, I swiped the tears off my face. Got ready to deal with Baker. Maybe I could explain all this shit to her? Girls sometimes liked guys who were all kinds of fucked-up. Felt sorry for them, felt important to hear all their problems. But that was opposite of sexy to me. I didn't want to be that shitty, whiny guy. I wanted to be the guy who made cupcakes and grilled cheese sandwiches and went to Story Island and didn't threaten her in any way. The guy Lana thought was so *good*.

I'd be lucky if I could just be Dirtbag Evan, though. Where the fuck was *he*, now that I was so close to getting down again? I'd already failed out once today, sex-wise, so I'd have to think of every sleazy thing in the universe, because I couldn't stay in this bathroom forever.

But when I came out of the bathroom, Baker wasn't there. There was a glass of water on the counter, which I gulped in two seconds flat. Then I stepped out onto the screen porch and saw Baker walking down the gravel drive, wearing those big brown boots she left by the door to slip on when she was in a hurry somewhere and her cutoffs she wore to mow the lawn. She was carrying a sack of groceries, and her eyes froze onto mine. And then Jim appeared behind her, carrying two more grocery bags. Then my father and Brenda.

"Hey, Evan," my dad said, a big smile on his face. "Brenda and I are going to make chicken stir-fry. You guys hungry?"

Dear Collette,

Something has happened to my father.

He does things now like talk. To other people. And cut up vegetables in other women's kitchens and make chicken stir-fry. I didn't know he even knew that stir-fry is cooked, that it doesn't automatically come ready to eat in a cardboard carton.

He takes me to buy clothes. Plays my video games. Wears red shirts. Has a favorite jazz station. Which he turned on while cutting up aforementioned vegetables. I hate jazz. But, still. Our house has always been quiet. There was no jazz, no music at all. No cutting up vegetables, no women teasing him about his shaved head or making him whiskey sours.

And by women I mean, Baker's mother Brenda. The way he and Brenda look at each other is so suspicious. Even if I hadn't just been the victim of the most epic cock-block of human time (don't ask, it's another punishment I deserve), I would have been uncomfortable watching my father banter with Brenda.

Speaking of uncomfortable, then I got to watch Baker's sort-of kind-of boyfriend Jim Sweet scarf down chicken stir-fry with his arm noodling around her shoulders as she stared at everyone but me and put on her best Student Council Vice President act.

Just when I think I might get used to this person my dad's become, I find out that we're going to move again. He doesn't tell me shit. Not that he ever has.

"What's so great about Boston, Adrian?" Brenda asked. "How can we convince you to stay?"

My father didn't say anything, and it was so awkward that I couldn't eat the goddamn cock-blocking chicken stir-fry anymore. Baker stared at her plate. I felt like there was a rope around my neck, tightening. It was quiet until Jim started talking about someone's birthday party. But I couldn't even follow the conversation because all I could think is we won't be here for anyone's party. We'll be gone, on to the next goddamn place.

Because that's what we do, my father and I. We're leaving. To Boston. To where you are. The girl who I wrecked and hurt, who I write letters that I never send. Aren't you lucky?

CHAPTER SIXTEEN

I was at Layne and Jacinta's, lying beside Harry in his bed with the Elmo sheets, reading him books about trucks while he sucked his thumb and coiled next to me in his monkey-print pajamas. Which was so damn cute that I could see why people have babies in the first place, even when they're still in high school like Jacinta was when she had Harry.

While clearing the table from the Chicken Stir-Fry Cock-Block of the Century (avoiding watching Jim with Baker on the sofa—his hands where my hands had been, hours earlier), Layne had called my cell and asked if I could come over and clean. He sounded embarrassed to ask, which made me want to help him even more.

I told everyone I had to run into town, and finally, Baker looked at me.

"Do you need me to come too?" she asked, a little too eagerly.

"Don't go out, babe," Jim said.

221

Babe. He called her *babe*. God. I knew Baker could tell how disgusted I was, but she had this trapped look on her face that might have made me feel sorry for her. If Jim Sweet's hand hadn't been all over her leg.

When I got to Layne and Jacinta's instead of handing me a mop, Jacinta asked me if I'd just get Harry to sleep while she and Layne cleaned. Harry wouldn't settle down because he was super wound up about his birthday party, but my droning voice must have done the trick, because halfway through the fourth book, Harry fell asleep with his sticky little kid hand clutching my T-shirt. I laid there listening to him breathing, adding "read little kid picture books" to the list of things that helped me fall asleep and the next thing I knew, Layne was poking my shoulder and saying, "Wake up."

I went into the kitchen where Jacinta was making sloppy joes in a crock pot for the party tomorrow.

"You think you could come over and do that every night, Evan?" Jacinta asked. "Me and Layne suck at getting him to bed lately."

Jacinta looked tired as hell and extra skinny in her jeans and bare feet. I wished suddenly I could give her something. Like a day at a spa where they give you champagne and a massage in your bathrobe and whatever the hell else women like.

Layne sat at the table, rubbing his face and looking at his cell phone with a frown.

"You want a beer, Evan?" Jacinta asked.

"No, I've got to head home. Got to finish the cupcakes."

"It's so awesome you're doing that," Jacinta said. "Even if Mr. Macho says you're a homo."

"I never said that!" Layne protested.

"Cleaning makes Layne pissy," Jacinta told me.

Layne slammed down his phone and swore.

"What? You *hate* cleaning," Jacinta said.

"No, it's fucking Lana," Layne said, getting up and looking for his keys. "I knew this would happen."

"What's going on?" I asked.

"Lana's out at Riverbend, totally wasted, and Randy Garrington just showed up," he said. "He's drunk too, screaming his head off. Lana's stuck in some guy's trailer."

My mouth dried up instantly. But my right hand curled into a fist. Thumb out.

"It's eleven thirty at night, Layne!" Jacinta said.

"This wasn't exactly *my* idea, Jacinta," he said.

"You want me to come with you?" I asked, hoping he would say no. But I knew I probably should take responsibility for Lana and the whole Dumpster dive thing. Though Layne would probably kill me himself if he found out about that.

"Hell, no," Layne said. "You might know how to punch, but I'm not delivering you to Randy Garrington on purpose. Just do me a favor—quit seeing Lana. I'm going to have a heart attack before I'm thirty because of shit like this."

"Don't forget the cupcakes tomorrow!" Jacinta yelled, as I followed Layne out the door.

***

The next day, I felt like I should at least say something to Baker. Since we'd almost done it, for Christ's sake. I wished there was some way to explain myself without having to go back to prehistory, to Remington Chase and Collette and my dead mother and The Cupcake Lady of Tacoma and the glaciers killing the dinosaurs. Speaking of wishing. My lazy morning-wood self spent a good amount of time wishing that Baker Margarete Trieste might magically appear naked right next to me, Evan McElhatton Carter, neither of us bothered by the demands of time and space and the male refractory period and non-monogramous agreements with guys named Jim Sweet. Eventually I came back to reality where I needed to finish frosting the goddamn Elmo cupcakes. I was packing them up in cake tins when my father waltzed in the kitchen and told me that we needed to go fishing. After the entire summer of living here, *now* he wanted to have a father-son moment out on the boat.

I was expecting a big talk. Not that we'd talked much since the day he told me about Grandpa Carter. He was nothing if not economical; he was where I learned it from. But I figured he'd at least tell me about Boston, all the logistical shit that he tended to focus on when we moved. Not the fact that he was forcing me to enter yet another hostile situation, with kids who wouldn't be my friends, with teachers who couldn't figure out my transcript, and coaches who didn't have space for me on their teams.

But instead, he talked about the weather clearing up. About Keir's sheep farm. About the Tonneson's septic system backing up the week earlier. Dumb shit I didn't care about. Especially if we were leaving.

"When were you going to tell me about Boston?" I finally interrupted.

He looked surprised. And a little guilty.

"Nothing's final about Boston, yet, Evan."

"Okay, well, school starts pretty soon, Dad. It might be

nice to know whether I should enroll somewhere or get my damn GED."

"You're not getting a GED," he said, sounding annoyed. "Colleges want to see a diploma."

I didn't tell him that college was completely foreign to me, that I couldn't imagine actually finishing high school. It seemed like I'd just continue on, one new shitty place after another.

"So, you just sleeping with Brenda until her boyfriend gets back from California?"

"Evan, Jesus," he said. "What are you talking about? Why are you so damn angry?"

"I'm not angry. I'm perfectly fine," I said. "About Boston, which you haven't said one thing about to me. And Brenda too. Go ahead and not answer. I'm asking a simple question. Because I don't know how this works with you now. Because we never make chicken stir-fry. And we never go to parties. And you never hang out with chicks. It's hard to keep up with you these days, Dad."

My dad pulled his fishing pole out of the water and set it down with a bang. "I don't really think this is any of your business. And I don't appreciate your tone."

"Right," I said. "None of my business. Who you sleep with. What was I thinking? Since I don't even get to know where we're going to live half the time."

I set down my fishing pole with a bang too and started pulling up the anchor. Because I'd picked a brilliant time for an argument. While we were trapped together in the middle of a lake.

"Do you have a problem with Brenda or something?" he asked.

"No, do you?"

"You're being childish."

He started the motor so it was too loud to talk. Instead of looking at him, I just examined my hands. The sprained left one had healed, but I didn't like to make a tight fist with it. The right had fading scars. I imagined using it on my father's blank face.

We docked in silence. My father cut the engine and gathered up the tackle and fishing rods.

"Okay," he said, standing between me and the shore. "I like Brenda. But ... obviously, there are issues there. I'm ... uncomfortable discussing it."

"Yeah, whatever, you're *uncomfortable*. Seems like you're *comfortable* enough hooking up with women who belong to other guys."

"What did you just say?" he asked, grabbing my arm tighter than I could remember him ever doing.

I didn't repeat it. I knew he'd heard me. I stared right into his blue eyes, pinched at the corners with wrinkles.

"You think you know the whole story, Evan," he said. "But you don't."

"Good thing you like to keep me so informed," I said, ripping my arm away from him and heading up the dock.

"Evan, wait . . ."

"I've got somewhere to be, Dad," I called over my shoulder. "But you can set me straight later. On the way to Boston."

Then I ran to Baker's cabin, because I knew he wouldn't follow me. Wouldn't ruin his image of jazz and stir-fry and whiskey sours and painted toenails in front of anyone . . .

Baker was at the screen porch table reading a book.

"Hey," I said to her, a little out of breath. "I need to leave. Go into town. Right now. You want to come with?"

***

Five minutes later, we were sailing toward Marchant Falls with sixty Elmo cupcakes in the backseat. Baker stared straight forward, her sunglasses on, her little white dress wrinkling over her tan thighs. I had all the windows open, and Baker turned up the radio, like she understood that I didn't want to talk.

I pulled up to Layne and Jacinta's house, turned off the engine.

"We don't have to stay. I'm just going to deliver the cupcakes, and we can go do something else."

"Okay." Baker looked nervous. But nervous-excited. I felt the same way.

"You decide what we should do, then."

"Taber just texted me about this party in town," she said. "Someone Jim knows."

"Well, then, let's go." Though I didn't want to do that at all. I just wanted her. Wanted to scoop her up and eat her. Wanted Jim to go away again. I couldn't really hate his guts, which would have been easier. I just wanted him erased, at least long enough for Dirtbag Evan—for me—to get what I wanted from her. Then I could be erased, and so could she.

"You're so nice, Evan."

God. If she only knew.

"Wait till you find me making out with some loadie chick tonight," I said. "Then we'll see how nice you think I am."

"Well, you're nice to me."

"I was a dick that one time," I reminded her.

227

And then I wanted to kiss her, but that seemed stupid, as I'd just mentioned making out with someone else and also that I was a dick. I *was* a dick. But damn, it didn't matter, because then her hand was on my thigh and she was kissing me and a second later I felt like persuading her to get over her car-sex aversion. Might have too, if not for bucket seats and Tim Beauchant banging his giant fist on the window and laughing his ass off.

"Jacinta needs the cupcakes, man!" he yelled. "Quit humping that chick already! This is a family-friendly event!"

I felt a little stupid, though there was no shame in being accused of humping a girl as cute as Baker, who Tim helped out the passenger door like he was some kind of gentleman wearing a cape and not a tattooed greasy-fingernail guy with biceps bigger than my head.

I introduced them as we hauled the cupcakes inside. And then we kind of just got rooked into staying. Not that Baker minded, being a social person, unlike me, the troll slinking under his bridge.

Harry's party was huge. Inside Jacinta scrambled around while old grandparents parked it on the couch and harassed-looking mothers stood around the food. Out back, Layne grilled hot dogs and guys who resembled some version of Jacinta or Layne hovered around a keg. Everyone smoking. I introduced Baker to Jacinta, and then Harry barreled in, shirtless with red Magic Marker scribbling all over his chest. He jumped up toward me and yelled "Cupcay!" I lifted him up and tickled his belly for a minute. Baker thought Harry was charming as hell and tried to talk to him, but he got all shy, and I put him down so he could rejoin the pack of kids. Then while Baker helped Jacinta, I went out back to get a beer and caught a bunch of shit for being the fag who made the Elmo cupcakes and met a bunch of Layne and Jacinta's relatives whose names I didn't remember. Then Jacinta came out the back screen door with a giant tower of cupcakes and we all sang Happy Birthday to Harry while I took pictures with people's cameras. The little kids took off like maniacs with the cupcakes, Harry screaming while wearing a firefighter helmet with frosting all over his face.

Layne put his arm around Jacinta, who was smiling.

"Told you the kids would love them," she said. "And no goddamn plates."

"Don't swear in front of your son," Layne teased her.

Everyone piled up paper plates with hot dogs and chips and sloppy joes and the backyard filled up with people eating and the little screen door between the kitchen and the patio slammed every twenty seconds from either moms getting more food or kids chasing each other. Tim started telling Baker about my boxing abilities and how it didn't matter that I was skinny, because of the size of the fight in the dog, which embarrassed the shit out of me, so I went to refill my beer and got caught talking with one of Jacinta's uncles about fishing and ice fishing, both forms of the sport that I knew jackshit about, but Jacinta's uncle was half in the bag and happy to explain it to me.

I was half in the bag myself by the time I came back to Tim and Baker. Baker was telling him about the history of the Beauchants in Marchant Falls, Marcus Beauchant being an esteemed fur trader and Indian ally, and the namesake of the Beauchant River, which she pronounced in the Frenchy way and which pleased Tim to no end. And I could tell that Tim was charming the shit out of Baker, because she kept laughing, and I didn't care, as long as he kept her laughing. Then Layne motioned to me, like, *I need to talk to you*, and we walked over to the keg.

"So, I don't think she's gonna show tonight," Layne said.

"Who?"

"Lana, you dumbass," he said. "Randy got to her before I could get out to Riverbend last night."

"Jesus."

"She went home with him," Layne said. "Nothing I could do without picking a fight with Randy." He pointed at Baker with his beer. "So. *She* your girlfriend now?"

"She's got a boyfriend."

"Too bad," Layne said. "Because you no longer have my permission to bang Lana. Because as long as Randy's around and Lana's an idiot, who knows what'll happen if he finds out about you guys. This is a small fuckin' town, Evan. He'll find out."

I flashed to behind The Donut Co-op. Was Lana really as dumb as Layne was saying? Dumb enough to fuck us both and tell Randy all about it? I knocked back the rest of my beer and poured another from the keg immediately. Then I couldn't sit still. I spent the rest of the party sucking down beer and chasing little kids and helping Jacinta with the food and talking to Layne's grandmother about the price of vegetables at Cub Foods versus at the Discount Food Mart in the strip mall on Shawton Street. It was a confusing conversation until Tim and Baker came over and Tim yelled, "Grandma, don't even lie, we all know you just like Discount Foods because it's right next to the porn store!" To which his grandmother laughed and lit one of those super-thin lady cigarettes.

The sun was down, and I was pretty damn drunk when the party ended. Jacinta held Harry on her lap in a lawn chair. She looked completely beat while he slurped on a Freeze Pop, which was spilling down his arm onto Jacinta's dress. Baker was playing hearts with Tim and some of the cousins. Layne lit a cigarette and sat down in a lawn chair beside me, slapping at mosquitoes.

"So, your hours gonna change when school starts, Evan?" Layne asked. "Or will you just quit on me, and I'll have to find two new dumbasses to replace you and Terry?"

"You fired Terry?"

"Kind of hard to work when you're stuck in county lockup."

"I might move to Boston."

"Why Boston?" he asked, exhaling cigarette smoke through his nose like an angry bull.

"I don't know. I don't even want to think about it."

"Well, *I* have to think about it," Layne said. "You're a good worker, and I'll have to bust ass to replace you. You think people would want jobs in this shit town, but most of them don't want to actually come to work. You're reliable, at least. Even if you fuck up the organic bananas still."

"Organic bananas are stupid," I said. "You don't eat the peel, anyway. Who gives a shit if there's pesticide on the goddamn peel?"

"The only difference is the price," Layne said.

"I'm sorry about Lana," I blurted out, because I was drunk as hell. "I shouldn't have messed with her. She's your sister."

"Half sister," Layne corrected.

"What's the difference?"

"Fuck if I know," Layne said. "She's as dumb as my real sisters."

We laughed and then Tim and Baker came over.

"Baker said her car's at the parking lot by the historical society," Tim said. "You need to go over there and jump it for her. I've got cables."

"Okay," I said. "But what if it's not a battery thing but something else? And I don't know if you've noticed, Tim, but I'm hardly in any shape to jump Baker's *bones*, much less her car."

Tim laughed. Baker's cheeks got super red, but she said she texted Jim and Taber to meet us there and to help out.

"Call me if you need a tow," Tim said. "No charge. You don't want to let that car sit there, though; the cops always tag the cars in that lot."

We said our good-byes to Jacinta, who was holding a now-sleeping Harry and looked ready to hit the sack herself, and Layne, who shook my hand and said, "You're an all-right guy, Evan. And I'm sorry about calling you a fag for the cupcakes. Harry fucking loved them."

"Don't swear in front of your son," Jacinta said tiredly.

***

Baker drove and I sat in the passenger seat feeling sloshy and talking way too much. About how the chocolate cupcakes turned out the best and how awesome Harry was and how I would love to have my own little boy someday and how Tim was my hero and how Baker should have sex with him instead of me, if she wanted to be non-monogramous so bad.

"It's non-mono*gam*ous, idiot," she corrected.

"Well, that's how Jim pronounces it," I said. "Maybe that's why you guys can't figure out how it works."

"Jesus, you're wasted!" Baker pulled in next to her Honda.

"Sorry."

"I'll forgive you, Evan," she said, patting my knee. "If you tell me the Cupcake Lady of Tacoma story."

I shook my head, and we jumped out to see if she had any tickets.

"Two of them, fifteen bucks each," she said. "Not great, but not terrible."

Then I kissed her. Because just then I couldn't keep my hands off her.

"Evan, Jim'll be here any minute," she said, pushing me off.

"So?" I asked. "You're not breaking your rules."

"But you're leaving."

"So are you."

She looked like she might cry. I didn't want to know what I looked like.

I thought of Collette in the library courtyard, pushing me back, telling me to focus on Monday. At least that'd been a possibility. Baker's face held the opposite of possibility. Like my drunk ass embarrassed her. Nothing I could do about that, of course. I *was* drunk, a mix of happy and angry and horny. And sad—Baker was deleting me out of her phone, and we hadn't even fucked.

She crossed her arms over her chest and shivered a little, and then headlights pulled up and blinded her. I turned around to see a rusty pickup. From the driver's side came a long-haired guy with cowboy boots, spitting chew into a Mountain Dew can. Randy Garrington. Had to be. Because coming out the passenger side and staggering after him was a tall blonde girl. Lana.

Baker stared at Lana's short shorts and long fingernails, and I felt crippled with shame. Lana was drunk. Even ten feet away, I could smell the goddamn Cherry Lick.

Randy, on the other hand, seemed completely sober. He looked amused at me, like I was wearing a Halloween costume out of season or something. He obviously thought he could take me. Which he probably could. Which pissed me the fuck off.

Now Lana was tugging on Randy as if to pull him back, though he wasn't even moving. She looked excited and thrilled, like she was enjoying starting shit between two guys she fucked. Lana, who never started anything, who I had to lead through getting naked? Lana, whom I felt sorry for?

"What the hell's going on?" Baker whispered.

I didn't answer her. I was getting madder and madder, and my arms felt like jelly, like I'd been hitting Tim's heavy bag, and though I was completely fucking drunk, I could tell Baker was adding it up. The loadie girl, this big guy looking me over. Which just made me madder. At myself.

"I told him not to come to the party," Lana said, her voice all sticky and whiny. "But he followed you from Layne's, Evan. Evan, I'm so sorry . . ."

"Just shut the fuck up," I said.

Lana froze, but Randy surged forward.

"You're a little punk piece of shit," Randy said, smiling. "Funny how you act so tough."

I didn't think, just swung back and hit him. Right in the face. He made a sound, sort of girly, which made me think I'd done it. The lucky punch. And then, while my right hand dazzled in pain—it wouldn't have surprised me if stars and sunlight started shooting out of it—Randy Garrington laughed. Wiped his mouth.

"Randy, don't . . ." Lana shouted, sounding thrilled again.

"You started this, girl," Randy said, easy as anything. "Now stay out of it."

I pushed him against his truck, and the Mountain Dew can flew across the parking lot. Baker started yelling behind me, but I didn't listen.

"You fucking cocksucker," I said. Then, because my right hand was completely obliterated, I hit him with the left.

Which did even less than the right. Randy just pushed me off until I slid on the loose gravel of the parking lot.

"You're not worth it," Randy said. "It makes Lana's panties wet to see a fight, but I'm not going back to lockup over some punk kid."

"Randy!" Lana whined, all outraged.

"Get back in the truck!" Randy yelled and Lana jumped. So did I. This was the first time he raised his voice, and then I just knew, by his instant pissed-off-ness, that I was *fucked*.

What people don't tell you about fights is how quick they go if you know what you're doing, but I wasn't the one who knew what he was doing. Maybe it would have gone different, had I let Randy dictate the whole situation, just backed off. But I was drunk and out of moves. So I just spit in his face. After that I was underneath him, my back screaming against the gravel while he whaled punches on my face and neck, and I flailed like crazy trying get him off me. Now both girls were shouting, and there was blood in my mouth. I flinched, sure my nose was going to break on the next hit, but then the pressure on my chest eased and Randy was off me.

But I wasn't the one who got him off me. Taber was. Taber lifted Randy Garrington off me, and I laid in the gravel like I'd become one with the parking lot. Faintly, I heard Taber slam Randy against the truck and yell at him, and then Baker was crouching beside me. Saying, "Evan, oh my god! Evan? Why did you do this? What's wrong with you?"

"Everything," I wanted to say. But my mouth hurt. Then Jim was there, saying, "Jesus, you okay, man?" Jim helped me sit up. Baker came running with a towel from somewhere and pressed it against my face. My nose wasn't broken, but it hurt, and my eyes were throbbing. I thought I might pass out. And then I did.

**

When I woke up, I was in Baker's backseat, feeling pain tingling out of me like invisible steam.

"Where's Randy?" I asked, my mouth cracking open fresh.

"Jesus," Jim said. "Get that towel, again, Baker!"

"Don't worry about him," Taber said, and he didn't sound dopey like usual. He sounded—as cheesy as it sounds—like a goddamn man who'd handled it. I shut my eyes, relieved I didn't have to be that goddamn man anymore.

"What the fuck were you doing here in the first place?" Jim asked.

"My car needed a jump," I heard Baker say.

"What the fuck was that guy's problem?" Taber asked.

"That girl," Baker said. "Was she the one Evan fucked at that party?"

"Evan didn't fuck any girl from that party," Jim said.

"Well, he's been fucking someone," Baker said, all pissy.

"I can't believe he hit that dude," Taber said. "That dude was fucking crazy."

"My mom told me it's not the first time he's been in a fight," Baker said.

I opened my eyes, wanted to protest, to sit up and explain that this wasn't who I was. But then Jim looked back at me, said, "He's waking up again." His eyes were serious and calm. "Easy, man, we'll get you outta here," he said, and I passed out before I could hear anything more.

Dear Collette,

What does it look like, real people getting down? Do they plan it? Do they think about how they must look while they're doing it? Do they think about other shit while it's happening, or are they strictly focused on the matter at hand?

Do they enjoy every second of it?

Do they even think about the other person? Or just about their own bodies? Or just about the other person's body and what it's doing?

Have you ever been with someone who acted one way and then you started the getting-down process and they acted different? Like a super-quiet chick getting all nuts and loud when you touch her? Or a super-funny dude who's always joking and then gets serious when it comes to taking clothes off?

Why do people do that? I know I do that. I feel weird about it. Shouldn't we always be who we are, no matter what (or who) we do?

For the record, you seemed the same as you were, both ways, whether half-naked or not. Sweet. Sexy. Nice to me for no reason I can imagine.

Later, Evan

CHAPTER SEVENTEEN

I barely got out of bed for the next few days. Only to eat and piss. I couldn't shower, not because of fear, but because I didn't think I'd be able to stand up without passing out.

One morning, my father came in my room. He looked furious and sad.

I didn't move.

"Get yourself cleaned up," he said. "I'm going to fill that prescription. When I get back, we're going to the going-away brunch for the kids."

I rolled over in my sweaty, nasty sheets and groaned, and he said, "Goddamnit, I'm serious, Evan. I've had enough of you lying around like this." He stomped down the stairs, and I heard the door slam.

The prescription was for crazy pills. Yesterday, Dr. Penny had called, and my father brought the phone to my bed. She went on and on about a million things, but I could barely listen. The main point was scolding me about getting into a fight. I didn't think she understood what had actually happened because she blamed me for learning to box. I wanted to say I was trying to defend myself, but I was too blown out to explain it. Finally, she said she was prescribing me some antianxiety medication. "For the trauma of the latest assault," she said.

I got up and stood around in my boxers. Looked longingly at *Under the Waves*, though I'd already finished it. The past couple of days, there hadn't been much else to do, since I couldn't get out of bed but couldn't sleep, either. My brain was a horrible mash-up of Randy punching me, of Patrick and Tate punching me, of my nose breaking, of my back slashed up by the rough gravel of the parking lot. Of Collette crying. Of Baker's face, completely shattered and shocked.

I didn't want to see everyone off—especially Baker—smelling like ass and blood, so I took a quick shower, my sore muscles practically vibrating as the shower walls closed in on me like a vertical coffin. I barely stopped to dry off before I dressed—there was still something really upsetting about coming out of the shower naked. A fear I could inhabit, but not for long.

***

It wasn't that I was the outcast of the Going-Away Brunch. Everyone was nice to me. Gentle, even. Like I was a retarded kid who might bash his skull on a rock at any moment. The only person who said anything about it was Tom. When he saw my black eyes and busted-up mouth, he said, "Fucking bummer, man."

Everyone at the brunch was nice enough. Still, I felt like my getting beat in a parking lot sucked just that much more joy out of what was already a sad day. Like I'd pissed in the pitcher of orange juice and spat in the egg bake out of spite. The whole thing would have been like a junior high dance as it was, segregated with the girls all giggly and squeaky and sad and happy at their table, except for Baker sitting at the guys' table, on account of how she and Conley still weren't speaking.

Baker smiled at me but didn't say much, which was weird for her—she was always talking her head off—but seeing as she sat between Jim and Taber, I supposed she was a little hemmed in when it came to conversation. Thinking of us almost doing it, of everything that had happened in the bathroom—me taking a shower, for god's sake—plus the chicken stir-fry and the parking lot beat down, it was a relief that everyone at our table talked about other dumb shit. It let me pretend everything was normal. Tom was talking about some guy on his baseball team who'd got in a fight with an umpire, but I barely listened. Just watched Baker eating her fruit salad and seeming as cool and comfortable as ever. I knew she wouldn't tell Jim about us. She'd kept Taber a secret long enough, and that was actually a big deal, a V-card level violation, while everything with me was lame and shameful, pointless even. It made sense that she'd want that memory to just dribble away.

The talk turned to other things. Sports, someone's party getting busted, the strip bar in Windham getting closed down for not checking IDs. I didn't say much, though. Just sat there looking at Baker, since it was my last chance to really do so, and feeling thankful for how Taber and Jim had saved me. Which made me feel like a prick, because at the beginning of the summer, I'd written them off as douchey assholes.

Okay, maybe they were douchey. Jim with his bleached teeth and "rebellious" pierced ears, Taber with his XXXL

"Abercrombie Sailing Team" T-shirt. It would have been easy to label them assholes, but for people I'd only known for a few months, they'd been pretty decent. And the way all the guys gave each other shit, talked about everything else besides my destroyed face, was about the nicest thing anyone could do for me at this point. I wondered if being a man was mostly about knowing when to shut up about something. If that was the case, then my father had trained me well.

***

I was at work when Brenda took Baker to the airport for Oregon, so I never said good-bye to her, and the rest of them left on their own timetable, which was fine with me. Tom was the only one I said good-bye to formally. I had his phone number, but we linked up all the other online ways, and I told him good luck with Kelly, because he'd mentioned at brunch that she had talked about going on the pill, which set off a shit storm of advice and teasing.

"I'll text you if anything happens," he said to me, all earnest, as he got in his dad's Suburban, and I waved and pretended my weepy eye wiping was just a reaction to the driveway's gravel dust.

As bad as it was to see Tom go, the day Brenda closed up the cabin and packed up for the season—she taught at Marchant Falls Community College—made me feel the worst. I sat in my room to give my father space, should he need to make some passionate plea to Brenda, which I doubted, since Keir was in the picture. But still. My father's lone farewell to Brenda seemed more pathetic than sad. I was surveying the shit I'd need to pack when he came into my room and told me we weren't going to Boston.

"What?"

"No," he said. "I can't bear it. I want to be here. I feel . . . it's good here. I hope that's okay with you?"

"Okay."

"Do you mind going to school in Marchant Falls?"

"I guess not," I said. Though I minded going to school anywhere. But all my friends having left, I felt back where I started. The Eternal New Guy. Nothing new about that.

"Have you taken your pills like Dr. Penny said?"

"Yes," I said. I didn't say that I wasn't sure they were working. I'd been taking them since the Going-Away Brunch, but I felt like I was getting crazier. I kept waking up in the middle of the night so jumped up that I'd have to do a ton of push-ups and sit-ups to shake off the excess energy thumping through my heart.

"It's a pay cut to stay here," he said. "Boston was good money. You might have to pay your own insurance, too, on the car."

"Fine."

"I think it's worth it, though."

"All right."

When he left, I considered how it was a big talk for us, even though it seemed so small. But I felt frustrated again. Leaving was something I knew how to do, even if I hated it. And now he wouldn't even let me have the satisfaction of doing that.

CHAPTER EIGHTEEN

My dad got a consulting gig in Minneapolis a week before school started, so when he left for a few days, the east side was even quieter than usual, with everyone gone and the docks pulled in and the diving platform put away, the buoy that held the chain bobbling sadly in the grey water. I spent my time running and working and stalking Collette online. I hadn't done that before, which was weird; even weirder was that I found her address and e-mail with frighteningly little effort. I stored it away with the notebook of magical letters to her I'd accumulated through Dr. Penny's therapy and told myself one day I'd be man enough to contact her. I'd brought up the idea of sending a real letter to Collette once, and Dr. Penny latched onto it and wouldn't let it go. Though even imagining that felt like sadness was coming down around me in buckets and I had no umbrella. I was Almost-Weepy all the time, constantly fending off dread. Being alone didn't help, either.

Dr. Penny said that was the crazy pills. I almost quit taking them, but she told me to be patient, to tire out my body so I could sleep, that it would pass. So every morning, completely keyed up, my legs jittery and spastic, I'd put on my shoes and run down the county road until I couldn't take it anymore. Then I'd walk back to the cabin and take the longest shower possible. My dad had arranged for a door lock to be added before he'd left for Minneapolis. And had talked about getting someone in to seal the cracks so there wouldn't be spiders, maybe even a full remodel. Somehow this made me feel more dread—dread that we were staying here. Like I couldn't escape anything anymore.

I'd agreed to school, though I felt mixed about it. I knew sitting alone in the cabin doing online classes or taking the GED would be even more depressing, though walking into a new place, a small town place, small like Remington Chase, where everyone might know what had happened to me with Randy Garrington, wasn't much better. Still, I started school on the first day with all the other seniors in Marchant Falls, which was weird; I often transferred midsemester and rarely started the term at a new place in September.

*** *

What kills me about teen movies is how they make high school into this endless string of insane, sleazy fun. Like every party involves a band and a throng of dancing people and every day is a pep rally for the big game where shit goes down between the head cheerleader and the dorky misfit girl who's actually hot once she takes off her glasses.

What movies never show is how goddamn boring high school is. The bigger the school, the less excitement, actually. A consolidation of kids from a whole bunch of littler towns,

Marchant Falls High School was a huge, prisonlike building. Grey and ugly, with no windows. Trying to find my classes the first week, it even sounded like a prison: English on A Block, science on B Block, etc. Strangely enough, my transcripts from other schools showed that I could take a lot of electives, and so I took a bunch of weird things. Physical Conditioning: basically gym, but you made your own fitness goals (which I had with Jesse, the one kid I knew). Ceramics: where a) kids tried to make bongs and b) kids hide the fact that they were bongs. My favorite class, though, mostly populated by the pregnant and the visibly high, was the simplistically named Foods.

Those first weeks were a blur of Class-This-Is-Evan introductions, which I hated, but I supposed were only good manners. Usually after being introduced like that, I just faded into the background, but in Foods, everyone was grouped together—the classroom was basically a series of mini-kitchens—so it was a little harder to ignore when a new guy suddenly appeared next to you while you made eggs in a frame or whatever the hell.

In Foods, I was in a group with two girls and a guy. A blonde girl named Jordan, who looked at me kind of shy but didn't say much and this homeless-looking guy who, when he bothered to come to class, mostly sat there reeking like he'd just woken up under a bridge and trying to eat everything before we could even cook it. The other girl was this pregnant chick who had a big fat Starbucks coffee milk shake thing with her every morning. She sucked on the whipped-cream–covered straw so hard that Homeless Guy said her baby was going to be born with the goddamn jitters.

One morning in October, we had a field trip in Foods. The teacher wanted us to learn how to comparison shop so we went to the Cub Foods just a few blocks away. Jordan and I were the only ones from our group who showed up. Pregnant Chick had a doctor's appointment, and Homeless Guy skipped. The teacher made us walk, which was fine, but field trips suck. They're so pointless. Not that learning is so important to me, but at least normal classes keep you from having to make small talk.

I pretended to be looking at something on my phone until Jordan went ahead of me, her shoes clattering on the sidewalk. I had so many dumb little tricks like that. Though I hated it, the awkwardness in being the Fucking New Guy was shockingly easy to cope with. There was a routine to it, at least: figuring if I'd be able to swim or do track (no to the first, maybe to the second); profiling which chicks might Say Yes and staring at them openly (left-of-normal girls with raccoon eyeliner sulking around the industrial arts annex, smelling like cigarettes, arty, hippie chicks in Ceramics, wearing no bras under their long flowy dresses, smelling like patchouli). All this while trying to blend into the walls.

But I didn't blend. People stared back at me, girls, too. I looked normal now, I guess, my old self, no ears sticking up, because I'd quit cutting my hair. There was a little bit of bruise left under my right eye, and though it made me feel like a liar, I was fine with letting people think I was a badass. At least I showered every morning, so I didn't smell like Homeless Guy.

My showering was a little weird. My father laughed at me when I emerged from the bathroom, a gush of steam rolling out behind me. It was like I was making up for lost time, all the luxurious hot water I'd missed. I'd bought a fog-resistant mirror on a suction cup so I could shave in there; I brushed my teeth in there too. And yanked it, of course. Maybe it was Dr. Penny's crazy pills or the new door lock, but I was coming to like everything about showering again: getting clean, coming out all pink and raw (though still checking the door lock, of course), looking at myself in the mirror, and making big plans for how I'd get huge so if anyone saw me shirtless again, maybe they'd notice that instead of just the scar on my chest.

***

Once we got to Cub Foods, we got a worksheet that instructed us to find various products and take notes on price and ingredients. The point of Foods was not just cooking but understanding everything involved in feeding a family. Jordan shoved a cart toward me.

"Ready?" Jordan asked. I nodded and pushed the cart while she walked ahead. I wondered if we'd see Layne. He told me the other day that Harry was starting preschool, so now they had to be extra careful about swearing.

Jordan took over the worksheet, all business. She was tall for a girl, had a cute enough face and short blonde hair, in one of those styles that looks like a boy's but better. She always dressed nice, nothing remotely slutty, and today she wore this huge blue sweater and jeans. Her shoes made this solid clip on the dirty linoleum that was hypnotic to me, I guess, because suddenly in the soup aisle, Jordan turned around and surprised me.

"We got the wrong bananas," she said. "We've got to go back to produce."

"What?"

"We're supposed to get regular bananas; I grabbed organic."

I smiled at this familiar mistake.

"I mean, who cares if they're organic?" Jordan grumbled to herself, her shoes snapping sharply. "Unless you're a freak who eats the damn peel?"

***

Grades-wise, I was doing pretty good academically. For me, at least. Though I sometimes ate with Jesse and some guys he knew, mostly I spent lunch in the library doing homework and reading. For English, I read *Jane Eyre*, which I hated, and *One Flew Over the Cuckoo's Nest*, which I loved. For Physical Conditioning, I focused on getting decent arms. In Ceramics, I pinched together a bunch of shitty bowls and stared at bra-less girls. And I made all kinds of stuff in Foods. Coffee cake. Corn bread. Stuffed peppers. Something called Taco Bake that looked like a bunch of tacos had been sent to their deaths but which tasted awesome. Jordan refused to eat Taco Bake. I got the impression she preferred finer stuff, but on Taco Bake day, Homeless Guy had some competition.

I began cooking at home too. Takeout food was so boring after a while. Plus our Foods teacher railed against the salt and fat in it and the wasteful packaging and how people didn't understand where their food came from, that Americans lacked a national cuisine. I didn't care about that shit, but I liked cooking. I'd get groceries after a shift at Cub Foods and test out the recipes on my dad, which he seemed to enjoy. Apparently, he now realized that sitting down to eat wasn't some silly thing lesser people did. He even talked to me while we sat at the table. Sometimes he talked about his work—he was consulting with a big financial company—other times he just asked the routine dad questions:

How's school?

Fine.

Are you doing any sports?

Maybe track in the spring.

Do you need anything? (Money? More crazy pills?)

No.

Though it was growing colder, he started taking walks around the lake in the evenings. He never invited me to go with, and he brought his phone with him, like he was doing something illegal, like calling his dealer or arranging for whores. When he came back, he seemed excited, a little punchy, but I didn't ask. Though I wasn't mad at him anymore, I wasn't loving him, either.

***

A week before Halloween I stayed after school to lift weights, and afterward, I walked to Cub Foods to spend the five-dollar gift card the store manager had given us the day of the field trip. I was standing in the candy aisle, trying to find a bag of something I could eat more than one of, when Jordan appeared.

"Finally spending your gift card, Evan?" she asked.

"Yeah. You too?"

"No, I gave mine to that guy," she said. "The one in our group? Who's always starving?"

I laughed.

"Want to go to a party?"

"Where?" I asked. So ridiculous—as if it mattered where!

"There's a girl who lives by me, from my old school," she said. "Her parents are out of town."

"Sure," I said.

Jordan lived in a nice neighborhood in Marchant Falls, big houses with giant porches with old-fashioned swings and lots of rustic-looking Halloween décor and people passing by with baby strollers or dogs, looking well-adjusted and content.

As we walked from her house—a giant thing with white columns that could have absorbed our cabin ten times over—Jordan carried the sack of assorted candy I'd bought and we kiddingly fought over the Starburst. Jordan had grown up in this neighborhood, and she lived with her mother; her parents were divorced. She had known the girl whose party it was since she was little, but since Jordan had gone to the Catholic school until this year, they hadn't hung out until recently.

The party house was even bigger than Jordan's, and the door was answered by this chick with a big mess of brown hair and boobs sticking way out of her shirt who was completely drunk ("JORDAN! You're HEREEEEEEEE!"). There were a bunch of people, not at mob levels, but every room had a different activity. Beer pong in the kitchen. Weed in the living room. Tequila shots on the back patio, which led to an empty inground pool full of dead leaves. I worried that Jordan would leave me, not knowing a soul, but she stuck by me like she was worried I'd nab the silverware. She got us some beer, which for some reason, tasted delicious with the Starburst, and then we went in the basement and played pool with this guy who wore giant black glasses and whom she knew and I recognized from my English class. I wasn't sure if Glasses Guy was her boyfriend—he treated Jordan the same way I did: polite, respectful distance. But I felt okay about it because he was scrawnier than me, the kind of guy who talked obsessively about music and philosophy.

Jordan beat me at pool, because I let her. Girls like being badass at shit, sometimes, and it was funny to see her happy when usually she was so serious, even in dumb Foods. Glasses Guy asked me where I was from, and I could see Jordan listening while she drank her beer. She did a weird thing whenever she took a sip, made this little "yuck" face as she swallowed, which sort of cracked me up, her bitten fingernails clenching the cup like someone invisible was forcing her to drink.

"My family's from Minnesota," I said. "But I didn't grow up here."

I ran through my list of places, and Glasses Guy stopped me at Washington, because he'd been to Mount Rainier once. So we talked about that for a while—he seemed like the kind of guy who'd get all into extreme shit, especially nature, because he couldn't do regular sports and had to make physical activity all deep and wise. I didn't mention that the few life lessons I'd managed to pick up in Tacoma weren't on a mountain but in a cupcake shop in the middle of the city.

Jordan kept getting me beer, and I wasn't drunk, but she was. She didn't act crazy, but bounced around more than normal, in a way that made her look like a little kid. She said we should go out back, and we sat on the lip of the empty pool, drinking and talking. About all the places I'd lived and how she'd never been to any of them. About Halloween costumes we'd had as kids and our favorite kinds of candy. Whether Starburst would taste good with different kinds of alcohol. Whether the pregnant chick in Foods class would feed her baby cappuccinos in a bottle.

Then she dipped her head under my neck. Which was a little surprising, but she smelled good. Not like anything drastic or specific. Just vaguely nice, some unknown girl product. So I put my arm around her very slowly, like she would vaporize if I pressed too hard, and she looked up and kissed me. She tasted like beer and orange Starburst.

This is good, I told myself, as her cold hands slipped under the neck of my hoodie. *My heart can speed up. That's normal when you kiss someone. Fucking relax already.*

But after a while, I couldn't sit there anymore, our backs to the house, where anyone could see us. I asked her if she wanted to get warm, and she nodded. But didn't lead me inside. We went into this little shed on the other side of a pool. We peeked in the window and saw it was full of lawn chairs and pool chemicals and deflated floaty toys. Good enough.

Inside, we sat on a lounge chair and Jordan pulled me on top of her and then there we were—making out. She had on this huge sweater—she always wore huge sweaters—with a giant rollover neck that threatened to swallow her head, and I couldn't feel much of her, but it was okay. Because I wasn't as drunk as she was, I went slow. As if I wasn't making out but defusing some kind of bomb.

But then her cold hands slipped under my shirt and pushed it and my hoodie over my head. Which was a little weird, and then I was freezing cold but whatever.

Her hand stopped over my scar, and I froze, because I knew what would come next.

"What happened," she said. Like she knew there was something wrong about me and wasn't surprised to find it, either.

So I told her, "I had my spleen removed. Two guys beat the shit out of me in the dorm shower at this fucking redneck boarding school in North Carolina."

I expected her to shove me off her and ask more questions. But she just kept kissing me, and slowly we continued to make out at the pace of ancient sea turtles. It was nice, but it felt like hours were passing and I thought about other random shit. The crickets chirping around us. Why Jordan had changed schools. If anyone knew where the hell we were.

If Jordan had any boobs under that massive sweater.

Maybe Jordan was like Lana, expecting me to lead her through things, too embarrassed to make her own moves. So I put my hands on her stomach, where she was so warm and soft, her belly button so small compared to mine.

"That tickles," she said.

"Sorry."

She laughed and I took that as a sign. Reached up to her bra and touched her boobs. Her bra was really smooth, but I couldn't feel anything. It was like she was all bra, no boobs. I couldn't help it, then—I thought of Baker Trieste's boobs in her striped bikini and a second later Jordan said, "Stop." Like she could tell I was thinking about another chick.

"I can't have sex, Evan."

I apologized. Jordan sat up. I put my clothes back on because I was freezing and felt like a prick who'd gone too fast. But I felt a little annoyed too. What, did she think we had to fuck because I touched her bra? Even if she *was* a virgin, Christ—how clueless could you be in these modern times?

"I mean, I've had sex," she said. "It's just . . . I can't right now. With you. With anyone. I'm in therapy. Something happened to me, I guess. So I'm . . . you're the first guy I've even kissed since it happened."

I didn't want to ask, but it seemed like the right thing to do.

"Since what happened?"

I thought she might be shy about telling me. But she didn't stop or stutter or run away. Just told me the whole story.

You don't have to rape a girl to fuck her up, it turns out. You can force her to give you head, though. Then seeing the asshole guy who did it makes her run to the bathroom in a panic and skip classes until one day someone hears her crying in the stall and the whole school finds out about it and the school calls her mother. Who then forces this almost-rape story out of her and sends her to therapy.

Jordan and I leaned back on the creaking lounge chair, our breath frosting out white . . .

"My therapist's Dr. Penny. She's a lady. A woman, I mean. Do you know her?"

"No, mine's a boy. A man, I mean. Dr. Richter. God, I shouldn't have drank so much. I can't really stand alcohol. God. I can't believe I told you all this."

"It's okay."

"So, what's your DX?"

"Huh?"

"DX, diagnosis. My mom's a doctor."

"Oh," I said. "I don't know. Dr. Penny never said. What's yours?"

"Anxiety. And post-traumatic stress. Though I think that's a little much. I mean, PTSD—it's not like I've been in a war or anything."

I curled my arm around her, and she nudged up to me.

"Yeah, well. It pretty much still sucks. I couldn't take a fucking shower in a bathroom for months."

She sniffed toward me, laughed. "You smell okay now."

"Pearl Lake was my bathtub all summer," I said. "A freezing bathtub."

"Did I just ruin everything?" she asked. "I wanted to have fun, I guess, and you're so nice. Thoughtful. The opposite of Jake."

"Jake?" I was trying to remember if that was someone I'd just met at the party.

"The guy who, you know . . ."

"Yeah. Oh." I stood and helped her up. "Let's get you home," I said.

We avoided the party and snuck around hedges like cat burglars, holding hands and laughing. Jordan was somewhat stumbly but never let go of me. But when I got her to her front door, she panicked, though.

"How will you get home? I didn't think, Evan. Are you okay to drive?"

"Don't worry about it," I said. "You should give me your number."

"You don't have to call me," she said. "If this is too weird. We can just pretend it didn't happen. Except we're in Foods, God! Evan, you don't have to . . ."

"I'll call you," I said, just to make her shut up, as it was making me feel like a dick. Which I was, technically, but it kind of killed me to hear her assume it. She gave me the number and I kissed her one more time and then she went inside.

I walked around Jordan's neighborhood awhile to sober up. I didn't realize how tense I'd been since the second Jordan talked to me in Cub Foods. How much work it was pretending to be a normal guy who went to parties and ate candy and played pool and listened to harrowing almost-rape stories. A good, attentive person who thought about others' feelings.

Finally, I circled back to my car and drove home, thinking about my options.

Quit talking to Jordan? Transfer schools myself? Tell her I have herpes? That I was bisexual? Drop Foods?

Or just pretend I could handle a girl who'd been hurt like her. Be a guy who didn't mind if he couldn't get laid anytime soon. Be *good.*

***

When I got home, my dad was standing in the kitchen, holding his cell phone.

"Evan," he said.

"Dad," I said, weaving around him to go upstairs.

"Hey," he said, stopping me on the shoulder. "Have you been drinking?"

I considered denying it. But what was he going to do? Ground me?

"Yeah, a little," I said.

"Where've you been?"

"At a party. Some people from school."

"I'm not pleased that you're drunk."

"I'm not drunk. Just a few beers."

"Still, you drove," he said. "Are we going to have the same problems like this summer?"

You mean, I'm going to fuck some girl whose ex-boyfriend is a psycho? I thought. *Or get cock-blocked by you and your split personality?*

"I don't think so, Dad," I said.

"You shouldn't drink with your medication," he said.

"Why, is there some side effect?"

"I don't know, but . . ."

"Don't worry about it," I said. "It was just a fluke."

"You're not in trouble again?"

"Jesus!" I yelled. "You're acting like I got someone pregnant. I just had some beer."

He looked stern, like he wanted to yell back.

"Were you drinking because of some . . . other reason?"

Now I was mad. Not drunk mad. Well, maybe a little. But Jesus Fucking Christ. Why the hell did I have to take crazy pills and go to therapy and write letters about my feelings and learn to *express myself* and *inhabit the fear* and *accept responsibility but not blame* and all the other famous Dr. Penny catchphrases while he could be the same clueless, closed-down bastard?

"Well, I'm at my seventh goddamn school. No friends."

"But you said you knew the people at the party . . ."

"It's nothing you need to worry about," I said. "Just forget it. Just turn on your laptop and tune out. It's fine." I started upstairs.

"Evan, goddamnit!" he yelled after me.

"I'm fine!" I yelled back, slamming my door.

The next morning when I woke up, the first thing I thought about was slamming my door like a goddamn drama queen. The second thing was Jordan and her phone number.

I laid in bed, remembering all the dickish options I'd considered. I thought about Jordan's yuck face when she was drinking. Her boy haircut, her cold hands. How easy it'd been to tell her about myself—she even took crazy pills too, she told me as I walked her home, though hers were a different brand.

I tried not to think about it too much while I showered and

dressed. Sitting on my bed, I could hear my father downstairs, and the idea of having to face him after I'd acted like a brat was awful. So though it was barely noon, I dialed Jordan and asked her if she'd want to hang out. Then I went downstairs and found the first piece of mail I could remember receiving since we started this whole moving bullshit.

Dear Evan,

Hey, how are you?

My mom said you ended up staying in Minnesota. How's gross old Marchant Falls High School? Are you enjoying the big pep rallies? I can just see you sitting there hating that. Our cheerleaders are always ugly for some reason. The girls you want play volleyball or soccer. Not that they're slutty girls. You will have to figure that out yourself. I have faith in you.

College life is very cool. My roommate is nice. Her name is Vanessa and she's from Alaska. She's very smart, and we dork out and listen to music together on Sunday mornings. She taught me to knit. Can you believe that? I'm not good at it yet, so no sweaters with your initials on them for Christmas a la Molly Weasley in your future, don't worry.

Here's an interesting fact. In my English class, we're reading A Clockwork Orange*! You'd think I'd stage a protest, but actually it's very good. The whole book has its own language. And it ends completely different than the movie. Alex grows a conscience—kind of—and settles down. Not the ending Taber and Jim would want. Well, maybe Taber. Jim likes everything all outrageous. It's his man thing, him wanting to be all badass when he's really just a nice guy. I'm like, you're a quarterback, dumbass, everyone knows you're in it not for violence but sex. He thinks he's so sneaky. I'm sure he's got* *some new chick there in Wisconsin. He won't admit it to me, still, like he thinks I'll break down if I know about him being with someone else. I mean, I don't know. I still like him and we talk on the phone sometimes, but it's just different. Everything's different. It matters, but it doesn't. You know?*

I want to apologize for something. For not saying good-bye to you. I mean, I know I did at the brunch and everything, but not really in a way that was nice. I mean, I really liked hanging out with you. All summer. It was cool and you were cool and I didn't mean to just leave as if we weren't friends. That day in the bathroom was weird. But good. Just bad timing, maybe? You're a great person. I know things haven't been great for you in the past. My mom told me some stuff that your dad told her, and I feel shitty now, about how I acted. Probably you don't want the whole world knowing about what happened to you last year. I'd be pissed at my mom if she told anyone stuff like that, and with your economical tendencies, I'm sure it's making you feel worse. But don't, okay? There's always someone who will be understanding, especially when it comes to bad shit. Really, ask my roommate. I've unloaded a ton of shit on her already and she with me too and it all just makes us stronger, right? Makes us better friends. Better people. I hope you won't feel weird next time I see you because I said all this. Because I'll be back next summer on the lake, and you better not try your Evan Carter avoidance bullshit. My mom and I are going to England in June for this research thing of hers, but we'll be back mid-July so I expect you to get drunk with me and tell me all about your views on my shitty lame high school . . .

The letter went on to tell me about her joining all these clubs and crap at college and there was also some weird story about camping and meeting these wilderness people who lived in a cave and built all their own tools out of mud and sticks and then she told me to write back and included some books I should "totally" read, as she thought they'd be "right up your alley" and it was nice, but too much like having Baker here, being bossy and parental and made me miss her. I was sick of missing people.

***

My dad and I were like two grizzly bears on the same mountain. Circling, snarling, trying to stay out of each other's way. He acted like he was this new dad, a tough guy, someone with expectations and plans. He wanted to know where I was going, who I was going with, what we were doing, when I'd be home. I told him mostly the truth, but I doubted he'd know what to do with the data I gave him. It was like he was just doing drills, practicing being a father.

Mostly I was with Jordan. Sometimes Jesse, when he gave me shit for being a pussy-whipped douche, but mostly Jordan. I went to her house after school; we ate lunch together; we hung out on weekends. For taking crazy pills and being in therapy, Jordan was fairly normal, though she didn't play sports or do much beyond reading. For entertainment, she liked to go for long drives where she blasted music and drove really fast. After school, we'd get in her VW and drive out into the country. Past farm stands selling pumpkins and apples. It reminded me of hanging out with Tom—so wholesome. We'd sit under trees until the sun went down, doing homework or playing Frisbee— she was unnaturally good at Frisbee—and sometimes making out a little, though always at a PG-13, sea turtle pace.

"We're worse than senior citizens," I told her one afternoon, when the weather turned and we ran to her car to get warm. "Too cold to be outside. We might as well sit in wheelchairs and bird-watch from the sunroom."

"Don't criticize me; I flunked my French quiz today." She started her car. "So, I'm *practicing self-care*," she added, all sarcastic. Her shrink used the same kind of dorky phrases as Dr. Penny, and so it was a little joke between us.

"Evan, please *validate and affirm my feelings*." She peeled out of the gravel turnout and floored it. "Evan?"

"Sorry, I'm just busy *inhabiting the fear*," I said back.

Fridays, Jordan's mother would come home from the hospital and pour a glass of wine and make really complicated foods from scratch, like apple pies with lattice crusts or vegetable curry. She said cooking relaxed her. Jordan thought this was ridiculous, but I liked coming around on Fridays to see what Jordan's mom would make. Sometimes I'd even help her out.

One night, after Jordan's mom made homemade pizza in the hearth on their deck, Jordan and I sat out there on a lounge chair under a big blanket. Stuffed full, I couldn't stop blabbering about how good the pizza was. Finally, Jordan just put her hand over my mouth.

"I get it, already, Evan!" she said. "You liked it."

"I know, but that cornmeal on the crust . . ."

"My mother can't hear you, you know, in case you're trying to get in her pants with all your compliments."

I told her to shut up.

"I mean, you probably could," Jordan continued. "She loves you, Evan. She thinks you're the best thing ever."

Compared to Jake, of course, was what went unsaid. Of course I was better than Jake, the Almost-Rapey Ex-Boyfriend.

Who I didn't enjoy discussing, though Jordan brought him up occasionally. Because she wasn't supposed to *stuff her feelings*; she needed to *let her trauma work its way out*.

"My luck with older women isn't too bad, actually," I said.

Jordan sat up, her face bright and shocked. "Really?" she asked, as if I'd just confessed to a murder. "How old was she?"

"I was fifteen; she was nineteen or twenty, maybe?"

Jordan was like a little kid, all excited.

"Oh my god! You've got to tell me everything!"

I sighed. But if I felt so unsure, why did I fucking bring it up?

"Wait, no. I'm sorry—you don't have to tell," she said.

"Yeah, I'd appreciate it if you'd *respect my boundaries*, Jordan."

"I don't know what I was thinking," she said. "*Sexuality is a personal matter for every individual.*"

"Thanks for *honoring my method of processing.*"

"It's important to have *a foundation of trust when sharing vulnerabilities.*"

For a while, we were like a machine that made psychological bullshit. Then the subject changed, and I forgot about the Cupcake Lady. Looked up at the stars and thought of how much brighter they were out on the lake. Concentrated on Jordan and her unidentifiable-but-good girl smell and how lazy and comfortable it was to sit under a blanket with a full stomach and nothing to do, nowhere to go.

But I wanted to tell her. There was something nice about telling a girl shitty things about yourself and having her laugh and ask you little questions, instead of being quiet, like I usually was. It made me feel like things in my life weren't just shitty. They were just stories, things that had happened. A woman in a cupcake shop. Mandy and the movie theater. Stacy and the rash cream. Collette during chapel. Lana and the Dumpster. Baker and the chicken stir-fry. Just stories.

CHAPTER NINETEEN

I never really thought about holidays before. Thanksgiving was hit or miss. Christmas we had presents, of course. Both times, though, for food, my father would hit up an upscale grocery store and pay for turkey or spiral-cut ham and all the sides. Cub Foods even offered meals like this, and the people who ordered that shit were usually about ninety-nine years old and one minute from death. The whole concept depressed me so I decided to cook for Thanksgiving.

Our kitchen was nowhere as nice as Jordan's mom's, but it was big enough. I thought I'd make turkey, stuffing, mashed potatoes, and some pie. Fridays at Jordan's had busted my conception of pie making as being difficult. I decided to do a pecan pie, since the gooshiness of fruit seemed too messy.

Thanksgiving week, I was looking online through a million recipes and turkey-roasting methods when Tom messaged me.

Kelly = my Everything Girl.

I messaged him back:

Nice.

To which he replied:

I know, it's good. But she thinks she's going to hell. And take my advice. Don't go to the same college as your girlfriend. Baker had it right with the non-monogramy thing. There's a million hot chicks here, and they all offer Everything right away. I'm dying here.

On Thanksgiving, I made two boxes of instant mashed potatoes (give me a break; I made pie crust) and we didn't have a serving bowl that fit all of it. I was considering other uses for mashed potatoes—could we spackle the walls? brick up a chimney?—when my dad came downstairs and told me that my Uncle Soren was on his way.

"What? Now? How do you know?"

"Because he just called me from the road," he said, looking somewhat happy but also nervous. "He's coming for Thanksgiving."

I nodded. My father nodded back. We were hell on the nonverbal communication, he and I.

"Looks like you've made enough food," he said, trying to sound jolly. "When's the turkey going to be done?"

"In a couple hours."

"I'm running to the liquor store for beer," he said. "If I can find one that's open. You need anything?"

"No," I said. He got his keys and left. I stood in the kitchen without moving for a minute. Soren? Here? Was this first Thanksgiving going to be a drunken throw-down, where my uncle would finally ream out my dad for being a wife-stealing bastard? Maybe I could convince everyone to get along, Pilgrims and Indians-style, just until we could choke down all this food I'd been freaking about making all day.

The nice thing about cooking is that you've got to keep moving. Stuff's heating up and other stuff needs to be started and you've got to set the table and make sure the pie won't come out burnt—Jordan's mom had coached me well on pie crust—and so I just kept working through my list of recipes like a robot. Hoping my uncle wouldn't think I was a pantywaist for fussing over it all. Maybe he'd just ignore me while he and my dad would have their big brother-to-brother moment.

I was half done with the stuffing when there was a knock on the door. I went to get it, flour all over my T-shirt, still in my bare feet—I'd been cooking since I'd woken up—and there was a man who looked just like me, so it had to be Soren. My uncle. Standing in the doorframe with a giant duffle on his shoulder, looking totally normal.

Looking just like me. With shorter hair, though, like he buzzed it every morning. I was sort of surprised. I'd imagined him some wilderness guy, bearded and scraggly. But then he was a marine, so I supposed he'd been trained to be tidy. Soren was as tall as me, and I could see under his jacket that he wasn't unsubstantial in the muscles department. Nothing like my dad, who was shorter than me and had a round little belly going.

"Evan," he said. "You've grown a bit."

"My dad's at the liquor store," I said. Like he was some door-to-door salesman, and I'd been given strict instructions not to let anyone in.

"Good, I hope he finds one that's open," he said. "I could use a drink."

Soren kind of shoved his way in and set his duffle on the floor and I just stood there, until he said he needed to use the bathroom. I went back into the kitchen and privately freaked out. Wished I could call Jordan. I'd told her about my Uncle Soren, but she was at her grandmother's.

"Adrian said you're quite the cook," Soren said, startling me. He nodded toward the disaster of food.

"You want a glass of water?"

"I can get it," he said.

"You know, your grandma was a cook too," he said, digging in the cupboard for a glass while I just kept standing there. He probably thought I'd been dropped on the head as a child.

"Yeah, I heard that."

"Well, it smells great," he said. "Been on the road for a while, and nothing but greasy gas station food. Awful stuff. It's been a while since I had a real meal."

"I didn't know you were coming to see us."

Soren shook his head and drank his water. It was the most manly method of drinking water I'd ever seen. I could even see the muscles in his neck working.

"Typical Adrian," he said. "Avoiding anything upsetting. I hope you've not inherited that from him."

My face felt hot, because, of course I had. I wondered now if my dad's trip to the liquor store was like those stories of fathers going out for a loaf of bread and never coming back. And I would have to live with Soren, the Scary Former Marine.

Soren sat at the counter across from the mess of food prep. Slowly, I went back to work, and he started talking. He'd been in Montana, with a buddy of his from the marines, helping build a house. Had meant to go back to California, where he lived, but thought some time at the lake was in order.

My hands busy, I relaxed a little, and Soren asked me a

bunch of questions. Did I like Pearl Lake? Did I fish? Did I like the little balcony on the second floor? He and my dad sneaked out of there sometimes, down the trellis. The trellis was gone now, he said, like he was sad about it.

"No, but I found enough trouble without it," I said. "It was kind of a crazy summer."

"Life on the lake is different, no doubt about it," he said.

***

My dad came back and he and Soren shook hands and I panicked, but then the worries of setting the table and getting all the food set out took over and there was no time for confrontation, for plates smashing or angry words. The three of us sat down and just shoveled it in. I realized I was starving. Hadn't even had breakfast in my quest to get everything made. My dad talked about his work a little, kept shuffling beers from the fridge to all three of us. I tried not to guzzle mine, but when I saw how quick Soren and my dad knocked theirs back, I figured what the hell. Kept up with them, then. We ate almost every bit of the mashed potatoes and all of the stuffing. The turkey sat in the middle of the table, and we just picked off it like vultures. Soren belched. My dad stretched.

"Good food, Evan," Dad said. "I'm impressed."

I ducked my head. "Better than takeout, I guess."

"Much better," Soren agreed.

We slumped the dirty dishes in the sink. My dad made coffee and Soren asked him if he had any whiskey and they both kind of smiled at each other and I watched them dose their mugs with it. I hadn't had whiskey in coffee since The Cupcake Lady of Tacoma, and the idea made my stomach turn.

"I guess we're on KP duty, A," Soren said. He kept calling my dad that: "A". I suppose that's the best nickname one can get from a name like Adrian.

"What's KP duty?" I asked.

"Kitchen patrol," Soren said. "Military slang."

"Isn't this the part when we fall asleep in front of the TV?" my dad asked. "And the women clean up?"

I tensed at the word "women." Had my mother been there, would she be pestering us to help her? Was I the woman in this whole holiday now?

"I don't see any women, so I say leave it," Soren said. And so we did.

Soren went to take a shower and was gone so long I wondered if there'd be any hot water left. My dad lay on the couch, and I turned on the TV. There was a choice of football and bad chick movies and more football. My father was fiddling with his phone, smiling at the screen, like he had gotten a good message. He seemed completely content, which was fucking weird. Maybe he was just drunk.

"How come you didn't tell me Soren was coming?" I asked.

My dad looked up quick. "Well . . ."

"Because you were avoiding him?"

"I just . . ." he stopped. "It took a while for him to convince me it was okay."

My dad went back to his phone, and I turned back to the TV, holding my bottle of beer tightly. At first I wanted to smash it on his head. But then I just looked at him, all bald and defenseless, his feet in socks in a curl beside me, and I felt like it was dumb for me to be mad.

Later that afternoon, after more football and a round of pecan pie that we all forced in with ice cream and more beer, my dad got up and said he was taking a walk. With his phone.

When the door closed, I looked at Soren and said, "He's going out to meet whores. Or get his drugs."

"What?"

"I'm just kidding," I said. "He does that a lot. Disappears with his phone. He might be a government agent. Breaking codes with computers. Who the fuck knows."

"I bet it's that woman. The professor."

"Brenda?"

"Yeah. She's been calling him."

"Really?"

Soren laughed a little. "God, Adrian never changes! Secretive motherfucker. Yeah, that's what he told me. We've been talking for the last few weeks. How else you think we're able to be in the same room without the fur flying?"

I didn't know what to say to that. I hoped it was just friendship, he and Brenda. Because the idea of Baker becoming my sister after I'd felt her boobs was pretty gross.

Soren clunked his beer on the coffee table, put his feet up. He was barefoot, too, like me.

"You know the whole deal with your mother, then? Or not?"

"No. Well, sort of. But not from him. From . . . well, you know that island? Story Island?"

He looked a little alarmed. And a little impressed, as I told him how I went out there with a girl, exploring the Archardt

271

House. How I found his name and my mother's name on the tree. And his book. I ran upstairs and got it for him. I watched him look through the blue book, and it was the first time I thought his easy composure might crack. I stared at the muted football game on the television and wondered if the thunder and lightning had finally come.

"Melina didn't want to stay in Pearl Lake," he said. "She hated it here. It didn't quiet her mind like it did me. Just made her restless. She was a curious girl. Not weird-curious. But just always reading, always looking past me, like she wanted something else. Not that she didn't love me. I knew she did. But I wasn't enough. Somehow, Adrian was."

I laughed. Thought of my dad. His boring clothes, his belly paunch, his bald head. "I don't get it."

"I never wanted college," Soren said. "I wanted a simple life. I moved out to the cabin after high school and just expected that Melina'd come with me. We'd been together since we met working at the Kiwanis Camp, when she was fifteen and I was seventeen. I just figured she'd go to college and then come back and play house with me. I'd catch our fish, and she'd cook them. That kind of bullshit. If you want any success with girls, Evan, don't take that approach, is my advice."

"But what did she see in *my dad*?"

Soren laughed. "Well, they were the same age, and they both went to school at the U in Minneapolis. And I suppose since it's a big place and they didn't know anyone else, that's maybe how it worked. I mean, my brother isn't an idiot. Just sort of slow when it comes to people. He doesn't see what's in front of him half the time. How things cycle back. Just like nature or the seasons. Doesn't think he should be stuck in a box like that. I mean, that lady he's talking to? That gay sheep farmer dumped her last month, and I'd bet money she's talking to Adrian wanting more than just a shoulder to cry on. But my brother's still acting like Melina'd be mad at him about it."

"Keir's really gay?"

Soren looked confused. "Who's Keir?"

"The gay guy."

Soren blinked, like it was a given.

"But Brenda wants to be with my dad?"

"That or she's just into phone sex," he said. I made a face, and he laughed.

"Anyway, he'll never admit it to you. He's ashamed of the whole thing with Melina. Thinks it's his fault she died. Like he deserved it, because he stole her. But she wasn't something to steal. She wasn't an object. She was a woman with her own mind. I didn't get that for a while. Took me a war to figure that out. Figure out I wasn't god's gift to womankind."

"You were in a war?"

"First Gulf War," he said. "Which lasted like two minutes, so don't get excited. That war wasn't shit compared to the next one. But one day, I was sitting in my rack, waiting for orders to move out and thinking about it. Melina was pregnant with you, and she'd written me a letter—she always kept in touch, even though I refused to attend their wedding—and I realized I was being an idiot. I was as bad as a girl. Romantic, thinking she'd come back to me. Stewing on Story Island the year she went to college and started being with your dad. Acting like Peter Pan out there in that crumbling old mansion. Like she'd see me fixing it up, and that would change her mind. And here, though I didn't like war and it was hotter than hell and we had a job to do, I knew it was no life to just sit around on the porch and watch the seasons change. There had to be more than one beautiful place on Earth, and I currently wasn't seeing it in Iraq. I had to quit wasting all this time."

"So, why did you guys not talk for so long after that?"

"Evan, I'm not a saint," he said. "It still ripped me up to think of her with anyone else. She was a beautiful woman, for one, and I was young, thinking I'd owned something because I didn't want anyone else to touch it. I said terrible shit. Told your dad he'd fuck you up without Melina to love you. Wrote him this big long letter about how his life'd turn to shit."

"Well, it kind of did," I said. "He's been dragging us across the country for the last few years. We're like nomads who live in condos instead of caravans. And just because I can make turkey doesn't mean I'm not fucked up."

Soren laughed. "You know, I have a son myself. Did your dad tell you?"

I just looked at him.

"Right," Soren laughed. "I shouldn't have to ask. Yeah, you have a cousin. He's five. Lives in California with his mother. We split up not long after he was born, but I still live out there, most of the time, anyway. Work's been hard to get lately, and his mother doesn't like me much. I rile him up with gifts and wrestling and whatever, and she gets all pissy."

"What's his name?"

"McElhatton," he said. "My grandfather's name. But we just call him Mac."

"That's my middle name."

"It's a good name," he said. "Your great-grandpa Mac was a good guy. Taught me so much shit. I don't know why any of that never trickled down to my asshole father." He turned toward the TV and jumped. "Jesus! Did you see that? Another interception. Unmute it, will you?"

I handed him the remote and laid back. Thinking again of this world where Keir was truly gay—Baker owed me twenty dollars for that, since we bet on it once, not that I'd ever claim it—and where my mother dissed a guy as awesome as my uncle for my dorky dad and where I had a cousin named Mac who lived in California.

"That's fucking insane," Soren said to the TV.

"Does Mac like football?" I asked.

"No telling what he might like. He's a wild little kid, though."

"I hate football," I admitted.

Soren groaned. "That's your dad's work," he said. "I bet you hate fishing too?"

"Kind of," I said. "We only went once this summer."

"Jesus!" he yelled up to the ceiling. "I've got a lot of work to do on you, kid."

"Focus on Mac," I said. "I'm a hopeless case."

He drank more beer and looked at the TV. "No, Evan," he said. "I wouldn't say that just yet."

***

Monday morning, before l left for school, Soren ran out in the driveway to say good-bye to me. He was only in a shirt, and it was freezing cold, but he didn't seem to care.

"It was good to meet you, finally," I said. "My dad told me about a lot of stuff you guys did, growing up."

"That's my necklace you're wearing, you know," he said.

"Really?"

"Melina gave it to me for a present when I was eighteen," he said. "But I sent it back when you were born. Thought you should have it. Since I wasn't sure I'd ever get to meet you."

I touched the circle necklace. Felt a little shy about it. Didn't know who to thank for it, just then.

"Well, I better go. I gotta get back and find work. Say what you want about your dad," he said. "At least he's always earned a good living."

"Yeah, great," I said.

"Hey, he's not perfect," Soren said. "And he's never gonna want to talk to you about Melina and everything. But I know he loves the hell out of you. He told me about how you got hurt at that school. He was losing it, Evan. Really losing it. I was the one who said bring you here. That was how we started talking again—he didn't know who else to talk to. So this summer was all my idea, and he thought it would work. Thought if you got enough sunshine and whatever else, that would make up for it. He's kind of slow, like I said. But he means well."

I nodded. He hugged me, and I didn't feel weird about it. It was a very manly hug.

"You've got my number," he said. "Keep in touch."

**

The rest of the year went on. The court date in North Carolina was pushed back from June to September, and my dad considered switching lawyers until I told him that I didn't care, the further away from it I got, the better. My dad and I had Chinese takeout for Christmas because neither of us could face the idea of dishes on the scale we had them on Thanksgiving, but then both regretted it when Jordan's mom invited us over the day after for their leftovers and dessert and it was all so good, we realized we'd been idiots to eat moo shu pork instead of making an effort.

Jordan and I rang in the New Year with the longest make out in human history, on her giant plush queen-sized bed at her house while her mother worked an overnight shift at the hospital. Jordan was still very cautious about this kind of thing, always stopping at certain points and shutting everything down, as if Dr. Richter was in her head, telling her to keep herself safe. Which was probably a good thing, given how after long make-out situations like that, I'd feel like a total fucking animal. No better than Jake, really. It was hard, ha-ha, trying to keep all that from Jordan, so she would never know Dirtbag Evan existed.

But we did a lot of other things besides make out. Jordan and I got into doing jigsaw puzzles in her breakfast nook. I learned how to make ratatouille. My muscles got somewhat decent from Physical Conditioning. One day in English class there was an awful pop, and I realized that my hearing—some of it, anyway—was back in my left ear. I walked around that day feeling like everything was too loud.

During spring break, Jordan went to tour her college, some all-girls place in Vermont. I spent the week being the laziest fucker alive. Lying on the couch and vowing to go for runs but never doing it.

***

After spring break, Jordan seemed crabbier and I didn't know what to do, besides imagine elaborate punch-out scenes between me and Jake that were likely to never happen. But mostly she was just so damn nice. I thought about her all the time. Not just sex stuff. But little things about her. How she automatically did her homework, no putting it off like I did. How she always ate a turkey sandwich and drank a bottle of grapefruit juice every day at lunch. How oblivious she was about sports and how she thought I was weird for running track. All that sweating for no reason, is what she said.

She always asked me what I was thinking too, which was thoughtful, I guess, but she'd get mad if I said I didn't know. I'd tell her bullshit, then.

"All right, I'm thinking about poetry."

"Shut up."

"I'm thinking about the epidemic of emerald ash borers."

"Come on!"

"Okay, I'm thinking about getting an Irish wolfhound."

"You are?"

"No."

"Evan, you bug the fuck out of me, you know that?"

Dr. Penny even started noticing that all I talked about was Jordan. I must have been boring her because one day she just flat out asked if I was "sexually active" with Jordan.

"No!" I said. "She can't. Won't. It's kind of this big fucked-up thing."

"What big fucked-up thing?"

I laughed. Dr. Penny swearing killed me, though she only did it to repeat something I said.

I almost didn't tell her the whole Almost-Rape story, but then I just did. I was better about telling her the truth now. And that story was easier to talk about than my weird father or my dead mother, in any case.

"Have you talked about sex?"

"Not really."

"Do you see yourself having sex with her?"

I laughed, a little embarrassed. "For real? Or just in my head?"

"For real."

"I don't know. I can't ruin it. I have to be good to her."

"This girl is not Collette, Evan," Dr. Penny said after a long silence.

"I know."

"You have to like her for her, not as if you're righting a wrong."

"Okay."

"Because it's not your wrong to right. You can't live out the past in this relationship."

"So . . . you think we should have sex?"

"No, I didn't say that," Dr. Penny sighed. "I'm saying that you should see Jordan as her own person. As an individual. With very different needs than Collette."

"Okay," I said. Not really getting what she meant.

"I think you should consider sending Collette a letter soon, Evan," she said. "I think it would be helpful to tell her some of these things you've shared with me."

"I don't want to upset her. I think even thinking about me would make her feel terrible."

"It's her choice to open a letter, Evan," Dr. Penny said. "She doesn't have to respond. Telling her how you feel would be an act of taking responsibility. Don't underestimate the good in this. For both of you."

"I'll think about it," I said.

Dr. Penny went on about closure, about how offering someone your true self was the greatest gift and blah-blah-blah. Then she gave me an assignment to write about something in the past that was painful and tell how I dealt with it, which wasn't anything I was in a rush to write. Though I knew she meant my dead mother, of course. She was waiting for me to tell that whole story out, and I just wouldn't and avoided the topic in our sessions as much as I could. The whole idea made me panicky.

Then I started getting panicky about Jordan too, thinking about her leaving for college. Not panicky in the sense that what the fuck was I doing with my life, where was I going to college. Me applying to college had about the same odds as me going to the moon, really. It wasn't just the idea of leaving, but more that everything was moving too fast and I just wanted it to stop. Or at least slow down for a little while longer.

I knew just where I'd slow everything down too. We'd have these marathon make-out sessions in Jordan's living room after school, before her mom came home from work, and they were slow and stuff but still really good. Nice. Relaxing. Every time, after it was over and I was getting my clothes on—Jordan liked to strip me down but rarely took off her own stuff, like I was some giant doll to play with, I guess—I'd think how shitty it was, that nothing good could ever just freeze and stay good. I mean, I'd have stayed in my boxers all afternoon if Jordan wanted. Forever, even. No sex, either. Just her and me and everything good and quiet.

And then, on cue, it was like Jordan knew that I wanted everything to slow down and stop. That I wasn't accepting reality. We were in Foods one day, and I was telling her the latest news from Tom—he and Kelly had broken up, Everything apparently not being Enough—and though I was joking about it, Jordan wasn't laughing.

"I guess that's just what sex does to relationships," I said.

Pregnant Chick rolled her eyes. Homeless Guy giggled.

"*Physicality is not a substitute for trust,*" Jordan quoted.

Maybe Dr. Richter was getting to her too, because soon after that, Jordan broke up with me. I was talking about my summer plans, about Soren bringing Mac to visit, when she announced she couldn't be my girlfriend anymore.

I thought, *God, I have an actual girlfriend!*—just as it was clearly no longer applicable.

She went into a long speech about going to college and maybe it'd be easier on both of us if it just ended now. It was shitty but made sense, because the whole time she was talking I pictured the entire sky filling up with storm clouds and I just wanted to run from it. And her.

"Okay," I said, not arguing. Then she cried, and I felt like a dick. As if I'd made the decision myself.

But then a week later, she showed up at my track meet and then we got dinner at Mackinanny's together and we ended up making out. We didn't talk about it, but soon we were in a pattern. She would break up with me, and though I'd feel panicked and crazy again, I'd agree. But then she'd show up and want to hang out like nothing happened. Sometimes I was the one who showed up. Either way, the world's longest make out would occur and we'd act normal until she decided she couldn't be attached any longer and I couldn't handle the sadness that always came after she said stuff like that. Clearly, relationships were a big ball of insanity.

After graduation, the school had an all-night lock-in where we did shit like play poker and get our palms read and eat pizza and play basketball and watch movies in the library. The whole point was to keep us from getting shit-faced and plowing our cars into trees, but it was pretty fun. At five in the morning, while eating cinnamon rolls and watching the sun come up, through the cafeteria windows, Jordan broke up with me again. I sleepily agreed. It was time; school was over. I tried to think about other things as I drove home that morning and collapsed into bed.

But a couple of weeks into summer, while my dad was in Minneapolis for work, Jordan texted me.

My mom's got an all nite shift at the hospital.

I paused the movie I was watching, stared at the text like it was from another galaxy. Pearl Lake was another galaxy this summer too. Mid-June and things were completely weird. There'd been no Midsummer Party, since Peggy Tonneson blew out her back. Brenda was in London with Baker until July. Soren was coming with Mac, but not until August.

So I texted back: *Come over.*

Jordan curled up by me on the couch, like she always did, like I was an extension of the furniture, something very comfortable and trustworthy. I asked if she wanted to watch something else, but she shook her head, and I could smell her girl smell, her skin fresh and damp, like she'd just taken a shower.

I wasn't sure where this was going, since it was only a few more weeks before she left for college. Still, once the movie ended, I leaned over and kissed her. Then I pressed my head against hers and stared at her. Giving her one last out. She could leave. She could talk to me. She could go into full make-out mode. Any of these would be fine—that was what I was trying to tell her with my eyes.

She said, "Let's go upstairs and listen to music."

Well, that wasn't on the script. But we went upstairs. She flipped through my playlists and then sat down on the bed.

"Hey, what's going on?" I asked.

I wasn't just asking because girls expect you to. I was used to her saying what she was thinking so it bugged me that she was quiet. She stared down at her bare feet, her bare arms in her tank top crossed over herself. She was so cute. Pretty. Crazy-hot, too, on my bed, with her girl smell. Everything about Jordan was just so *good*.

But I wanted to be good too. Really *be* it. Not just give the appearance of goodness. Or drown her in hot sex urges, so she'd be flattered, mistake that for goodness, like some other girls had. I wasn't just thinking about getting down with her.

Okay, maybe I was. Because inside, I was the same Evan Carter. The Dirtbag profiler. The guy who yanked it often enough thinking about Jordan-shaped objects. Lots of other girl-shaped objects too. That Evan wasn't loyal, but he was constant. And that Evan wasn't going away, not entirely.

But that Evan wasn't the one who'd stayed with Jordan over half a dozen breakups.

The Evan now sitting beside her on his bed? *That* Evan could lounge under a blanket with her looking at stars without getting handsy. That Evan did jigsaw puzzles and made shepherd's pie and still locked the bathroom door before he stripped to shower.

Both of these Evans wanted to see Jordan naked, of course. But only one of them didn't mind if it didn't happen.

Which probably explained why it did.

Jordan switched on the nightstand lamp, turned off the overhead light, and said, "Just come here for a second."

So I did, instantly next to her at pretty much the speed of light, because it was awesome to know what direction this was going. She lifted my hoodie off me, then my T-shirt. She touched my scar, softly, and then ran her hands down my arms, which I was secretly proud of since they were finally bulking up. Not to Tim Beauchant standards, of course, which maybe explained why she didn't linger there. Maybe girls didn't give a shit about arms? Or maybe just Jordan didn't. It wasn't something I wanted to dwell on, because I was rattled enough by how bossy-yet-quiet she was acting.

"Hey," I said. "What the hell's up with you?"

"What do you mean?"

"We can't keep doing this forever," I argued.

"We can't keep doing *anything* forever," she argued back and then pushed me into in standard make-out mode. Clearly I'd been arguing for no reason.

She stripped off all my clothes, until I was in my boxers, which was also awesome, but also made me instantly calculate the hours between now and when she left, the math of which was full of Almost-Weepiness, a feeling so big and terrible that our multiple breakups began to make sense.

From all our afternoon make outs, I'd gotten over feeling like a dork about being the only half-naked one. It was her thing, and I never said anything about it. So it shocked me when she took off her own stuff. I tried not to look surprised at seeing her bra and panties, which had a matching blue-dot pattern that was cute, not meant to be sexy. Which made them instantly sexy to me, of course.

"Let's get under the blankets," she said.

Under the blankets like little kids, we looked at each other in the half-dark. Smiling like we were getting away with something. Her shy hands tickled me—she enjoyed making me squirm. To make her stop, I pressed her to me, and she was so still, I wondered if she might fall asleep. But then she started kissing me again. Slow, like always. She smelled and felt so good, but I avoided the bra and panties zones, as if they were something priceless and untouchable from a museum. She didn't do the same for me, though. Her hands dipped down my boxers and she kind of sighed when she felt my hard dick— *Jesus*—and I wanted to apologize and almost did, but she pulled back and I breathed out, slowly.

She whispered, "I keep doing this because I really like you, Evan."

Which made me almost lose it. I wanted to cry. Crush her with happiness too.

"I like you too," I said, my throat filling up with a salty lump. Then I kissed her, as if that would make all the Weepy go away.

All sweaty together under the blankets, I wanted it to both stop and keep going. The huge sadness seemed to get closer. Tears rained down my throat, my nose. Twice she asked me if I was getting a cold or had allergies. Both times I pretended not to know what she was talking about. Finally, I got up to piss. Something I'd never done when getting down with a chick. Which was probably good—pissing with a boner's tricky. But I had to do something about the Goddamn Weepy.

In the bathroom with the door locked, I looked at myself. Flexed in the mirror. I had become a total strutting douche about my muscles, though I was private about it. For some reason, just seeing myself, alone, made me feel a little better. Made the fucking Weepy recede, at least.

Back in my room, under the blankets, my hands discovered a now all-the-way-naked Jordan.

"Is that okay?" she asked.

"Jesus, don't be crazy."

"I *am* crazy, Evan."

"You know what I mean."

"I have condoms," she said. "If you want to."

"Do you want to?"

"Yeah. But only if you do."

"Jesus!" I said. "Yes. Of course I do. But only if you want to."

"We sound like total idiots."

"I don't care."

"They're in my bag."

I didn't feel right telling her I had my own condoms. My own condoms felt somehow unlucky. So I grabbed her bag and handed it to her. Regardless of which Evan I was, neither one enjoyed rummaging through a girl's purse.

She pressed a condom square on my chest, like a little medal, instantly activating Dirtbag Evan. I didn't want to be gross and grabby, but Jesus Christ she felt great. She felt like relief. Like the antidote to Weepy. I struggled to be cool. Slow and gentle. I decided that this had to be good, since it was her first time since the Almost-Rape. But then she crawled on top of me and completely took charge. Which was surprising. And unbelievably hot.

And pretty much flushed away any ideas of me being *good*. I didn't last long and once she pitched herself off me and I'd gotten back to life, I felt dumb about it. We laid there breathing and listening to the faint noise from the waves coming through my open window. I rolled over, wanting to amend things somehow, but the only thing I could think to say was, "Sorry." Which is a shit thing to say to a girl after you've done it with her, really.

So I just stared at her, the first girl I'd ever brought home to my bed. Though my father was often absent, physically and mentally, I had avoided bringing girls back to my rooms in all the anonymous condos. Only Collette had been in my bed, but I never thought of the bed in Connison as really mine. I always saw myself as a kind of adventurer, exploring the exotic, potentially hostile habitat that was a girl's bedroom. Piles of clothes on the floor. Candles and jewelry on the dresser. Posters and pictures on every available surface. Parents lurking nearby.

Jordan's own bedroom was like that, and her bed had nicer, fancier sheets than mine and probably better mood lighting than my stark reading lamp too, but looking at her naked on my boring, needing-to-be-changed white sheets, with her short hair all rucked up and sweaty, it was like seeing something so perfect. Beyond seeing her naked, which, of course, was nice. But it was like I also could see *her*. All of her. Jordan, Almost-Raped girl, turning into a story. But something more than just a story too.

She whispered that this wouldn't be our only opportunity; though I knew the math on that, I nodded into her neck. I waited for the huge sadness to roll over us again, but it didn't come. Not even when she cried a little and then laughed, called herself stupid for crying. My head still hiding in the soft skin of her neck, I said that she was beautiful. And good. And, yeah, crazy, but so was I, so we were perfect together. Which was probably a stupid thing to say, but I couldn't help it. Then I pulled the covers up, because the breeze from the window was suddenly cold, and though my bed was just a twin, nothing like Jordan's giant deluxe one, we fell asleep together.

***

The next morning, I woke up thinking about Collette. Though I hadn't dreamed of her, not in a while. It was very Dirtbag Evan to think of other girls with one in my bed, but the truth was that I never really stopped thinking about Collette. The letters to her in my notebook under the bed, next to the gross lotion, the unlucky condoms. I'd written the last letter just a few days earlier.

I sat up, with an idea, but Jordan woke up and pulled me back to her. I almost stopped her, because the idea was so strong, but Jordan had some ideas of her own. So we did hers first. In my bed and on the floor. Also, my tiny shower. She had lots of good ideas.

Jordan's final good idea was that I should make her breakfast. Do girls always have their good ideas the minute you've realized you've got something important to do? But since there was nothing in the fridge, I used that as my chance. Got dressed, gathered up the Collette letters. Put on my shoes and grabbed my keys.

"You're not running away and never coming back, are you?" Jordan asked.

"You're not going to college and never coming back, are you?"

"Evan . . ."

"I'm kidding. I'm just going to grab some stuff at the grocery."

There was a post office branch in Cub Foods, so I slid the notebook into a cardboard mailer, paying extra so it would get there sooner. Then trying not to think about it too much, I dropped it in the outgoing slot.

Layne was in produce, looking pissy. Some idiot had set up the strawberry section wrong. He waved to me, shaking his head, and I waved back. Then I got a cart and filled it up with everything I could think of to eat for breakfast.

Dear Collette,

    It's June. Everyone's due back to Pearl Lake soon, but until then it's weird and quiet. I'm a little nervous to see everyone again but mostly excited. I thought about contacting you so many times, but I just can't. This is my compromise, just text on a page, something that takes a while to get sent, something you can put down or tear up. I'm guessing it's hard enough to forget that shit and that my dumb ass is probably insignificant in comparison, but I didn't want to pile on, you know? I've always wanted to talk to you, I guess, even though I didn't know why. I don't know why it's important that you know all this.

    What will you do with the rest of your life? I've been thinking about what I'll do with mine. There's no college plans, no good job in my future. I'm your basic loser at this point. But I don't care. I'm wondering if the answer's in my Uncle Soren's belief in cycles. That we grow when other things die. That water rises, then falls. That circle necklace, the one you asked about the day we first skipped chapel, was his. My mother gave it to him, but Soren gave it back when she chose my father.

    My dad, of course, was no help on the whole cycle thing. Cycles, yes, he said, but circles have no exit. What the fuck does that even mean? Maybe it's math genius speak for "I don't want to agree with my brother." But this isn't what I want to tell you.

    I've never told anyone about the Cupcake Lady of Tacoma. The first redheaded girl I'd ever touched. She was the first Everything, actually. Before Dirtbag Evan existed and took over. She managed a shop called Hey Cupcake! in downtown Tacoma. Some relative of hers owned it. She was taking a year off before college, and I was fifteen. She hired me as counter help, but later, when she realized I was a decent worker, she took me on as a baker's apprentice.

The Cupcake Lady of Tacoma was very quiet, like me, so we worked well together. Which sounds terrible—someone preferring your void over your voice—but once I realized that she wasn't waiting for me to say anything, I felt really comfortable there. Just watched her mix batter and whip frosting, so quiet. A lot of cute chicks came into the shop, some of them older than the Cupcake Lady too, and none of them subtle about flirting, even though I wore a goddamn pink apron that said HEY CUPCAKE! on it. But I had no game to speak of with girls back then. Every day after school, I went into that shop that smelled like butter cream frosting and was quiet, but not alone. The Cupcake Lady didn't even hum while she worked. It made me feel calm.

One night we were at the shop late. I had cocked up a special order due the next morning for someone's bridal shower, several dozen white cupcakes. The problem with all-white anything is that it's just that much harder to hide any mistakes, and the bride-to-be wanted them arranged on tiered cake plates where you could see every angle. It was ten o'clock and we still weren't done and the Cupcake Lady made us Irish coffees. To wake us up and amuse us, she said. I'd never had Irish coffee; I'd never drank any alcohol prepared in a kitchen on purpose like that.

Irish coffee made me chatty. I sat on the counter while we waited out the oven, and I just started complaining. I'd never done that before, but the Cupcake Lady just listened while I kept knocking shots of whiskey into my cup.

I was telling her about everything in the world that bugged me. The idiot kids at my school. The stupid way customers acted all sinful about eating our cupcakes. That I had no mother and that my father was never home and that I ate from takeout menus seven nights a week. How my dad looked at me funny when I told him I liked baking stuff.

The Cupcake Lady sat beside me on the counter. Put her arm around me. That's the way it goes sometimes, Evan, she said. Sometimes the elevator, sometimes the shaft.

In my whiskey haze I kissed her. The Cupcake Lady froze, but then she kissed me back, which was pretty amazing to me at the time. Pretty amazing to me now, actually. Then the timer went off, and she jumped down to pull the cupcakes out to cool. Then she set the timer again. And we kissed, while the cupcakes cooled, her face red as her hair.

When the timer went off, she handed me a bag of butter cream frosting, and we got to work. Once we finished frosting everything, she sent me to her office in the back, where she kept a sofa if she had an early morning or a late night. I thought that maybe she didn't want to deal with me anymore, that she wanted me to sleep it off. She was an adult; I was a dipshit high school kid. I wanted to say I didn't mean it, that I'd go home.

But then she was there, saying, Shh, Evan. It's going to be all right. This won't last forever. It feels that way, but it won't. And then there was sex, but I'll spare you the awkward details. I can barely stand to think of what a dumbass I was myself. I mean, the whole thing was so different from other times I'd been with girls, and not just because I was a virgin. Probably my mouth was dropping open in shock, but she never acknowledged my dumbassery in any way. When it was over, she told me to sleep. But I couldn't. I just wanted to keep touching her. Finally, she told me to go home and I did. I walked all the way home, like a billion blocks in the dark, but I didn't care, because I was so happy. Not just because of sex. Because of how she listened. Because I loved her and knew she loved me too. Because who would put up with my virgin idiocy otherwise? This was my excellent life, then: selling cupcakes in the front of the shop, sleeping with her in the back. Getting paid on top of it. What a dumbass.

The next time I came into work, she barely acknowledged me. I thought maybe she'd act different when we were alone. But that night when we closed up, she wouldn't even look at me. I thought I was maybe fired. It was terrible. I mopped the floors with tears in my eyes like a little boy. I considered making a big show of quitting. Leaving my pink apron on the counter, stalking out. Daring her to fire me. All sorts of dramatic scenarios. But I was too pussy to even talk to her. We just went back to quietly making cupcakes. A month later, we moved.

Yes, I know why she didn't fire me. Why she was embarrassed. She knew what she did was wrong and did it, anyway, but I was too dumb about love to get that. It wasn't the sex part that bothered me, though I will never, ever forget how that went, especially the parts where I was a shaking, drooling idiot. What sucked was how she was good to me for no reason and then suddenly not. I felt like a dumbfuck. So small. When we moved, I was glad to escape.

This story compares to yours in no way, Collette. Don't think I'm trying to say I know how you feel. But it brings me, circling back— ha-ha—to my Uncle Soren. I used to imagine Soren as some kind of freak, someone you'd see mumbling in an alleyway or hopping freight trains, but it turns out he's a pretty cool, smart guy. Still, I'm not sure life goes in a circle, like he thinks. But when I bother to pay attention, it seems like there are patterns, at least, things that match up. So here's a shitty thing that happened, and I've told you for no reason. Beyond you're a girl with red hair who was good to me, for no reason. And then a shitty thing happened to you. But I hope people will be good to you too. I don't know what I plan to do for the summer. Or my life. The only thing that really sounds good now is going to Story Island and reading through Barrett Archardt's old books. If I read anything interesting, I'll write and tell you about it.

Later, Evan

ACKNOWLEDGMENTS

A few words of thanks.

My family, for being incredibly kind as I've shirked my tasks as wife, mother, daughter and sister in order to write. Thank you for sending me to writing camps and college and especially for listening to me as I lurched from euphoria to neurosis and back.

Mary Blew, for patiently guiding early drafts of this story.

Jim Heynen, for encouraging me to write and for leading me to The Rainier Writing Workshop at Pacific Lutheran University.

Kirstin Cronn-Mills, for her excellent brain-storming and friendship.

Michael Hettich, for his beguiling poem.

Maria Blum, MSW, for her insight and expertise on trauma and therapeutic practice.

Several readers also offered much help: Melinda Brown, Kari Fisher, Sid Johnson, Holly Keller, Meagan Macvie, Kristin Mesrobian, Laura Bradley Rede, Heather Reinert.

Much of what I learned about lake ecology I owe to Bruce M. Carlson. His book *Beneath the Surface: A National History of a Fisherman's Lake* (Minnesota Historical Society Press, 2007) is a great source on the topic.

Laura Rinne, for the beautiful cover art.

Finally, thank you to Andrew Karre. I don't even know how to say this in a couple of sentences. You're just so damn nice, for one thing. But also: your patience with me, your way of seeing what I could not see, your giant literature-soaked brain. I am very lucky to know you.

ABOUT THE AUTHOR

Carrie Mesrobian is an instructor at the Loft Literary Center in Minneapolis. *Sex & Violence* is her first novel. Visit her online at www.carriemesrobian.com.